THE VACUUM OF SPACE

JULIA HUNI

IPH MEDIA

The Vacuum of Space Copyright © 2019 by Julia Huni. All Rights Reserved.

Previously published as Murder is Messy, © 2018

All rights reserved. No part of this book may be reproduced in any form or by any electronic or mechanical means including information storage and retrieval systems, without permission in writing from the author. The only exception is by a reviewer, who may quote short excerpts in a review.

Cover designed by German Creative

This book is a work of fiction. Names, characters, places, and incidents either are products of the author's imagination or are used fictitiously. Any resemblance to actual persons, living or dead, events, or locales is entirely coincidental.

Julia Huni
Visit my website at http://www.juliahuni.com

Printed in the United States of America

First Printing: Jul 2019
IPH Media

CONTENTS

One	1
Two	3
Three	9
Four	13
Five	17
Six	21
Seven	25
Eight	29
Nine	33
Ten	37
Eleven	41
Twelve	51
Thirteen	55
Fourteen	57
Fifteen	67
Sixteen	71
Seventeen	77
Eighteen	81
Nineteen	85
Twenty	89
Twenty-One	95
Twenty-Two	99
Twenty-Three	109
Twenty-Four	115
Twenty-Five	119
Twenty-Six	123
Twenty-Seven	133
Twenty-Eight	139
Twenty-Nine	147
Thirty	159
Thirty-One	165
Thirty-Two	175
Thirty-Three	179
Thirty-Four	189
Thirty-Five	195
Thirty-Six	205
Thirty-Seven	209
Epilogue	215
An Excerpt from Space Janitor Two	217

Acknowledgments	223
Also by Julia Huni	224

In Memory of

*My father, Jerome,
Who introduced me to Norton, McCaffrey,
Adams, and Zelazny*

and

*My mother, Kathleen,
Who always said I should write.*

ONE

A TELLTALE FLASHES on the alert board, bright red against the dim light of the room. I toss the last of my Slami'n'Chēz wrap in the trash and shove a station boot against the desk drawer, scooting my chair across the room. Arriving at the console, I wipe my fingers on my grey station coverall and tap out a command.

"Bot 43H, again," I mutter. That bot has been a pinhole in my air supply for the last week. It keeps hanging up on Level 72. Diagnostics show nothing, every time, which means I'm going to have to climb into the access and see what's going on. Probably gum. Those idiot upper-lev women insist on spitting the stuff on the deck; don't they know it makes them look like dirt-side trash? And it's impossible for the bots to handle. You'd think after hundreds of years, someone would figure out how to clean up gum, but it still takes a human with a scraper to get the mess off the deck.

This time, the bot is on Level 67, but it still could be gum. Diagnostics show nothing, again, so I fire up the on-bot cam. A fuzzy lump appears on screen. The fuzziness is due to the crap resolution — standard maintenance bot equipment. I stare at the screen and try to sharpen the image. The good news: it's way too big to be gum.

My stomach cramps suddenly as the Slami'n'Chēz launches an attack on the Tasti-bun I ate for breakfast. I take a deep breath through my nose and force the nausea down. I knew that wrap looked a little dodgy, but it was only two days past its freshness date. Note to self: no more vend-o food.

I pan the camera to the right and barely make it to the trash can before the

Tasti-bun surges back out the way it went in — pushing everything else I've eaten today ahead of it. After a few minutes of heaving, my stomach settles down to an uncomfortable rumble. I wipe my face on my sleeve, rinse my mouth with a swig from my water bottle, spit in the trash, and do some deep breathing. Another drink and some more deep breathing, then I slowly turn back to the screen where my mind finally comprehends what my stomach instinctively knew: that lump is a very dead body.

AFTER ANOTHER TRIP to the trash can, I stumble into the bathroom. Running cold water over my wrists and splashing more on my face seems to help, so I do that for a while. The body isn't going anywhere, so there's no rush, right?

By the time my hands are numb, I'm ready to make the report. Back in the Maintenance Control Center, I bring up the in-station comm and tag the Ops Supervisor.

"Ops, al-Rashid-Thompson," says a familiar voice as my boss, known among the maintenance group as "Rash" although we'd never say that to his face, appears on the screen.

"Maintenance, Moore," I respond. The required self-identification always seems silly to me: our names are pasted right up there on the screen under the vid, but today the rote exchange is comforting. "Request confidential," I add.

Surprise crosses Rash's face, but he leans a little closer to the camera as he taps in the secure call sequence.

"Confidential protocol established," he says as the purple tell-tale begins flashing on my screen. "What the hell's up, Triana?"

"I found something, uh…." I swallow hard and then launch into the whole story. I'd swear I can hear heads swivel toward him when he hollers, "Zark!" but with the confidential protocol turned on, I know it's just my imagination.

"OK, you sit tight," he says in a low voice. The rest of the Ops Center can't hear me, but they can hear him. No one's invented a Cone of Silence, yet. "I'll notify Security and I'm sure they'll contact you, soon. Did you record the vid you got from the bot?"

"Of course," I snap. "It automatically records, and we're not allowed to turn it off."

Rash smiles tightly, "I know the rules," he says. "But I also know you. Make sure you've got the vid."

TWO

THE DOOR CHIMES. I check the read-out: Security. That was fast; way faster than I expected. I look down at my chest to make sure there's no stray vomit or spit splatters and hit the "unlock" button. The door whooshes open, and four rigid, black-clad, mirror-helmeted agents stride into the room, executing precise turns and taking up obviously pre-assigned positions at parade rest. The Maintenance Control Center is not very big, so having four military types stomping around in here is a little claustrophobic. I jump as one bumps my chair with his burly elbow.

"Triana Moore?" barks the one by the door. He has the most stripes, so I guess he's the leader.

"That's me," I reply.

"I'm Agent Baker," he says. "Secure the room."

For a few seconds, no one moves, then I realize he's telling *me* to lock the door. I smack the screen, miss the button and try again. The door whooshes and the light over it flashes to red.

Agent Baker pulls off his helmet and reveals a mass of tightly curled purple hair, a nose stud, and long, dark eyelashes. Oops—Baker's a woman. She must have the galaxy's strongest compression bra—there is no hint of a curve under the tight-fitting, black material. Distracted, I glance at the other three, wondering what they've got hidden under all that Lether clothing.

"We got a report of a dead body," Baker states, her eyes never leaving my face. Again, there's an awkward silence as I try to figure out if she's asking me a question or giving me a report. I've found it's best to talk as little as possible when dealing with Security, so I wait. "Where is it?" she finally demands.

"Level 67, D Ring, Slice 7." I give her the location in standard station reference, not sure security agents would know where maint-grid 67-243.8 is. Most people don't.

Her jaw tightens, and she jerks a hand toward the big screen. "Show me."

I call up the 3-D station schematic. Station Kelly-Kornienko, or SK2-142 as we're formally known, is built on the standard cylindrical template. We have 83 decks, each laid out in concentric Rings. The center of each deck is named the concourse; it's where float tubes and public areas are found. Offices and workspaces fill the middle Rings, with the wealthier and more powerful occupying the outermost Ring A. There are ten Radial corridors which run from the concourse out to A, and each Radial bisects a "Slice" bearing the same number. Yeah, Slice. Like a slice of an 83-layer cake.

I zoom in to Level 67 and rotate it to Slice 7. Swiping it bigger, I insert a little green arrow on grid 243.8. "It's in a bot duct; not accessible to most station residents," I say.

"Do you have visual? How did you know it was a body? Have you touched it?" The questions quick fire out of her mouth.

I stare at Baker. "Have I touched it?" My voice jumps an octave. "Who in their right mind would touch a dead body?" My stomach lurches, but I grit my teeth and breathe in hard through my nose. No way I'm going to ralph in front of the Iron Maiden. "Besides, it's on Level 67, and we're on 2." I stab a finger at the schematic floating on the screen.

"Give me a copy of that schematic," she says, "then show me the vid."

When I tap the copy button, she holds out her left hand. The fabric of her glove glows a little near the base of her middle finger as her holo-ring wakes. "Do you want the full 3-D?" I ask. "It's a pretty big file."

Baker doesn't answer, she just gives me the stink eye and makes a "give it to me" gesture with her fingers. I touch the screen and flick toward her hand, where the rotating green "Loading" icon fades in over her palm.

Turning back to the screen, I pull up the recording of my discovery and a current view from the bot-cam. Then I tell the whole story one more time. Baker asks a few questions, while the other agents apparently turn to stone around the room. When I'm finished, the Loading icon is still flashing in Baker's palm, although it's cycled to blue, indigo, violet, and on through the whole rainbow at least twice by now. I smirk a little, but bite back my "I told you so." Even I'm not dumb enough to piss off Sec agents.

Much.

Anymore.

A tiny copy of the schematic pops up over her hand and Baker zooms in to the green arrow. She rotates the view a couple times, zooming in and out, and suddenly I realize she has no idea how to find this location. Don't Sec agents have to pass some kind of station orienteering course? After a few more minutes, she grinds her teeth. Really, I could hear it.

"You will take me here," she commands. "Now. Litovsky, Smith, you'll run the lock-down here. Chen, with me." The statues snap to attention and one of them marches to the door. I scoot back in my chair.

"I can't take you," I say. Don't want to, I mean. "I can't leave the MCC unattended."

"Litovsky and Smith will be here," Baker grinds out. Clearly, she is getting tired of me. Well, the feeling is mutual.

"Regulation 4930.35 states a Maintenance Technician must be on duty in the MCC at all times," I recite. I have no idea what reg says that, but I'm pretty sure one of them does.

Baker grinds her teeth, again, and jams a finger at the comm board. "Get the Ops Sup on the line. I'm sure he'll authorize an exception."

She's right. Rash falls all over himself "yes ma'am"-ing Agent Baker. Three minutes later, we're on our way out of the MCC and heading toward the float tubes.

I DON'T LIKE the upper Levels. Everything above 40 is full of ultra-wealthy visitors, and even richer residents. They all wear trendy clothes, no one seems to have an actual job, and it all smells like Pashun Froot air freshener instead of the slightly metallic, sweat sock aroma of the lower Levels. Dampers mute the conversational noise to a dull hum, and noise machine tracks tinkle in the background. Constantly. The shops and restaurants are priced for people with more money than brains. And if you're wearing a station coverall, you're invisible. I mean really. I've been walked into, shoved out of the way and even mowed down by an old geezer in a float chair.

It's different this time. The upper-levs may ignore station crew, but the black

Security uniforms get their attention right quick. People loitering in the corridors all find something urgent to do somewhere else as soon as we step out of the float tube. I swallow a laugh as a sharply dressed guy stares at his holo-free palm, gives himself a dramatic head slap, and darts into a nearby store.

Agent Baker isn't as reserved. Her snort of laughter rings through the now deserted hallway. With her helmet on, even her laugh sounds androgynous and strangely robotic. The helmets must have some kind of voice changer in them because Chen sounds identical when he speaks. The fleeing guy looks back over his shoulder and promptly crashes into a whole rack of lingerie.

"I love coming up here. They run like rats from a gassed compartment!" Baker laughs again, punching the other agent in the arm. Chen staggers a bit but quickly catches his balance. I give Chen another look. I had assumed male, but maybe Chen is a woman?

Baker snorts one more time, then pops the station schematic up in her palm. "Lead the way, Moore."

Without bothering to look at her holo, I turn right. A hundred meters down the hallway, I turn left at the corridor leading to the outer Rings of the station, and right again at D Ring. A few hundred meters down, I wave my holo-ring at a door marked "Authorized Personnel Only" which whooshes open.

"This is grid 243," I call out over my shoulder as I trot through the narrow space. I don't know if they can hear me over the clanging of their boots on the metal floor. Their boots were designed for the carpeted areas, I guess. Or for audio intimidation. "Sub-grid 8 is this way."

As we approach 8, a putrid smell fills the corridor. I try to pull the collar of my uniform up over my nose. Bot 43H is right where I expected, diligently advancing and retreating as it tries to find a way around the, uh, obstruction. I press back against the wall so Baker and Chen can get by, carefully keeping my eyes away from that still lump blocking the corridor.

The duct is narrow; Chen lurches against me as he pushes past. Definitely a guy. He's wearing so much body spray, I can smell it through his supposedly impermeable uniform when he's this close. I guess a thick cloud of Black Hole for Men is better than Parfum du Death.

"Get this bot out of here," Baker growls.

"I'll tape off the area," says Chen.

I flick a few commands on my holo-ring and hit the send icon. The bot trundles past me back toward the garage. "There's no need for tape," I say. "Only the bots come out here, and they'll roll right through the tape. I can block this section for as long as you need."

Baker's head turns toward me. I hate that I can't see her face behind the mirrored visor. I start to sweat as she stares, and realize I've broken my own rule: say as little as possible to Security.

"The tape is to keep nosy maintenance workers out, not bots," she finally says. "Litovsky and Smith will block the bots."

I open my mouth and close it again without saying anything. When did Sec agents learn to program maintenance bots? Usually, that kind of work is beneath them. And who knows what they'll muck up in the process.

"Maybe I should go back and help them," I say, trying to breathe through my mouth. The smell is bad enough but thinking about its cause makes my stomach heave again. I inch back down the hall, my back still pressed against the wall.

Baker's helmet turns toward me again. I freeze, my eyes impossibly huge in that mirrored surface. After another long moment, she nods.

"Chen will escort you back."

I finally blink as she turns away. "I know how to get back," I mutter.

"Chen will escort you back," she repeats. Even through the voice changer, I can tell it's a command. I shrug and turn away. Chen can escort me if he can keep up.

Just before we reach the door, Chen grabs my arm. A wave of dizziness washes over me and I stagger against him. He holds me upright and leans in. His visor clears and concerned grey eyes peer down at me.

"Are you OK?" The voice still sounds robotic, but it's comforting to see his face instead of my own warped reflection.

"I guess." My own voice is faint and quavery. "Maybe I'm just in shock or something."

He nods. "Let's get you back to your office so you can sit down."

―――――

BY THE TIME we get back down to Level 2, I'm feeling better. The other two agents let us in and I sink down into my chair. The screens look normal, and the bots are performing fine. I gulp down half a bottle of water and lean back in my chair.

The agents stand immobile again, but Chen's faceplate is still transparent so I can see his lips moving. That's why they spend so much time as statues—they're talking to each other on a private circuit! Thinking back, Baker's silences seem much less threatening now that I know she was talking to Chen. I wonder what she was saying.

I wave my hands in front of Chen's helmet. "Hello! I can see you! What are you talking about? Can I get back to work?"

Chen starts, eyeing me. He says something else I can't hear then smiles, a professional looking smile. Probably learned it in agent school: how to disarm anxious citizens. I shake my head and try to focus on Chen's voice.

"... we're done here." He's staring at me, like a doctor presented with a mysterious illness. "Are you feeling OK? You still look a little pale. I can take you up to the clinic if you want."

The words are kind, but I get the impression he's anxious to get away. Who wants to babysit a nauseated witness when there's crime fighting to be done? I pull myself out of a strange vision of Sec agents wearing tights and capes and nod at Chen.

"I'm fine. Or I will be as soon as I get back to work." I flex my fingers and roll up to the console.

Chen blanks his helmet visor. Even though I know what he looks like, he's so creepy with the shiny mirrored face. The other two pick up their bags, toss a couple wrappers in the trash and push in their chairs like good little children. I still can't tell who is who, but I really don't care. I just want them to leave so I can take a nap.

"We'll contact you if we have further questions," Chen's robot voice tells me. I nod and wave the door open for them. Hopefully, they won't have any more questions, at least not today.

I finish my programming, then flip on one of my favorite old vids. Bot monitoring is a lot of sitting around; you only have to work if something goes wrong. Like they find a body. Ew. I shudder and turn up the sound, singing along with the corny theme song, letting my mind drift off to twentieth-century Earth.

THREE

A SUDDEN DROP in the noise level of the bar draws my eyes to the door. The reason keeps my attention. Thick dark hair with just the perfect amount of curl, ruggedly handsome features, broad shoulders and sharply tailored clothing that hints at a well-toned but not muscle-bound body.

"Wow," I lean over to yell into Kara's ear as the sound ratchets back up to normal. "Check out the dude at 7 o'clock! Ain't he shiny?"

"Shiny?" Kara drawls. "Is that from one of your *Ancient TēVē* vids?" She swivels on her stool and her lips make a shocking pink O of surprise. "You're right. He *is* shiny. 'Shiny' is perfect," she purrs. *"He's* perfect." She swings back around to check her hair and makeup in the big mirror over the bar, her eyes darting over to keep the newcomer in view at the same time.

I glance at my friend as she pulls a long lock of pink and gold hair down over one eye and pushes her boobs further up out of her hot pink camisole. If it were any tighter, she'd pop right out. She winks at me, her violet eyes catching the light, then licks her lips, knocks back her drink and aggressively turns her back to the man walking toward the bar. Next to her, my reflection with its drab blue eyes, grey coverall and shaggy brown mop of hair is barely noticeable, even though I tower over her. Somehow, I just fade into the background.

I focus on the shiny guy in the mirror and realize he is staring right at me. For a long moment, I look deep into his chocolate brown eyes.

"Is he still coming this way?" Kara hisses at me. I start, breaking eye contact with Mr. Shiny, and look down at Kara. She gazes past me and bats her eyelashes at the guy on my right. He nearly spits out his drink in surprise.

I glance back up in the mirror, but the shiny guy is gone. I quickly scan the room and pick him out again. "Looks like he wants to talk to the bar-master."

Bars that we can afford to frequent don't have bartenders. Instead, they have bar-bots to serve the drinks and a bar-master who sits up on a catwalk, monitoring the room and the credit flow. If anyone gets out of line, he calls security without getting physically involved. It's a pretty floaty job if you don't mind working the night shift. Of course, we're in space, so night shift is just a designation anyway. I tried that job for a week; too much human interaction. And drunks get cranky. Maintenance bots just run into gum once in a while.

"He looks like station security to me," I tell Kara. "Probably looking for someone who's outstayed his welcome. I wonder why he isn't in uniform?"

Mr. Shiny climbs right up the access ladder, his pants just tight enough to show off his equally shiny backside. He gestures smoothly at the bar master's holo-screen, flashes a holo-ID, says a few words. The master's usually grumpy face gets even grumpier and he waves his arms around in a menacing fashion. Eventually, he huffs and starts tapping away. After a couple seconds, the bar-master points. At me.

"He's coming over here!" I squeak. Kara rolls her eyes, jiggles the girls a little, and rubs a bit of whiskey between them. Completely distracted, I ask, "Did you just use your drink as perfume? Does that work? Hey, that was my drink!" I grab the glass and put it in front of me on the bar.

"Mine's always the fullest," she says with a brilliant smile and turns to watch Mr. Shiny in the mirror. Sometimes I wonder why I like her so much.

"Triana Moore?" His voice is smooth and shiny, too. Flipping his hand open, a holo-ID appears for a second. It looks pretty official, but he snaps it closed before I can read anything. "I'm Special Agent O'Neill. I need to ask you a few questions about a confidential matter."

I narrow my eyes and look him over, totally faking a cool I don't feel. He's tall, at least he's taller than me, and even better looking up close. "You'll need to transfer a copy of that ID to me; I didn't get a chance to properly read it," I say in my best upper-lev voice. Unfortunately, it comes out sounding like someone added helium to the station scrubbers.

O'Neill stares at me as he flicks his hand open again and transfers the data without looking. His chocolate eyes look less melty; more like stone. Or frozen chocolate.

THE VACUUM OF SPACE

I could really go for some chocolate right now.

My holo-ring vibrates just as Kara decides it's time to jump in the game. She flicks a long lock of hair over her bronze shoulder and slowly rotates on her barstool, giving the agent a multi-angle view of her, um, assets. "Maybe *I* can help you with a confidential matter," she says in her low sultry voice. How does she make everything sound like a proposition?

I let Kara do her thing and call up his ID. Standard station security ID, verified by the station OS. It lists his department and job title: Special Agent for the Board. Holy zark, this guy works directly for the station Board of Directors! I look up at him and compare his face to the photo. He's so naturally shiny that even his ID pic is good. Figures. It also lists his name: Tiberius O'Neill y Mendoza bin Tariq e Reynolds.

"Seriously? That's your name?" I blurt out.

Names tell a lot about your social and financial status in this neck of the galaxy. The really top-lev guys have a single last name, like Gates or Huateng. There are only a handful of top-lev names, and everyone knows them. The only way to get one is to be born with it or contract in. The station board of directors is filled with single-names.

Then there are the rest of the upper-levs: they're like this guy. Depending on how high up his family is, he could have a whole string of lesser names that wouldn't fit on the ID. It's like they're trying to make up quality with quantity. And they're all hoping to find an unattached top-lev who's willing to contract them through the glass ceiling. Although, those contracts rarely last more than a few years, and the expiration always includes a name reversion clause. Makes you wonder why they even bother trying.

The further down you go, the fewer names you have until you reach the bottom, where we only have one again. Of course, *most* people only use their primary last name except in very formal situations. Like contracting ceremonies or station identification.

Is there just a tinge of red in his face? "Yes, that's my name, Technician Moore," he says, stressing my one name. Jerk. "You need to come with me."

"I don't make a habit of leaving bars with strange men."

"Look," he says, leaning in until we're almost nose to nose, "you can come with me voluntarily, or I can bring you in as a person of interest." He stares into my eyes, menacing, then turns away. "Are you coming?"

"I'll *come* with you," Kara says, her voice like velvet. Seriously, how does she do that?

O'Neill gives her a quick glance—there's a hint of a smile on his face. Surprisingly, it's not the I-always-reel-them-in smirk I expect, but an actual glint of humor. He gives her a quick wink. "Maybe next time," he says. Then he walks to the door without waiting to see if I follow.

I do.

FOUR

OUT IN THE CONCOURSE, O'Neill waits for me. We're on Level 4, which is mostly bars, restaurants, and entertainment. It's busy this time of day; even on the station, most lower-levs work the day shift and spend their evenings partying. Although the concourse is crowded, people leave a wide island of space around O'Neill. He's obviously not from these parts, and no one wants any trouble.

When I reach him, he turns and leads the way to the float tubes. "Can't we just talk here?" I ask, hanging back.

"No." He doesn't even bother looking over his shoulder.

He takes my elbow as we step into the float tube together and waft up. And up, and UP. We finally step out on Level 82. Right, Board Security Offices are right at the top of the station, just below the top-lev penthouses. The walls are a super-pale yellow, with none of the usual track marks marring their perfect surface. Everything from 80 up is maintained by real humans; no bot could keep the walls that clean without a single scrape or scratch. It smells better, too; real vanilla and tropical flowers. I don't know how they do it; it's a heavily guarded secret the human maintainers won't share with us bot-jockeys.

O'Neill strides across the deserted concourse and enters a narrow hallway. I mentally track our path as we wind deeper into the inner Rings; his office is in a side corridor on grid 126.9. The door slides open at his approach, and I don't get a chance to see if his entire name is printed on the panel. This is Level 82, so I'm sure it is.

He gestures to a chair, (a real wood chair!) and steps around the desk to sit down. The office is twice the size of the MCC, even though it's obviously used by only one person. The huge, (also wood!) desk sits in front of an even larger, although probably sim-wood, credenza. A couple pictures lurk in the shadowy corners of a full-wall bar on my right, and a huge vidscreen covers most of the left wall. Right now, it's showing a sandy beach with swaying palm trees and lapping surf.

Behind me, two comfy-looking chairs sit on either side of a small glass table. Two mostly empty glasses make me wonder if his own cozy little cocktail hour was interrupted to come question me. Bet his girlfriend was pissed. Somebody important must have demanded instant answers.

"At oh-eight twenty-three this morning, you reported a dead body to your supervisor," O'Neill says, consulting a screen in his desk. "Is that correct?"

"Yes," I reply. "I guess I did. I think I showed the agents where it was."

O'Neill looks up from his screen. "What agents?" he asks.

I think for a few seconds. "I can't remember their names. I think the boss was Baker?" Strange, I usually have a really good memory, but everything about today is kind of foggy.

"Baker," he says, making a note on his screen. "How many agents?"

I think back to this morning. The memory of finding the body is clear—strong enough that my stomach rolls uneasily. Then I called Rash, and it starts to get foggy.

"Four? I think." In my memory, I am surrounded by tall black forms with mirrored faces, crowding into my MCC. The room shrinks as they loom over me, but the details are vague. The feeling of dread and claustrophobia is all too clear.

O'Neill makes another mark. "What else do you remember?"

"I took the agents to the body," I whisper. "I remember the float tube, and a guy covered in lingerie?"

O'Neill's head pops up, staring at me with amazement. "The body was covered in lingerie?"

"I, uh, no, that was someone else." I close my eyes and try to focus. "I took them into a maintenance corridor. Ugh, the smell!" I swallow convulsively, sweat springing out on my forehead. My eyes fly open, searching frantically for a recycler hatch. Or a vase. Or even a potted plant. I barely make it to the ornate, no-doubt-historically-accurate-replica trash can by the end of the desk.

I kneel by the can for a few minutes, until I'm sure my stomach is steady again. It's probably a good thing Kara stole most of my drink. As I sit back on my heels, O'Neill gets up and hands me a napkin and a glass of water. Fine white linen and real glass. I wipe my face, take a drink and slowly retreat to my chair.

"Sorry about that," I say, glancing up at O'Neill. "I don't usually barf in strangers' offices."

The brown eyes watch me closely, unsmiling. Then he steps over to his credenza. "You only barf in friends' offices?" he asks over his shoulder, straight-faced.

I stare at him, then snort, trying to stop a laugh from coming out. If I start laughing right now, hysteria is probably not far away. "Yes," I reply. "Only friends. And my own. I remember that."

He returns with something in his hand. "I'm going to need a blood sample," he says, holding out a MedChek.

"What the—"

"Relax," he says. "I think you were drugged. It would explain the memory loss, and the other, uh, loss." He gestures to the trash.

I guess if you ralph in a shiny guy's office, the least you can do is give him a blood sample. I hold out my arm. The MedChek snugs around my elbow and a needle pricks my arm as it takes the sample. The androgynous voice, specially programmed to be calm and authoritative, says "Analyzing," and the device loosens and slides down to my wrist. O'Neill puts the MedChek away and sits back down at his desk, staring at me again.

"So, nice office you got here," I say, looking around, trying to avoid his eyes. He raises one eyebrow. I wish I could do that.

A soft ping draws his eyes back to his screen. He taps his finger on the desk and reads to me. "CaptioPraevus. A black-market drug that erases recent memories. Can be calibrated very finely. Disappears from the system within twenty hours. Alcohol is contraindicated," he adds, and his lips twitch. "Common side effects: dizziness, vomiting."

I roll my eyes. "Thanks for the timely warning."

"It's administered via aerosol, which would be perfect for a Security agent wearing a helmet. Standard issue helmet has micro-filters built in. No risk of collateral damage."

"Wait a minute," I say. "Are you telling me those *agents* drugged me?"

"They weren't agents," he says. "They were accessories to the crime. And I need your help to catch them."

FIVE

I STARE at him in disbelief. My mouth opens, but I can't think of anything to say, so I close it again.

"You're a maintenance tech," he says. "You know every inch of this station. You can access places no one else is supposed to go, and no one will question you. And from what I've heard, you're a computer genius." He leans across the desk, gazing into my eyes. I feel a magnetic pull. "I need your help."

"Maybe you should tell me what's going on," I say, shaking my head against an overwhelming desire to say yes to anything he asks. "How did you know I was drugged? Who were those agents? Who was the body?"

"Are you hungry?" he asks. "I got called back to duty before I could have dinner. I'm starving."

I stare at him, then very deliberately turn my head toward the trash can. I can't believe the smell isn't making him sick, but here he is talking about food!

"Sorry," he replies. He grabs the can and takes it out into the hall where I hear him toss it into the recycle chute. His office supply budget must be extremely generous. "I'm going to get some pizza. Is that ok with you?" he asks as he returns to his desk.

"Sure," I say with a shake of my head. I guess he has an iron stomach.

"Baker!" I gasp. "The Iron Maiden!"

"What?" O'Neill glances up from his screen where he's probably ordering everything on the menu.

"Agent Baker," I say. "She had purple hair and a nose ring. Like Natasha Iren."

"The singer?" he says.

"Yeah, Baker looked like a Natasha super-fan. And she had an iron personality, so I named her the Iron Maiden. It's also a band from Ancient Earth." He stares at me like an exhibit of alien animals. "It's just what I called her inside my head," I mutter.

"Do you always give people nicknames?" he asks. "What do you call me, inside your head?"

"Shiny." It pops out before I can stop myself. I clap my hand over my mouth.

O'Neill smiles. It's a nice smile, showing his straight, white teeth and crinkling his eyes a little. Just as his chocolate eyes start to look a little melty again, he looks away.

"Would you recognize her if you saw her again?" he asks.

I shake my head. "Maybe. I don't know. All I can remember is the hair and the ring. Just plain gold, like Natasha's. But I can get you a picture, if you need one," I say with a shrug.

"Thanks, I've seen Natasha Iren before," he says, going back to the menu on the screen. "Are you sure you don't want some pizza?"

"No, I can't eat pizza right now," I say, "but do they have any chocolate? And I didn't mean Natasha, I meant Baker."

His head snaps up, "You can get a picture of Baker?" His voice is loud and rough with excitement.

"Sure, we record everything in the MCC," I say. "Did you order the chocolate?" I lean forward and tap the desk.

His shoulders drop a little. "They wiped that. I've already accessed the vids from the MCC, and there's a 42-minute gap, starting when you answered the door."

He's watched a vid of me at work? I guess that's why he made eye contact with me when he walked into the bar this evening before he confirmed my identity with the bar master. Not my vid star good looks or sparkling personality. No, he recognized me from a grainy MCC video. I drop my head into my hands. A video of me barfing. And now he's caught the second show. Great way to make an impression, Triana.

"I don't normally puke this much," I say, not looking at him.

He laughs, a sympathetic, don't-worry-about-it kind of laugh. "I think you had a good reason. Both times."

Super. He *did* see the first one.

"OK, back to business," he says. "Everything I'm going to tell you is confidential."

I nod.

"This is the third body that we've heard about." He gets up and paces around the room as he speaks. "Each time a body is reported to Station Security. Each time, when they send an agent to investigate, there's nothing. The first time it happened, Security figured it was a prank. The second time, they found a single surveillance vid showing the body. The phony Sec agents somehow missed one frame from a rotating camera; the rest was wiped."

"So, you don't even know who was killed?"

He swings around and points at me. "Exactly. In fact, there's no evidence a crime had been committed at all. Except that one frame showing the body. At that point, it was still a Sec thing; they weren't even sure if they would bother investigating. But a family friend of one of the Board members disappeared the same day. They assigned *that* case to me, and in my research, I came across the Security notes on the missing body."

"And, of course, if it involves a friend of a Board member," I say, "it has to be investigated."

"Right," he says, nodding in agreement. He stops by the small table and picks up the half-finished drinks, shoving them through a panel at the back of the bar. The upper Levels have AutoKich'n that can create and serve food right in your compartment and clean the dirty dishes, too. Apparently, at this Level, you can get one in your office.

"Aren't you going to finish that?" I ask. In the lower Levels, we'd call that alcohol abuse.

"It's not mine; I had a meeting earlier." His tone is all business; clearly, meetings over drinks are not uncommon at this end of the station. Not his girlfriend, then. A little curl of warmth unfolds in my chest.

"So, did the body belong to the missing person?" I ask, dragging my thoughts back to business.

"No, that was totally unrelated. She just decided to go dirt-side using a fake ID." He shakes his head. "She's partying in Atlantis and didn't want her family to find her. Anyway, my case was closed, but I couldn't help wondering about that missing body. And the Board member encouraged me to continue." He flicks his holo-ring and pulls up a picture. I turn my head away; I really don't want to get sick again.

"I enhanced it as much as I could, but it isn't good enough for a software ID.

Based on the hair and clothing, she was a young woman. If I had some idea of where she came from, I could start asking individuals, but at this point, it's a like a diamond in an asteroid belt. So, I put it in the back airlock, until today's report came in."

The door chimes. O'Neill walks across the room and opens it. A man in a white uniform stands there, holding out a tray. The smell of melted cheese, freshly baked crust, and spicy sausage wafts into the room, making my stomach growl. I guess I've recovered from the drug-induced nausea.

The server puts the tray down on the table and retreats to the door, holding out his hand. O'Neill's holo-ring wakes and he flicks a tip toward the pizza guy. Board Security jobs must pay well; I can barely afford bot-cooked take-out. My stomach growls again, louder than the door whooshing closed.

"Sounds like you've changed your mind about the pizza," he says, waving me toward the table. "I guess all that vomiting made you hungry."

I give him the stink eye and stalk over to the food while he heads to the bar to pull out the now-clean glasses. When I get to the table, I stop cold. On the tray, next to the pizza, a gold-rimmed plate holds an assortment of gorgeous truffles. I bite my lip. How can I be mad at a guy who buys me chocolate? And not just a Choklat bar; these look like they came from Dolce Amour, the upper-lev chocolatier.

"Help yourself," he says as he sits, handing me a glass of sparkling water. He sets his own glass on the table and grabs a slice of the pie. He takes a huge bite, drops the slice on his plate and sinks back into his chair with a sigh.

I perch on the chair across from him and take my own slice. Wow. That is the best pizza I've ever had. Thinking of this morning's Tasti-bun almost makes me cry.

O'Neill nods his head. "I know," he says, taking another bite. Maybe he does.

SIX

"Your report, or rather, the report filed by the Ops Sup, tripped my surveillance query, and popped up on my screen immediately." Agent O'Neill has eaten half the pizza, and I've done a pretty good job on the other half. He pops open a zero-grav brew and pushes the plate of chocolates toward me.

"This job seems to involve a lot of drinks," I say.

He rolls his eyes. "If I don't drink on the job, I never get to drink at all," he jokes. "It's just one beer. Besides, I have these if I need them." He grabs a bottle from the shelf against the wall and holds it out so I can read the label: BuzzKill, anti-intoxication pills. BuzzKill is one of the biggest companies in the galaxy, selling their drunk-reversers everywhere except New Deseret and the Quaker homeworld. Like real pizza, they're super expensive on station, but upper-levs don't have to worry about that.

"Unfortunately, I was in a meeting with a Board member." His nostrils flare as he returns to his narrative. "Don Said insists we set our holo-rings to 'do not disturb' so I didn't get the alert until almost noon. By the time I got to talk to al-Rashid-Thompson, one of our faux agents had already stopped by with a dose of Captio. The Ops Sup couldn't remember who had reported the incident, or even that it had happened. There was no record of your call or his. In fact, I didn't even know about you until this afternoon.

"Since I had a copy of the original call, I knew which Level to look on. Unfortunately, al-Rashid didn't report the exact location. But I was able to find several people on the Level 67 concourse who confirmed the presence of a female station worker with two agents this morning. No one could give me a good description, though, not even what color coverall you were wearing. I ran some data sorts on the cam feeds from 67 and got a shot of you as you came off the float tube. The ping came in just as I was about to get dinner, and that's when I started pulling MCC feeds and your records."

He holds out his hand and a vid of me pops up in his palm. The huge, stylized 67 on the wall behind me pinpoints my location as completely as the coordinates running across the bottom of the vid. As I watch, a helmeted Sec agent steps out of the float tube behind me and steps to the left. A black-clad arm pops out from just outside the vid and punches the agent in the shoulder, making him stagger. After a moment, I trot out of the frame, the agent following.

"There's another agent!" I cry, pointing at the edge of the vid where the arm appeared. "Can't you find him on another camera?"

"Doesn't help," O'Neill says. "They're wearing helmets."

"Oh, yeah." I sit back. I choose one of the chocolates, then eye him speculatively. "So, how are we going to find this murderer?" I take a bite of the truffle and my eyes roll back in ecstasy.

I hear a sexy chuckle and open my eyes. O'Neill is smiling again, but this time it is the I-know-how-to-get-what-I-want smile. "You tell me. You're the tech expert."

I refuse to let an argument interfere with my enjoyment of this incredible sensation, so I close my eyes again and savor each bite. Agent Tiberius "I'm too shiny for my shirt" O'Neill y Mendoza whatever-it-was can just wait. As I'm licking my fingers, I hear him sigh.

"You'd better stop that—I'm really trying to focus on my work," he says.

My eyes pop open; his are glued to my mouth. "I-I wasn't, uh, sorry." Heat floods through my face, and I grab a napkin, avoiding his eyes. Even after years of knowing Kara, I'm not any good at the sexy tease act that seems to come so naturally to her. I certainly wasn't trying to do it just now! Although, maybe I've just discovered the key. I'll have to remember this for future reference.

"Hey, station to Moore," O'Neill waves his hand in front of my face.

"Sorry," I say, scrambling for a casual tone. "Uh, call me Triana."

"OK. You can call me Ty," he replies.

"Not Tom?" I ask.

"Tom? Why Tom?"

"Tiberius, O'Neill, Mendoza. It spells Tom."

THE VACUUM OF SPACE

"No, not Tom." He shakes his head. "I can see that keeping you focused is going to be a full-time job. How are we going to catch this killer?"

I cross my arms and stare off into the distance, chewing my lower lip. How can we catch an unknown killer when all the evidence disappears within hours of being discovered? A huge yawn forces its way out of my mouth.

"Look." I yawn again. "I've had a really full day. I discovered a body, threw up, got poisoned, got intimidated by Sec agents, worked a full shift, drank too much—"

"Barfed again," Ty chimes in.

I huff. "Yeah, very funny, I barf a lot. Anyway, I'm exhausted. Can we save the station tomorrow, instead?"

"Sure." Ty stands up and holds out the gold-rimmed plate. "Do I need to buy more chocolates?"

I tip the four cubes into my pocket. "Oh, yeah."

SEVEN

THE NEXT DAY, I get a text from O'Neill.

Citrus Nebula, Level 38, noon.

It's Saturday, so I have the day off. Kara came in late last night, long after I returned to our tiny compartment. She's still deeply asleep when the text comes in, so I shower as quietly as I can. I throw on a clean t-shirt and soft pants, pull a comb through my hair, leave a note in Kara's queue, and let myself out.

I've got some time to kill, so I run down to the MCC. Juan Kalincezk is on duty, with his usual Saturday morning hangover. When I show up with a huge cup of coffee and a Tasti-bun, he's happy to let me in.

"You got the jumbo, extra spicy bun! You are a lifesaver! I love you and will bear all your children!" He grabs the coffee and chugs half the cup.

I hand him the bun and drop down into the extra chair. "Well, I'm not sure how your wife would feel about that. Do you mind if I log in and check something?" I ask.

He shoves his chair away from the console as he unwraps the Tasti-bun. "You can check anything you want. I'm going to eat this and take a nap."

Saturday maintenance schedules are generally pretty light, so napping is almost expected. That's why Juan volunteers for this shift.

I scoot up to the console and log in. O'Neill was right; there's no recording from yesterday morning. I run through the logs for yesterday and run a search on files created yesterday morning. Still nothing.

"Could you stop pounding so hard on that!" Juan moans.

"Sorry." I check my messages then log into my partitioned space and copy those files to my holo-ring. "I'll let you sleep. Hope you feel better soon."

I leave Juan to his nap and head up to 38. I've never been to the Citrus Nebula; it's a bit out of my price range. Their specialty is brunch, so I'm not sure why we're going at noon. Seems a little late for brunch.

I'm early, so I wait outside in the concourse. People watching is excellent on the mid-Levels. Across the way, two lower-levs wander by, mouths open as they gawk in the window of a jewelry store. A gaggle of wealthy looking teens ignores each other, staring at their holos. The tallest one trips over a shorter one, recovers his balance, and walks on without taking his eyes off his palm. The shorter one doesn't even notice.

Over by the restaurant, a family of four stops to look at the menu posted outside, a toddler screaming bloody murder. I hold my breath until they pick up the screamer and move on. I don't want to share an enclosed space with that today. Despite my minimal alcoholic intake and subsequent purge, I'm still a bit hung-over. As the family marches away, an attractive couple exits the Nebula. She's wearing what must be a designer tunic and the wildly expensive gladiator sandals Kara was drooling over in one of last week's zines. He's dressed casually in a loose shirt over linen slacks. They stop and the woman wraps her arms around the man and attacks his neck like a vampire. A wash of ice pours through my body and I stare, mouth open like the lower-lev gawkers. The man is Ty O'Neill.

Hoping he won't notice me, I slip into the sporting goods store behind me. Who am I kidding, he was way too busy to notice me. I sink down on a crate of hoverboards. Why do I care? Sure, he's shiny, but he's way out of my league. And he wants to work with me, not date me. But no matter how many times I tell myself that, I still want to cry. Or gouge her eyes out.

I jump up and pace around the ZeroGrav Sports display. Get it together, Moore, you have things to do! You're too busy for shiny jerks and their top-lev daddy's girls. I come back around and kick the crate I was sitting on. It slams into a whole stack of self-propelled zero G volleyballs, sending red and blue balls zinging every direction, careening off everything in their path.

One ball knocks into a huge pile of Velcro climbing gloves. Another bounces off a ceiling strut and narrowly misses me before plowing into a rack of workout gear. I grab crazily at the sliding pile of gloves and get hit in the back of the head by another ball. Stumbling, I fling out a hand and hit a tower of Super-Bounce parkour shoes. As the tower starts to sway and teeter, I put my head down and power out the door without looking back.

Across the concourse, O'Neill is waiting in front of the restaurant. I take a deep breath, imagine pulling his girlfriend's bright blue hair out by the roots, then breeze up to him with a mega-watt smile. "Are we going in, or standing out here all afternoon?"

He blinks at me a couple times, then gestures to the door. "After you." He pauses when shouting erupts from the sports store, but I grab his arm and drag him into the Citrus Nebula.

Inside, O'Neill points me toward a booth in the back. I'll bet the vampire didn't have to sit by the kitchen. I drop down into the seat and focus on the table screen.

"How are you feeling today?" he asks, tapping the coffee icon. A tiny cube-shaped bot immediately trundles over. It stops at our table and telescopes up until it reaches table height. A hatch on the side opens and a stream of coffee pours into a ceramic mug. O'Neill grabs the handle and slides it toward me, raising his eyebrows.

"Actually, I was hoping for one of their famous mimosas," I say.

"Sure. The effects of the Captio should have worn off by now." He pulls the coffee back to his side of the table and taps another icon on the screen. Another bot replaces the first one, dispensing a tall stemmed glass. I take it and pour half down my throat.

O'Neill looks at me for a moment, then stabs the mimosa button again. "May as well stock up while the bot is here," he says drily.

I raise my glass in salute and sip this time. It's really too good to pound down like that. Besides, with an empty stomach, I've already got a buzz starting.

"So, what's the plan, Tom?"

He glares over the rim of his mug and sets it down with a thump. "I thought you were going to come up with the plan."

"I've got something better than a plan." I smile brightly. "Gimme your hand."

I reach out and grab his left hand. It's warm and strong, but the skin is softer than mine, with no calluses. I slide my thumb across his knuckles. I hear him suck in some air, and I freeze. What the hell am I doing!? Remember the vampire woman! I flip his hand over and flick a finger against his holo-ring.

"Did I tell you that I am very cautious?" I activate my own holo and pull up files, keeping my eyes focused on my palm. "Some people call it paranoid. I have my system set to make backups. Private, hidden backups. Completely partitioned from the station OS. This morning I stopped by the MCC and got this."

I open a vid, fast forward, freeze it, and swipe it to his palm.

"Is that—"

"Yup." I sit back and take a celebratory sip from the second glass. "That's Baker. And this," I fast forward again, "is Chen."

EIGHT

"You're brilliant!" O'Neill says.

I smile, my yes-I-am-too-bad-you're-an-idiot smile. I've gotten really good at that one over the years. He doesn't appear to recognize it.

"I'm going to cross-reference these through the station ID database." He nods at the table screen. "Order whatever you want for lunch."

As he sorts through the holo-screens, I scan the menu. Eggs; real chicken eggs, not synth eggs. Bacon, also real. Pancakes, syrup, butter, fried potatoes, whipped cream, fresh fruit. I order it all. I'm really hungry. I hope his girlfriend didn't already clean out his account.

Ty continues to work. I amuse myself guessing what level each patron lives on, the clinking of plates and utensils and the low murmur of voices almost lulling me to sleep. My head snaps up when the food arrives. Bot after bot scoots over and deposits its delicious load on our table. The smells of cinnamon, coffee, butter and bacon almost make me faint.

Ty finally looks up, eyeing the table. "You shouldn't have ordered for me," he says. "I'm not hungry."

"This isn't for you," I reply with dignity, digging in. He'll just have to wait until I'm finished if he wants to talk; this amazing food deserves my undivided attention.

After I return the first three plates to the waiting bot, I realize O'Neill is staring at me. "What? Do I have something on my face?" I flip over my spoon, but the plaswear doesn't offer a good reflection.

"I've never seen anyone eat that much food," he says in a stunned voice.

I snort. "Upper-levs are too worried about getting fat," I say. "They don't work as hard as we do."

"You sit at a console all day," he says.

I shrug and tap my temple. "Maybe all this brilliant thinking burns a lot of calories. I guess your girlfriend doesn't think enough if she has to be that careful about what she eats." Oh, zark, did I just say that? I guess the food didn't make up for the third mimosa.

He looks at me strangely. "What? Who said anything about a girlfriend? I said I've never seen *anyone* eat that much. Not even when I was on the double grav weightlifting team back in college. What are you talking about?"

I shrug again, trying for nonchalance, but my shoulders hunch in guilt. "I got here early and saw her leaving."

O'Neill turns bright red. "She's not my girlfriend. That was the granddaughter of one of the board members. Some of those spoiled top-lev kids think they can have anything, or any*one* they want, without even asking."

"Would you have said yes if she'd asked?" I can't believe that came out of my mouth! I shove a blintz into it.

His lips twitch. "Maybe if she'd used the magic word. She is kind of hot in an artificially amped up way."

I roll my eyes and swallow the blintz. Men.

"Let's get back to business," he says. "I'm on the clock. We can explore what I'd say yes to at another time." He smiles—the sexy smile again. My heart starts pounding in my ears, and I miss his next few words.

"—find a facial match in the database. If that happens, we'll arrest them, question them and hopefully find our perp. If not, and I'm not too optimistic, we'll have to wait for another murder. And we need to figure out some way to get to the scene before they sanitize it."

"I used to work in Comm; I'm sure I can find the loop that relays the calls to Baker and her team," I say. "You just need to get me access to the Comm systems."

"I don't want to do anything that will tip them off," he says doubtfully.

I give him a level look. "I'm very good at what I do. They'll never know I was in the code."

"Think highly of yourself, don't you?" He ducks when I take a mock swipe at him with a leftover piece of bacon.

"What if we insert a delay?" I point the bacon at him. "I can set it to alert you first. After you investigate, we'll let the call revert to them."

"Won't work," he says. "Baker actually answers the calls. She talks to the witness."

I chew thoughtfully on the bacon. "How about this—after your guys have done their forensic magic, someone can pretend to be the witness and call it in. It doesn't matter if the body's been removed, right? You can set up a decoy to fool them long enough to get them to the site, then swoop in and arrest them." In my excitement, bacon crumbs spray out of my mouth. Fortunately, O'Neill is staring off into space while I talk; I whip out my napkin and wipe off the table screen before he notices. "You must have an aspiring actor somewhere in your office. We can set up a virtual box that will fake the ID info, so they won't know it's your people calling!"

His looks at me, puzzled. "My people?" He shakes his head. "I don't have 'people,' not on this job. My patron on the board was very clear: it's just me, at least until we have some evidence. Then I can call in forensics. I'm making an exception for you because I need you, and you're, well, you aren't likely to be connected to the killer. Any theater experience in your background?"

I shake my head a bit wildly, ignoring the jab at my less-than-stellar social standing. "Oh, no, I'm not getting involved in that. I'm tech support, not talent. Besides Baker would recognize me."

"Now who's not being creative? You'll just report it to the Ops Sup, and he'll do the actual call. He won't know we've already been in to investigate."

"Won't it look suspicious if I keep finding bodies?" I shudder and wish I hadn't eaten so much after all.

"Hopefully it will only be one more body. We'll come up with something. But speaking of suspicions, we have something else to discuss." He looks squarely into my eyes. "We have no idea who is involved in this; no one can know we're working together. Which means you can't keep showing up on Level 82 unless we've got some kind of cover story."

My stomach twists again. "Maybe you can come down to 2. I don't like the upper Levels anyway."

"That's also problematic; I have no reason to be down there. Unless," he leers ridiculously, "I've got the hots for you."

I drop my fork.

"Triana?" O'Neill's voice sounds distant. I blink, and he's sitting across the table from me again. "You kind of went away there for a minute."

I open and close my mouth a couple times. "Do you really think anyone would believe you and I are," my voice tapers off, "together?"

"Why not?" He takes the last mimosa and raises it toward me. "You're attractive, in a lower-lev way. We don't even need to make up a cover story—we met when I came to interview you for the case. You had no memory of the body, but we felt an immediate connection and decided to spend some time together." He claps his hand dramatically over his heart as he speaks.

"How many of your Board Security co-workers have dated anyone from below Level 40?" I ask coldly. Attractive in a lower-lev way?! Who the hell does he think he is?

"Well, none of them," he admits. "The unattached agents are all trying to hook a top-lev so they can contract into a single name."

"Aren't you?" I ask, distracted from my indignation.

He grimaces. "I've dated a couple top-levs. They're all like that girl you saw earlier. They think they can have anything they want. I don't want a single name badly enough to endure that kind of high-maintenance selfishness."

I know what he means, but I still feel an odd stir of anger. He can't possibly know *all* the top-levs. How can he make that kind of generalization? On the other hand, I have heard the stories. And seen the shuttle-wreck vids.

"Fine." I push back from the table. "You can come slumming with me. But you'd better have your credit all warmed up; it's going to cost you."

NINE

I END up in O'Neill's office again to do my programming magic. Although I'm uncomfortable with our new cover story, it's easier to reach the code I need through his all-access Board security console rather than setting up a stealth account. I thread my way through the firewalls and find the comm loops. A clever but not impossibly sophisticated loop is reassigning any calls with the keywords dead, body, murder, killed, or bloody (and a gazillion permutations of those words) to a mobile comm node. I trace the node to a location on Level 53 but suspect it's just a relay hidden in a closet. If I were setting it up, the call would bounce through multiple wireless nodes before landing at an illegal, unrecorded, and untraceable holo-link. They're supposed to be impossible to create, but I know firsthand that's just not true.

"We could go up to 53 and look at this node," I tell O'Neill, "but they probably have a camera watching it. We'd end up busting our cover."

He's pulled one of the armchairs into the middle of the room and is watching a high-grav Lacrosse match beamed in from Armstrong while eating a Tasti-bun. All that amazing food down in Citrus Nebula, and he decides to wait and eat a Tasti-bun. I'm beginning to have serious doubts about this guy's mental stability.

He glances away from the screen for a millisecond. "You're probably right. I trust your judgment."

"Why?"

He looks at me, surprised. "Why are you right?"

"No, why do you trust my judgment?" This has been gnawing at a tiny corner of my brain since we met. "You know nothing about me, why do you think I'm a trustworthy partner for this whole thing? You could get anyone on this station. Why me?"

He turns off the match and swivels his chair around to face me. He stares at me for a few beats, then shrugs. "I told you I have no idea who's involved in this. Someone with wealth and connections must be bankrolling the whole charade. Someone who can afford to hire a programmer and a team of imposters for weeks on end. Any of my co-workers have the connections to set this up, so I can't bring in any other Board agents." He leans forward.

"Before I went down to talk to you last night, I pulled your personnel records." He starts ticking things off on his fingers. "You consistently score in the top percentile on intelligence and skills tests. You've worked in a lot of different places on the station, which means you know a little bit about almost everything. Your inability to hold down a job concerned me a bit, but your personnel reviews all have high scores—even your exit interviews are positive. And then there's the fact that you reported the body, so chances are good you have nothing to do with the murder."

"You read my personnel files?" My voice comes out squeaky, like an animated mouse.

He waves a hand. "Standard procedure. You know I have access to everything on the station. But really, it came down to a hunch. When we talked, I got a feeling you'd be an asset." He shrugs again. "Sometimes an agent has to trust his instincts."

"So, that's it, you're going to stake this whole thing on gut feeling?" I ask. I guess he didn't look too deeply into my records. There are some, uh, gaps, that might make him nervous.

"I have to trust someone. And you seem like a good bet." He raises his eyebrows at me. I nod and he turns the vid screen back on. "Ah, zark! I missed a goal!"

When I've finished programming, I realize he isn't as naive as he sounds. He makes me walk him through every script and call, checking it against the current code. He clearly understands more about coding than I'd thought. Finally, he nods, clapping a warm hand on my shoulder.

"Do it."

I upload the new code, replacing the existing. "Done," I say. I get up from the desk and walk across the room. I stretch my arms, rotate my shoulders;

inserting new code into a live system always makes me a little tense. One mistake and you crash the whole station. I grab a soda from his fridge.

"Wanna test it?" I pop my holo-ring to life and make a call to Station Security. The AI answers.

"Please state the nature of your problem," the pleasant, androgynous voice says. If you didn't know this is an AI, you'd think it was a real person.

"I've found something," I stutter, trying to add drama to my voice. Behind me, O'Neill claps a hand over his mouth, stifling a laugh. "I think it might be—there's so much blood!"

"One moment, please, I will transfer your call to an agent," the voice says. "Please do not disconnect."

Long seconds pass, then a telltale flashes on O'Neill's desk and the call comes through. He slaps the screen and says, "Agent O'Neill."

I glare at him. "Really, that's the best you can do? I'm over here getting hysterical about a little blood and you just tell me your name?" My voice echoes through the desk speakers, filling the room. I flick my holo-ring and disconnect.

O'Neill shrugs. "That's how I answer the comm. Do we need to delete the records from that call?"

I shake my head. "I've redirected that, too. It will record here," I stab a finger at his desk, "but not in the station OS archives. Just so you know, what I've done is kind of—" I wrinkle my nose, looking for the right word, but ultimately give up. "Illegal."

His lips twitch. "I doubt Baker will take us to court."

TEN

"Where've you been?" When I return to our compartment, Kara is flipping through a holo-zine while her nail polish dries. Her nails are hot pink with alternating green and blue diagonal stripes. She's wearing a tunic that barely reaches her thighs in a sheer, glittery abstract print of the same blue and green, over a nearly invisible, flesh-colored mini-sheath. Strappy pink sandals match both her nails and the streaks in her hair.

"Had a date," I say with a shrug. I may as well start the cover story now. Kara is generally incapable of keeping a secret, so telling her will spread the rumor faster than anything O'Neill could devise. But I've got to be cagey.

"*You* had a date?!" Her disbelief would be insulting, except I wouldn't believe me either. "And wore that?"

I look down at my saggy t-shirt. Oops. I shrug again. "It was kind of spur of the moment. How was last night after I left?"

Not to be distracted, Kara peppers me with questions as if *she* was a Sec Agent. "Who was it? Where did you meet him? Where did you go? What did you do? Do you like him? Are you going out again?"

"Douse your boosters, girl! We just had lunch."

Kara heaves a dramatic sigh, then asks again, one word at a time. "Who. Was. It?"

I heave my own sigh. She's going to be impossible when I tell her. "His name is Ty." I escape into the bathroom.

"You can't hide in there!" she hollers through the door. "I can wait out here all evening!"

That isn't true; it's Saturday, so she has a date. Kara always has a date on Saturday. And most other nights. I wait until she hollers again then come out, trying to look reluctant. It isn't hard; I am reluctant. She's going to be so excited, and it'll just be a lie.

She tips her chin toward the couch. "Sit. Spill. I'm not going anywhere until you tell me everything."

I sit. "The shiny guy last night—" I start, but she cuts me off.

"Yeah, I want to hear about him, too," she says waving her hand around. "Date first." Why does nail polish take so long to dry? And why is it so stinky until it does? And why does she jump to the conclusion that the shiny guy has nothing to do with my date? Oh, yeah, because she knows me.

"Actually," I begin again, smiling a little.

Her eyes widen. Really, she jumped right back faster than I expected. "*He* was your date?! Come on, tell me everything!"

I recite the story I practiced all the way down from 82. "He thought I witnessed a crime or something. It was weird. He kept asking me questions about some call I supposedly made yesterday. Anyway, after I convinced him he had the wrong person, I figured he'd send me away. But he ordered pizza and asked me to stay. And oh, Kara, the pizza! It was—" I can almost smell it again, "—so amazing."

Kara fixes a disbelieving look on me. "You had a date with the shiniest guy we've ever seen, and all you can talk about is the pizza? That is SO you."

"Seriously, if you'd tasted it! And the chocolate! He ordered Dolce Amour, and *they delivered it* to his office!"

"Wow, that must cost a bundle! Did you thank him properly?" she asks, shimmying her shoulders a little.

"I'm not going to sleep with a guy just because he buys me chocolate," I sputter. "Even expensive chocolate!"

"I'd have slept with him for nothing."

"You sleep with anyone who asks," I reply.

"Prude!"

"Slut!" We both laugh.

"So, you saw him twice in two days; that's something."

"He's pretty busy and today was his day off," I caution. "I probably won't see him again for weeks—or at all."

"All the more reason to take advantage of the opportunity when it comes around," she says, fluttering her eyelashes. She looks like she has a pair of demented butterflies on her face. "So, I gotta bounce. I've got a date, too. Don't wait up!"

I don't bother asking her for details; she dates a new guy almost every weekend. Sometimes several different guys per week. "Stay safe," I say. Somewhere on this station, there's a killer. But I can't tell her that.

She rolls her eyes. "Yes, Mother. Got my holo-ring right here." She waves her hand in front of my face, gives me air kisses, and skitters out the door.

I stare at the closed door for a minute, then follow her out. When I reach the float tubes, I bounce down to Level 2 and wave my hand at the MCC door.

Juan is still on shift, so I let myself in. The system will log my entrance and exit, but there aren't any rules against dropping by the office, as long as we don't cause any trouble. Let's face it, monitoring bots can get boring, and the Ops Sup doesn't mind if we keep each other company. Of course, Juan is out cold, with his feet up on the console and head hanging over the back of the chair. I knew he would be. Juan's hangovers are legendary, and measurable on a scale of one to ten. This morning I estimated he was easily a seven, and anything above a five results in an afternoon "nap."

I slide his feet a few centimeters to the left and open a window on the screen. This afternoon I let Ty believe I needed his account access to break into the system, but there's nothing farther from the truth. I have a virtual backdoor programmed into the MCC console and can rove the system undetected from here. But there's no reason for Security to know that; especially not Board Security. Ty may be shiny, but he's still an unknown quantity.

I build a tracking loop and attach it to Kara's holo-ring ID. I set it to ping to the node that our perp set up on 53 but coded with an encrypted bounce that will send it to me. I've always wanted my own undocumented bounce node but they're really expensive. And super illegal. I don't have the right contacts to get one even if I had the credits. Using the murderer's illegal node to keep Kara safe from him seems like poetic justice.

Not that I'm really worried about Kara; the three murders Ty heard about were all on the upper Levels. Of course, the evil little voice in the back of my head taunts, those are only the ones he knows about. There could be others. Kara is my best friend, and I will do just about anything to keep her safe. Adding an illegal tracker to her holo-ring is nothing.

ELEVEN

THURSDAY NIGHT, Kara drags me to the rec center on Level 6. Dmitri, her man of the week, works in the Multi-Grav sports center where they have some kind of obstacle course set up. I'm less than thrilled to be here, but Kara is convinced I'm pining over Ty.

"It's only been four days," I mumble. The truth is I kind of expected to see him before now, just as part of the cover story. Even though we aren't really dating, I'm disappointed he hasn't come down to see me.

"Forget him! Move on!" She drags me to the sign in. We wave our holo-rings at the registration pad, and it logs us. The door beside the panel slides open. Kara hustles me through.

Inside, there are four gazillion guys and three girls. Now I understand why she was so anxious to attend. And why she insisted I put on makeup for a sports event. Kara flips her hair over her shoulder and glides toward a muscle-bound guy with ridiculously high cheekbones wearing skin-tight shorts and nothing else. He's dusting chalk onto his hands when she shimmies up to him. He pulls her in for a fast kiss, then swings away to bark at a bald guy passing out water bottles, leaving white chalk handprints on her SkinSuit encased butt.

"You might want to dust off your backside," I say when she comes back. Grinning, she smacks the chalk away, giving a flirty little look over her shoulder at the six guys whose eyes are glued to her glutes.

"Look at all these prime specimens," she coos. "And no competition, at least not for the straight ones." She ruthlessly ignores the three women. The two burly gals look pretty cozy, anyway, and the third one, a tall, skinny girl with a long, green-tipped ponytail, is draped over a bland guy in the corner.

"Has it occurred to you that there may be a reason there are so few women here?" I ask.

"What do you mean?"

"Well, most of these guys seem to have a lot of upper body strength." There's a fellow bench pressing an actual bench over by a blue door marked Multi-Grav. Two other guys in matching skin suits are doing chin-ups on a bar mounted to the wall.

Kara surveys the room. "Yes, yes, they do," she purrs. She nods at a skinny guy in a bright green sweat suit. He's chugging a red drink out of a huge bottle. "What about that guy?"

"He masses nothing," I say. "He can probably float in low grav."

She snorts, a delicate little puff of air. Kara can sneeze, snort, burp and probably even fart in a delicate, sexy, lady-like way. My mother would love her. "This is a beginner's course. How hard can it be?"

I have a bad feeling, that doesn't improve when Dmitri blows his whistle. "I'm flashing back to my high school gym class," I tell Kara.

She rolls her eyes. "Come on."

"Ok, teams of two," Dmitri announces loudly. I turn to Kara, but she's no longer beside me. She's across the room, wrapping both her hands around Dmitri's massive forearm. I sigh, disappointed but not surprised. The skinny guy with the sports drink approaches and smiles at me, flashing a mouthful of old-style metal braces.

"I'm Errol," he says, holding out a chalky hand for me to shake. "Looks like we're the last two."

I look around, and sure enough everyone else has paired up. "That was fast. I'm Triana."

Errol grins. "Most of these guys are here every week. Lot of 'em are training for the Vac Games."

I stare at him. The Vac Games are a big deal. Teams come from all over the system to participate in the specially built GameStation over in the L4 position. "You mean they *want* to be in the Vac Games, or they really have a shot at it?"

"Well, most of them are posers," Errol admits, "but Lugo and Wei are frontrunners this year, and Vladlena and LaTanda represented Station Kelly-Kornienko in the games last year." He points to the matchy guys at the pull-up bar, and the two cozy women who are now strapping on goggles.

I gulp. "I thought this was a beginner's course," I say.

Errol gives me a double take. "Ha, you had me there for a minute!" His laugh is nasal.

Over by the blue door, Dmitri consults his holo-ring. "T minus thirty seconds," he suddenly hollers. "Johnson and Lee, you're up first!" A digital countdown appears over the door, and the two women stride up, grim expressions on their faces. What has Kara gotten me into?

The entry door whooshes open and conversation stops. Two vid-ready guys strut through the crowd, which parts for them like the automated doors. The darker one is wearing a silver and red skin suit; his pale companion is decked out in identical green and gold. Their hair is perfectly styled, their complexions are poreless and smooth, their muscles ripple smoothly under the tight, flexible clothing.

"Top levs!" Errol whispers. "That's Nicolai Bezos and Bobby Putin."

I turn away and roll my eyes. "What are they doing here?"

Errol shrugs. "They show up every few weeks to do a run. They're pretty good. Nothing like Lugo and Wei, but not bad." He scowls. "It's not fair they've got all the money and power, plus bodies like that."

A snort escapes me. I clap a hand over my mouth, but no one seems to have noticed. "They paid for those muscles and the looks. Guys in that economic bracket can buy anything."

"Do you know them?!" Errol's voice swoops up an octave.

"Don't be ridiculous," I snap. "I've seen pictures, though. Putin was a skinny, acne covered dweeb as a kid."

"Oh." For some reason, he looks disappointed. "I thought he just grew out of that phase."

I laugh again, but it's covered by Bezos' loud voice. "We'll go first. Bezos and Putin." He points at the list hovering over Dmitri's hand as Putin pushes past Johnson and Lee. Dmitri's lips tighten, but he waves them toward the door just as the countdown reaches zero.

The top-levs burst through and the door slides shut behind them. Dmitri turns to Johnson and Lee. "We'll just give them a few extra seconds," he says. His voice is level, but his nostrils are flared. "In case they didn't have time to warm up." Johnson mutters something and Dmitri and Lee laugh.

Every 30 seconds, the door swooshes open. The first three times, Dmitri waves a hand through the opening to trip the sensors and lets it swish closed again. Finally, he sends Johnson and Lee through, wishing them luck. After that, he sends another team through every time the door opens. The room empties out as competitors surge through the door in pairs. The clock ticks through its endless thirty-second cycle. I hurry over to Dmitri, Errol hot on my heels. Kara gives me a little finger wave. I ignore her.

"Dmitri?" He glances at me and turns his attention back to his holo-ring. "Uh, I think there's been a mistake. Kara thought this was a beginner's course, but obviously, it isn't. I'm going to have to bow out; can you give Errol here a new partner?"

"Zhang and Onogbosenge!" Dmitri yells. Two huge guys barely wait for the door to open before they're barreling through. Dmitri glances at me again. "Too late for substitutions. You'll have to run."

"What?! You mean run the course? I can't."

He shrugs. "Smith-Porter and Gonzeles!" Ponytail girl and her boy toy hustle through.

I turn at a yank on my sleeve. "You can't quit," Errol's nasal voice grates. "I need a partner!"

"You'd be better off without me," I protest. "I've never done this before. You don't want to be stuck with me."

He glares at me. "You think you're too good for me, don't you?" he whines. "I've got skills! Wait till you see my vertical! I may look small, but that's an advantage in there. I practically float."

"Kara, help me out here!" I cry, but she just smiles. Never again! Next time she suggests I join her for something, I'm going to hide. Or shove her into an airlock.

"Go on, Triana, it'll be fun."

"Logan and Moore!" Dmitri bellows. One of his huge hands lands on the small of my back and he shoves me through the door.

Stumbling over the door track, I fall in slow motion. I throw out my hands; in low-grav you have time to catch yourself. Just before I hit the ground, a force yanks against my belt and I stop.

"Up, up!" Errol shrieks, his voice climbing a couple octaves. "The clock started when we crossed the threshold! Let's move!" He lets go of my belt, and I'm so close to the ground I don't have time to put my hands out. My nose slams into the thin padding.

"Ouch! What did you do that for?" But Errol is leaping away down the long, double-height hall in huge graceful arcs, following the giant yellow arrows painted on the floor. I brush the tears out of my eyes and push off, following his skinny, bright green ass.

At the far end of the hall, another huge yellow arrow points upward. A series of holes are cut in the right wall, like windows stacked up three levels high. A holo of a svelte athlete bounces up the wall, demonstrating the technique. Errol jumps up into the air, bouncing off the left wall and twisting in midair to bounce off a narrow strip between two windows on the right. He looks like a character in a virtual game, but nowhere near as smooth as the holo. After three bounces, he disappears through a window with a flashing gold frame.

"Come on!" he calls, hanging out through the opening. "Wall bounce!"

I stare up at him. Right, wall bounce. I'm going to kill Kara. Behind me, the door whooshes open and two guys dressed in mismatched stripes come barreling down the hall. Zark. I back up a few steps and race at the wall. Just before I slam into it, I squeeze my eyes shut and launch myself upwards.

I hurtle upwards faster than I expected and frantically curl my legs up into a fetal position. Wham! I slam into the wall. In a panic, I push off with my feet, like a kick turn in a swimming pool, twisting around to face the other side. I open my eyes and I'm going head first into one of those strips of wall. I throw out my arms and they collapse as I slam into the wall. I manage to get an arm hooked over the window above it.

Above me, Errol sticks his head out again. "What are you doing?" he cries. "Stop goofing off and get up here!"

Below me, footsteps thunder, but I don't want to look down. In the low-grav, I can pull my legs up to my chest with surprising ease. I take a deep breath and launch myself across the hall again. Another twist and swimming turn and I'm bouncing off the left wall and sailing through the window head first into Errol's gut. We both go flying across the room and slam into the far wall. He shoves me off and leaps up.

"Stop screwing around!" He spits the words at me. "Get your act together and let's win this thing."

He is seriously deluded.

Errol sprints off down another dark hall, lit only by the glowing yellow arrows. Wham! The floor shakes as something slams into the wall behind me. A meaty hand grasps the edge of the window. The next team is close behind. I chase after Errol.

I step through a door and my knees collapse under me. "This is the high-grav section," Errol gasps, crawling across the floor ahead of me.

"Really? I hadn't noticed." I'm lying on my stomach, the side of my face pressed against the hard floor. "What do we have to do in here?"

Errol slowly raises a hand and points to the left. His right arm shakes from holding up the weight of his body. He gets his left hand back on the ground before he collapses completely. I turn my head. No.

About twenty meters away, a set of steps leads to a small platform. How the hell am I supposed to climb up those steps? I'm barely able to crawl on a level surface! But it gets worse. On the far side of the platform, there's a trampoline, a pool of water and a wall with tiny handholds starting about two meters up. The holo athlete is back, and she bounces effortlessly off the tramp, over the water and clings to the wall. Without a pause, she swarms up the wall like a spider.

I let out a groan, and hear it echo behind me. I manage to turn my head just far enough to see the two burly guys from the team behind us go plodding past. They're both still on their feet, but each step looks like they're slogging through quicksand. Ahead of me, Errol starts swearing.

Red stripe dude stumps up the steps and trips on the top one. Unlike the low-grav obstacle, this one doesn't give you time to catch yourself. He slams, face first, into the step and smashes his nose. Red heaves himself up, blood pouring down his face. He groans, takes a couple of stumbling steps across the platform, and flings himself onto the trampoline.

Bad idea. He doesn't get enough height and splashes right into the pool. Water sloshes, but only a few listless drops make it over the side. Now *his* partner starts swearing.

"What the hell, Homer! We talked about this last week. You need to stop, ground yourself, gather your energy, focus your chi, engage your core, and then leap into the abyss!" His diagonal green stripes are quivering with indignation, but his dramatic gestures are subdued by the gravity.

Homer drags himself out of the pool and mutters something obscene about his partner's chi. A hidden door behind the platform slides open, revealing Dmitri with his whistle. He blows it, of course. My head starts throbbing. Behind him, Kara blows me a kiss. Seriously, why do I like her?

Homer and his furious partner stumble out the door, which closes seamlessly behind them.

"Yes!" Errol, propped against the bottom step, pumps a fist into the air. Or tries to; it only gets up to his chin. "Let's do this!"

Still seriously deluded. I crawl toward the platform. Errol sees me coming and cheers.

I have no memory of how I got through that obstacle. A second ago I was crawling up the steps, and now I'm halfway up the wall. My arms and legs are shaking so much I can barely grip the tiny knobs protruding from the wall.

I could let go, right now. Fall back into that pool of water and step out the door back into normal gravity. I think longingly of a hot shower, a glass of wine and some pizza. Of course, it wouldn't be like Ty's pizza. I'm not sure I can go back to lower-lev pizza. Still, any pizza would be better than this.

Above me, Errol crows in triumph. "I made it! The gravity's much lighter up here. Come on Triana! Push!"

"I'm not having a baby," I grumble, but he doesn't hear me.

"Push! Push through it!"

The little guy is annoying, but somehow, I can't let him down. I make a herculean effort and push up with my legs. (Oh, I get it now! Push!) I force my body higher up the wall, my hand creeping up to grasp the next little knob. Suddenly, my fingers feel free, like they'd fly away if I don't hold on to them. Low-grav! I shove off with my right leg and launch myself upward.

It felt like a launch. I think I only moved up about ten centimeters. But it was enough to wedge my toes against the next protuberance. I take another deep breath and shove my left arm higher.

After what seems like three hours, I'm above the gravity line and I bounce up the remaining handholds as if I'm pulled up by strings. I push off with my feet and almost float through the window into the next level where Errol is dancing in excitement.

"I've never gotten this far before!" he screams, throwing his skinny arms around me. "This is awesome!" He jumps back and rips off his green sweatpants, which part at the seams like a stripper's. Underneath, he's wearing skin-tight shorts of the same color. The effect is not flattering.

"I thought you were an expert at this? What about your crazy vertical skills?"

Errol tosses his pants into a corner, looking deflated. "I was afraid you'd quit on me. Dmitri really talked you up before the competition, so I figured…." His voice trails off under the strength of my glare.

"Dmitri talked me up? Let me tell you something about your friend Dmitri." I start winding up. "He just wants some alone time with my roommate. He knows NOTHING about me!"

Errol backs away, his eyes wide. "Let's just move on, ok? Only seven more stages to go!" He smiles hopefully.

"Seven?" I ask faintly, but he's not waiting around to talk anymore. Once again, I'm following his skinny green ass.

He really does fly through the low-grav. I'm starting to get the hang of it now, and imitate his effortless long, loping style. We round a corner and he stops short. I slam into him from behind, not so graceful as I thought.

The next obstacle looks like an enormous hamster habitat or one of those kids' play structures. Huge, brightly colored transparent tubes twist and turn, climb and drop across an expanse the size of a shuttle hangar. Some of the tubes rotate in place, others end in large spheres that spin and move. The huge hydraulic arms moving the structures hiss and thump as they work, creating an almost rhythmic noise.

About halfway up, Smith-Porter and Gonzeles, the ponytail girl and her boyfriend, are negotiating the obstacle. Close to the top, Zhang and Onogbosenge squeeze through the tubes. Zhang has just pushed himself into the final sphere. It twists and turns as it moves across the wall toward a hole marked "Exit."

Beside me, Errol is practically quivering with excitement. Or dread. Maybe both. He points at Zhang. "See the holes in the sphere?" he hollers over the noises. "He has to avoid those as it turns, or he'll end up down here on the ground and disqualified!"

Through the green plasglas, I can see Zhang doing some fancy footwork to avoid a gap that just spun to the bottom of the sphere. He grabs the edge of the hole as the sphere rotates upward and launches himself through the hole and into the exit, feet first.

"That's what I'm talking about!" Errol hollers, pumping his fist as he runs out into the room. He stumbles and in slow motion falls flat on his face. The floor of this room is thick, soft foam, too soft to walk on easily. I take an experimental bounce.

"Hey, Errol, like this!" I cry, bounding across the space to the entrance tube. A scream fills the air, I whip around, almost losing my balance. Onogbosenge plummets through a hole in the tube he was climbing, arms flailing. He drops slowly to the ground like a big, angry leaf, and bounces three times before getting his feet under him. Above, Zhang pops his head through the exit hole, swearing.

There's a lot of swearing in this game.

Errol and I seem to have an advantage in this obstacle. We're both tall and wiry; the tubes that must be constricting for a guy like Zhang are easy for us to swarm through. I hit the first twisting tube and brace my hands and feet on opposite sides of the tunnel, spinning with it as I climb. In the low gravity, being upside down really doesn't faze me, so I keep on, steadily moving through the stage.

Up, down, up, up, down, left, right, spin, twist. I've lost track of Gonzeles and Smith-Porter but hear a muted cheer ahead, so they must be through. A few minutes later, my head pops up into the green sphere at the top. I lay half in and half out of the sphere, exhausted. My arms and legs are shaking, and I'm dying of thirst.

"Get in the sphere!" Errol screams, right behind me. "It detaches from this tube! If you don't move, we'll both fall to our doom!"

I roll my eyes. "I saw Onogbosenge fall to his doom; it wasn't that terrifying." Errol ignores me and shoves against my butt. "All right, hands off! I'm going already!"

We both land in the sphere and slide down the slippery side just as it detaches from the tube and starts rolling erratically. Errol screams as I slide directly toward one of the openings. He grabs my leg and I jerk to a stop, narrowly missing the hole. The sphere changes direction and another hole appears in our way. I'm sliding right for it when I have an idea.

"Let go!" I yell at Errol, shaking my leg as violently as I can. He clings like a burr, then finally drops my leg. I slide down again, twisting over onto my back and using my hands to direct myself. I reach the hole and jam my legs across it, so I'm wedged into the hole with my butt on one side and my feet on the other. Errol slams into me, but I manage to keep both of us from falling through.

The sphere spins, and now I'm hanging from the side of it, still jammed into the hole. My legs shake with exhaustion, but the exit is spinning crazily toward us. I only have to hold on a few more seconds. To my left, Errol has followed my example and is wedged into another hole.

The exit swings into view, and I collapse my legs, falling through the opening and onto the foam exit pad. I throw myself inwards, barely getting out of the way before Errol lands right beside me. I don't think I'll ever move again.

Errol leaps to his feet, performing a crazy, impossible dance. His legs and arms flap around like a huge flightless bird and he's yelling something about crushing the competition when he steps too close to the edge and falls out the exit hole. A high pitched, nasal wail echoes through the air.

I drag myself over to the exit and poke my head out. Errol bounces in the thick foam, his long, gawky arms and legs spread wide. It looks like he's crying. I roll back into the room and lay still. Staring up at the ceiling, I hope Dmitri will let me rest a while before I have to exit the course.

"That was remarkable." A smooth voice sends warm shivers up my back. Ty steps into view and offers me a hand.

"I'm just going to lay still for a while," I say. "What are you doing here?"

He leans over and grabs both my hands. I briefly consider fighting him so I can stay on this comfy foam, but it seems like more effort than it's worth. I let him pull me up, the low gravity making it easy.

"Your friends Kara and Dmitri let me in. You really killed it on that last stage," Ty says. "Too bad your partner let you down."

I laugh as I limp across the room toward the door. "If he hadn't fallen, I might have pushed him. You didn't tell me what you're doing here."

As we near the door, he slides an arm around me and leans in to whisper. "I came to see you." His warm breath tickles my ear, making me shiver. "We have a cover to sell."

Oh, right, the cover story. My chest turns to ice.

He pulls me a little closer. "I brought you some more chocolate."

A trickle of warmth drips through the ice. Some guys really know the way to a girl's heart.

TWELVE

TY AND I settle into comfy chairs in the viewing area of the Multi-Grav stadium. Each seat is fitted with Holo-Wrap technology which lets you throw multiple views around you. You can also link seats, so viewers can share the same views. Kara is seated on Ty's other side, and already has a dozen holos stacked around us like a huge bubble. She presses her breast against Ty's arm as she reaches across him to point at a holo on my left. I give her the stink eye. She gives me a repentant look and a grin, then leans away. Ty doesn't react. Is he immune to Kara? I didn't think that was possible.

"Gonzeles and Smith-Porter are doing really well," Dmitri says. "They're almost keeping up with Lugo and Wei." He's standing above and behind us in the control station, monitoring the entire course. A handful of disqualified competitors are scattered through the viewing area, each engrossed in his own holo-bubble. Zhang and Onogbosenge sit on opposite sides of the room, obviously ignoring each other, but Homer and his flamboyant partner are nowhere to be seen.

Errol slinks in and takes the empty seat on my left. I hit the link button and let him into our screen set. Ty glances over, gives Errol a nod, winks at me and turns back to the screens.

"That sucked," I whisper, not looking at Errol.

"Yeah, we were robbed!" he replies. "I knew that stage would be awesome; I've always wanted to try it. It's not fair we were DQ'd for me falling—we made it through the stage!" He's getting loud.

"You know the rules, Logan." Dmitri scowls down at us. "No checkpoints in the Multi-Grav. This is a professional level competition."

"Yeah, but we were way better than Gonzeles and Por —"

"No buts, Logan. If you want to compete again next week, I suggest you shut your mouth." Dmitri glares until Errol breaks eye contact and slouches back down into his chair.

From beyond O'Neill, Kara squeals. "Check it out: you had the best score for that stage tonight!"

She has a stats screen up in front of her. She swipes it to the center of our viewing area and filters the data to Stage 3. Sure enough, at the top, it shows Logan and Moore, with Johnson and Lee a close second, Porter-Smith and Gonzeles right behind them.

"We beat the pros?!" I squeak.

"I told you we were better than Pee Ess and Gee!" Errol crows, jumping up to do another little victory dance. "We would have pounded them in stage five!"

"Stage three is tough for a lot of the more muscular athletes," Dmitri says from behind me. "But usually the skinny ones don't get through stage two."

"Hey!" Errol hollers, puffing up his scrawny pectorals. He looks like a pre-teen trying to intimidate a space marine. "I'm not skinny, I'm wiry! We were robbed! That should be us in there." He stabs a finger through a holo of Gonzeles and her partner sliding between laser beams in the zero-grav dome.

I gulp, glad to have DQ'd before reaching that stage. Zero-G makes me hurl, and I've done enough of that this week.

"You know, if we start training, we can—" Errol begins.

"No." I cut him off. His face falls. "Sorry, Errol, but this was my one and only foray into Multi-Grav games. You'll have to find someone else."

I stand, pushing right through a holo of Lee and Johnson scaling some sort of tower. Half turning, I look at Kara. "I'm heading home. I'm too tired to even sit here."

Ty rises, too, and smiles at Kara and Errol. "It was a pleasure meeting both of you," he says, giving them a half bow. Errol ignores him, still spluttering about his zero G prowess.

Kara leaps up and gives me a hug. "I'm sorry," she whispers. "I really did think it was a beginner course."

"Yeah, right," I whisper back. "And keep your hands off my guy."

"He barely noticed me," she says with surprise. Kara seems unable to turn off the sex goddess act and is genuinely confounded when a man treats her with indifference. To be fair, most men are immediately entranced by her charms. "He must be crazy about you; I think he's a keeper."

My smile twists a little and I pull away. Any guy not swayed by Kara is either gay or totally in love. Or completely focused on his job. "I'll see you at home."

Ty reaches out and takes my hand, drawing me toward the door. His firm fingers send a shiver up my spine again, even though I was just thinking about how phony our relationship is. As soon as the door slides closed behind us, I pull my hand away. "What's happened? Why are you really here?"

Ty cocks his head at me. "Nothing's happened. I had some free time and thought I'd check in. It's what I'd do if we were together, right?"

"Yeah, I guess so." I start toward the float tube. "Well, you've made your appearance, so you can get back to real life, now."

He follows me across the concourse. "Why are you so anxious to get rid of me? Most people think I'm pretty good company."

I stop short. Why *am* I so anxious to get rid of him? He's attractive, entertaining, generous. Maybe I should just enjoy the game. I turn and look up at him. He smiles. I smile back. "What did you have in mind?"

We go back to my compartment and he waits patiently while I shower and change. When I emerge from the bathroom, he's watching lacrosse on the vid screen again. He flips it off immediately and jumps to his feet. "What'll it be? Dinner? Dancing? Making out on the couch?" He wiggles his eyebrows.

"You wish," I retort. "Why don't you turn the match back on, and we'll stay here and watch. I'm too tired to go anywhere."

His eyes widen. "You are an angel from heaven," he says. "I don't suppose you have any beer?"

I grab a couple bottles from the fridge in the kitchen corner and drop down on the couch, handing him one. "It's not what you're used to," I say.

He takes one and clinks it against mine. "It's cold and it's wet," he says.

———

A VIBRATION against my upper arm wakes me. I open my eyes. The room is dark except for the vid screen. The match is still on, but the volume is low. I freeze when I realize I'm using Ty's thigh as a pillow. To be honest, it isn't a great pillow because it's solid muscle. Just thinking about his rock-hard thighs makes me blush. I hope I didn't drool.

His holo-ring vibrates again. "Agent O'Neill," he answers. A voice call. Zark. I sit up, turning to stare at him. He jerks his head toward the vid screen, and I shut it off. The room is dark now, except for his ring casting a pale glow—red for a private call. I hear one side of the conversation, but I can guess what the person on the other end is saying.

"Where are you?" He leans over and pulls his shoes back on. I look at the clock: 1:15 am. Kara's not home; no surprise there.

"Are you hurt?"

"Is anyone else hurt?" Now he's on his feet, striding toward the door. "Hang on a sec."

His ring shifts to blue to indicate a call on hold. "This is our call. Body on Level 8. I'll call you when I know more." He reaches out, and pulls me close, kissing me hard on the lips. Then he's gone.

My knees go weak and I collapse back onto the sofa. I take a deep breath and remind myself: *enjoy the game, Triana, but don't forget, it's just a game.*

THIRTEEN

A MOMENT LATER, it sinks in. Kara and Dmitri were on Level 6 last time I saw her. The Multi-Grav stadium takes up two slices and three Levels, so the body could easily be near it. I flick my holo-ring to life and frantically pull up Kara's location. It takes forever to load, bouncing from that node on 53. Every murder mystery vid I've ever watched flashes through my head, all starring Kara as the dead body. I start to hyperventilate, and my guts liquefy.

Finally, Kara's location loads—Level 3. Thank God. I sag back on the couch.

AT 2:23 am a text from O'Neill jerks me out of my stupor.

Going as planned. We'll talk tomorrow.

I finally go to bed.

FOURTEEN

EARLY THE NEXT MORNING, I sit in the MCC. My brain throbs dully, and I can't stop yawning. Even after Ty's text, I couldn't sleep, one gruesome scene after another popping into my mind. The bots are all running as programmed, so I rummage through Juan's stash for some painkillers. He's got an amazing variety of drugs—over the counter, prescription and illegal—hidden in a small box attached to the underside of the console. Only someone opening the console for hardware repair would find it, which means every tech in the MCC knows it's there. Most have borrowed something at least once.

I stick an OTC pain tab under my tongue and grab a glass of water. I can't stand the thought of vend-o food, but I still have a couple of the chocolates Ty brought me last night. Even if they don't settle my stomach, they'll make me feel better while I'm eating them, right? Maybe I'll eat them after I sit here for a while.

My eyes have just drifted closed (really, it was only a few seconds) when my holo-ring buzzes. It's O'Neill. "What happened?" I've barely got the connection open before the question bursts out of me.

"Can I come down?" he asks.

"Sure. I'm not going anywhere."

A few minutes later, he's at the door, a small carrier in hand. He looks tired, less shiny than usual, but still handsome and well groomed. By contrast, I look like zark, even though I'm pretty sure I got more sleep than him, plus a shower and clean clothes. I buzz him in, and he hands me a bag: a Cynn'mon Roll from

Citrus Nebula! This guy is going to make some woman very happy. Not me, I remind myself.

"Did you stop for breakfast on your way down?" I ask.

He shakes his head. "Had some delivered to my office. I've got a couple Sec Agents finishing forensics and they'll be hungry when they're done. Usually, we'd have it delivered to the scene, but we don't want to tip anyone off. Baker and company could have spies anywhere."

I shudder. Dead bodies and Cynn'mon Rolls. Yum. I supposed Sec Agents get immune after a while. "So, give me the sanitized version of events, 'K? Don't worry, I've got a disrupter on just in case anyone is listening." I don't tell him I keep one running all the time down here. Not that I have secret conversations here often, but I don't like the idea of anyone listening. Period. I told you I'm cautious, right?

He narrows his eyes at me, then shakes his head. Sitting in the extra chair, he leans back and closes his eyes. They're darkly shadowed and just a bit bloodshot. He rubs his hand over his face, then sits back up and pulls two cups of coffee from the carrier he set on the floor by his feet. He hands me one and sips from the other.

"Level 8. A teamster from the barge dock was going in for a mid-shift workout and found the body in the zero-grav chamber. Just floating there with a broken neck."

"Zero-G?" my voice pitches up sharply. "We were there last night!"

"It gets worse: the body was Arianna Gonzeles."

"Green ponytail girl from last night?" I spill my coffee on my coverall. Fortunately, it's made of stain- and water-repellent fabric; that's why it's the perfect clothing for me. O'Neill hands me a napkin and I blot up the coffee.

"Yeah. We'll be questioning her partner, of course. And everyone else at the stadium. After," he points at me, "we deal with Baker and crew."

I set my coffee down. The Cynn'mon Roll is now sitting like a lump of ballast in my stomach. I know I must do this, but I don't want to. "I can just call Rash, right? I don't have to talk to Baker."

He rubs his hand over his face again. "We'll follow the same procedure you did last time. But she probably will, too, which means she'll come down here to question you, and have you show her the place."

"But wait a minute! I have no reason to find a body in zero-grav!" I jump up from my chair. "None of my bots go through the Multi-Grav areas."

"Frak!" Ty rubs his hands through his hair, making it stick out crazy. I stare;

I've never seen him look so rumpled. He shakes his head, and it all falls magically back into place. See what I mean? Shiny.

"OK, what's the closest your bots get to the Multi-Grav?" he asks.

I drop back into my chair and pull up the schematics. "Here." I zoom in on Level 8 and point to a corridor behind the stadium. "There's a hallway here that we clean, and they take this back way to the far side of the station."

"Perfect, that's better than the real location anyway. I'll put agents here and here," he stabs at the screen. "They can close in after you take Baker to this location. Can you put a bot there; make it look like it's been stopped by a body?"

I stare at the screen. "There's a weird little alcove here where they sometimes hang up," I say slowly, zooming in a little closer. I pull up the bot program and find number four. "I can re-route four over this way and get it trapped in the alcove. You can't see it well from this side, so if I bring her in this way…."

"Will anyone notice?" His eyes are closed again, and he sounds like he isn't really paying attention to what I'm saying.

"No, the schedule is pretty fluid. If there's an accident or damage, we re-route. Besides, Rash never worked down here, so he won't know this isn't routine. But won't Baker know this is the wrong spot?"

"No, I don't think so. She doesn't seem to know anything about these murders until they're done. I don't think she's involved in the killing; she's just covering up for someone." O'Neill's holo-ring vibrates, and he checks the screen. "Ok, my guys have finished their work. Let's do this."

He makes a voice call and explains the plan. Based on his responses, I can tell there's some disagreement, but eventually, he convinces them. In the meantime, I tune out and focus on finding my inner chi. Or something like that. Some chocolate would help.

"Triana."

My head jerks up at the sound of my name. "2017! Internet Neutrality! Affordable housing!" I shake my head. "Sorry, flashback to history class."

Ty gives me a weird look and hands me my coffee again. "Drink up, it's time."

I take a deep breath and call the Ops Sup. O'Neill steps into the bathroom and partially closes the door. I can still see him, but the camera can't. He's texting; probably putting his agents into position.

"Ops, Patrick." A female voice answers.

"Where's Rash?" I blurt. "I mean, al-Rashid-Thompson?"

On screen, a woman's face appears. She has blonde hair scraped back into a tight bun, and deep grooves at the corners of her eyes as if they're perpetually narrowed in suspicion. Her lips press together. "Identify yourself," she snaps.

Flustered, I shake my head. In the bathroom, O'Neill grins. "Uh, Moore, this is Triana Moore, down in the MCC."

"Technician Moore, you obviously need remedial training in communications," she says in a tight voice. "I will make a note of that. Supervisor al-Rashid-Thompson is on an unscheduled leave. What do you have to report?"

I open and close my mouth a couple times. "I found a dead body," I finally get out, my voice squeaky.

Patrick's face blanches and her jaw tightens. Behind her, every head in the room has swiveled toward me. "Initiating Confidential protocol," she grits out. A second later, she speaks again, in a low, furious voice. "Confidential Protocol established. What the hell do you mean by blurting that out over an open channel, Technician?"

A chill washes over me. Just what I need, an angry Ops Sup. "I'm sorry ma'am, but a bot on Level 8 got stuck, and when I turned on the camera I saw a person. I think she's dead!" I wail. In the bathroom, O'Neill's fingers are dancing over his holo-ring. I shove my left hand under the edge of the console just as a text pops up on it.

*We didn't make a vid! *

Zark.

"Send me the vid from that bot, Technician," Patrick demands.

"Yes, ma'am." I fumble around, muttering to myself as I log in to my secure partition and pull up the vid from last week. I quickly adjust the wall color and wipe the date.

"What is taking you so long?" Patrick's voice sounds tight and hard. Her nostrils are flaring and there's a deep groove between her eyebrows. "You obviously need significant re-training in every area. Sending a vid to Ops is as easy as flick, flick, swipe!"

I'm sweating, and my fingers are slipping as I swipe. I grab the location data from the current bot feed and insert it into the vid I'm doctoring, all the while keeping up a whiny refrain of excuses to distract Patrick. Finally, the vid is ready, and I swipe it up to Ops.

The woman on screen draws herself up and glares at me. "I am Chief Inspector Rhinalda Patrick Inaldin Wang von Krieken," she announces. A station ID with the distinctive red bar across the top flashes on screen. "This Operations branch is under a no-notice inspection and I find your performance appalling. After you speak to station security over this other matter," her hand waves as though murder is a minor detail, "you will be relieved by another technician and will not stand duty until you have completed thorough remedial training and recertification. You will not mention this inspection to *anyone* unless you wish to be terminated." The screen goes blank.

"If anyone looks too closely at that vid, they'll know it's a fake." My hands are cold and I'm shaking. "The angle is wrong, and there's no alcove."

Ty comes out of the bathroom and squats down, wrapping his arm around me. I lean against him. "I watched you doctor the metadata," he says. "You were amazing. Very cool under pressure. I'm sure the vid will fool anyone who isn't intimately familiar with the back corridors of this station."

"I'm going to get fired!" I wail.

"You won't get fired. I can fix that. Inspectors work for the Board." He rumples my hair, kisses my cheek, and stands. "I'll take care of Patrick. But now it's time to get ready for act two; Baker should arrive soon. I've got to get out of here."

I check the vids on the corridor outside and send Ty on his way as soon as it's clear. Not five minutes later, Baker is at my door. I take a deep breath; time to pretend I've never heard of her before. I watched my secret copy of the MCC vid from last week, but I still don't really remember last time. I guess that will help me make it real. I slide the door open.

Four Sec Agents are standing outside my door. They stomp in and take up positions at evenly spaced locations. I wonder what they're expecting; are they guarding me or the room? And from who? Or is that whom? The room feels closed in with this many big bodies, so I stay on my feet.

"Triana Moore?" barks the one by the door.

"That's me," I reply.

"I'm Agent Baker," she says. "Secure the room."

I stare at her for a minute, then realize she wants me to lock the door. Why can't she just say that? I squeeze around one of the agents and swipe the lock screen. The door slides shut and the red light above it glows. Baker removes her helmet and gives me a glare.

"Did you report a dead body?"

"Yes, I did. Excuse me," I say to the agent standing in front of my chair. He takes a half-step to the left, and I sit down. "My bot ran into it on Level 8.

Here's a vid." I pull up the vid I sent to Patrick, hoping Baker won't recognize it from the last time. These corridors all look pretty much the same, even to me.

"Do you have a live feed?" she asks. "Where is it?"

I ignore her first question; of course I don't have a live feed. Or rather, I do, but I suddenly realize I can't show it to her. There's not really a body there. Zark! We really didn't think this through. I pull up a station schematic and swipe into the location where the bot is now waiting.

"Right here," I tell Baker, pointing. Her purple hair is really quite shocking. I can't believe I've forgotten meeting her before. "Level 8, Slice 6, B Ring. It's kind of stuck in this little alcove. I can show you where it is."

Baker's eyes narrow. "Are you allowed to leave the MCC?" she asks.

"Uh, no, I can't, actually." Zark! I just remembered the vid from last week; I'd tried to get out of showing her the body by quoting some bogus regulation. Sudden inspiration hits. "But the Ops Sup is supposed to be sending a relief tech down."

Baker exchanges a look with one of the other agents. That might throw a crimp in their plans; they'll have to drug two of us this way. "My agents will stay here; you can show me right now."

What did I say last time? Oh yeah, I referred her to Rash. I sure as hell don't want her calling Patrick, so I'd better come up with something else. "Uh, let me ask one of my coworkers."

"I spoke with Supervisor Patrick when she called in the report," says Baker. Of course, she did. I mentally smack my forehead. She gestures to the door. "Lead the way. Litovsky, Chen, stay here. Smith, you're with me."

As I lead the way to the float tubes, I wonder if they trade off who stays behind to wipe the feeds or if Chen is being punished for something. We wind our way out of the maze of corridors to the concourse. We waft up to Level 8 and I skirt around to Slice 6. We turn right at the Radial and work our way out to B Ring. I wave my holo-ring at the bot duct door and lead the way toward the alcove. I stop suddenly and point.

"It's right there," I whisper. "I'm just going to wait here, ok?"

The agents' heads turn to each other; they must be talking on a private channel. Then Baker's robot voice booms out. "Smith will take you back to the MCC."

I duck around them and scramble down the hall. "That's ok," I call back over my shoulder as I trot away. "I know how to get there." And I don't want to get drugged again. They let me go; probably Chen has a dose of Captio waiting for me back at the MCC.

I round a corner, and almost run into O'Neill, pulling a helmet on over his perfect hair. He gives me a wink and then blanks the helmet visor. I slow down, but he jerks his thumb at the door. About halfway there, I hear shouting, so I turn around and sprint back to the corner.

I poke my head around the corner, but I've missed most of the excitement. Smith and Baker are standing near the bot with their hands on their helmets. Ty and another suited-up agent have weapons drawn and pointing. I inch forward.

Smith and Baker are on their knees. "You're under arrest." O'Neill recites their rights, continuing to point the weapon at them, while the other agent straps their hands behind their backs. Then he steps forward and removes their prisoners' helmets.

Smith, a young, blond guy with a bad haircut and acne, looks scared. Baker grins. "Took you long enough," she says.

"What do you mean?" says Ty.

She laughs; a loud, harsh bark. "I'm afraid you'll have to figure that out on your own." She jerks her head back, gasps, and her eyes roll back. Her body jerks once, twice, again and again, faster and faster. She pitches over, slamming into the deck, convulsing horribly. It seems to go on forever. Finally, one last massive heave and she lays still, a dribble of blood leaking from the corner of her mouth.

Smith has curled over into a fetal position, whimpering.

"What the hell?" O'Neill yanks off his glove and presses his fingers to her throat. "She's got a pulse. Call the medics!" His partner goes still, in that way the Sec Agents do when they're talking to someone.

O'Neill swings around and sees me at the end of the corridor. "What are you doing here? I told you to go." He doesn't even wait to see if I comply, he just turns back to the phony agents. I shrug. If he was serious about me leaving, he'd have made more effort. I ease closer.

"What the hell happened to her?" O'Neill has Smith by the collar and has dragged him up off his knees. "Tell me!" He releases Smith's collar. The guy drops to the floor, stuttering and babbling incomprehensibly.

"He's just a kid!" I tell O'Neill, glaring at him. "Back off a second."

O'Neill glares back, but I ignore him. I crouch down next to Smith and put a hand on his shoulder. "Are you ok? Not feeling sick, are you?" Smith stops talking nonsense and freezes. After a second, he shakes his head.

"I'm going to help you sit up, ok?" I grab his arm, still strapped behind his back, and help him roll onto his backside and finally into a sitting position. He has tears running down his face, and his skin is grey. "Do you want some water?" He nods. I look up at O'Neill.

Even though I can't see his face through his visor, I know O'Neill rolls his eyes. His head turns toward the other guy, and after a moment, his partner produces a water pac and hands it to Smith. The boy takes a couple sips and heaves a sigh.

"It must be the drug," he whispers, jerking his head toward Baker without looking her way. I turn my head and can see her lifeless feet and legs. Fortunately, her head is out of view right now. O'Neill checks her pulse again.

I look back to Smith. "What drug?"

He shrugs a little, but his jaw tightens. "I think it's the same stuff we gave you. She said it would make her forget, so the enemy couldn't make her talk."

I look at O'Neill, but I just see my own reflection in that stupid visor. "The enemy?" I ask.

"Yeah," says Smith. His voice is getting a little stronger. "She said enemy agents might try to make her talk. But you aren't enemy agents, are you?" He looks at me, his eyes clear and curious.

"What do you think?" I ask.

"I think he's station security," he says, jerking his chin at O'Neill. "I'm not sure what you are. But I don't think you're an enemy agent. I'm starting to think we're the bad guys." His voice trails off with a little whimper.

There's some commotion in the distance, and soon a medical team in full hazmat gear is trotting down the corridor toward us. They stop by O'Neill, and then two of them kneel by Baker. The third comes over to us and switches her visor to clear.

"I'm Medic Cortanza," she says, and she squats down next to Smith. "I need to check your stats. How are you feeling?"

I get up and wander over to O'Neill as Cortanza gets to work. "Did they grab the other two?" I ask.

O'Neill pulls his helmet off and nods. His helmet hair disappears and his usual bouncy waves spring into place. I wasn't even wearing a helmet, and I know my hair doesn't look that good. Life is not fair.

"I told you to leave," he says, but it doesn't sound like he's mad.

I shrug. "You needed me," I reply. "I got Smith to talk."

O'Neill shakes his head, but his lips are twitching. "You didn't get much out of him."

"He told me about the drug!" I cry.

"I think they would have figured it out." He waves at the medics, all three now gathered around Baker.

Cortanza's head snaps around. "What drug?" she asks.

It's my turn to smirk. "It sounds like Baker took some Captio-, uh, Captio-something," I don't look at O'Neill.

"CaptioPraevus," he fills in. "They've been using it on victims. We think she might have taken a larger dose so she's unable to remember who hired her."

"How large a dose?" Cortanza asks, her voice alarmed. "That stuff isn't lethal, but it can have horrible effects in large amounts."

O'Neill's lips tighten and he points to her now still body. "I guess she took enough to cause seizures."

FIFTEEN

"Chen and Litovsky confirmed Smith's story," O'Neill tells me as we sit in his office Saturday morning. After the arrests yesterday, I went back to work, but Juan was there waiting for me. Patrick had called him in to relieve me. He wasn't happy, and neither am I. O'Neill says he can fix it, but he doesn't want to tip our hand until we catch the murderer. He figures Patrick might have been sent here by whoever is trying to shield the perp.

Ty spent most of yesterday questioning the three prisoners. Baker is in the clinic, full of tubes and wires, not responding to anything. She has minimal brain activity but is breathing on her own. The other three were talking, but not telling us much.

"Baker directed everything. She was the only one who communicated with their boss. She brought the other three to the station, found them places to live, paid their salaries and called them up when they needed to work. Of course, they claim they didn't know they were doing anything wrong. Baker gave them some crap story about how they were undercover agents working for internal affairs or something. They didn't ask too many questions; the money was too good." He sips his coffee and leans back in his chair.

"We found a needle-equipped capsule sewn into the collar of Baker's suit. She activated it by jerking her head back into the collar. There were traces of CaptioPraevus in the capsule and enough in her system to make her forget a year—if it worked that cleanly. I guess Baker didn't know if you take enough to forget more than a few days, you risk stroke and brain injury. The docs say even if she somehow recovers consciousness, she won't be able to speak. Or have anything to talk about. She'll be lucky if she can feed herself someday." He shakes his head.

"Anyway, the three musketeers claim Baker said she had the means to make sure she couldn't 'turn traitor' and give away their employer. The only thing they can tell us is Baker was in charge and she called the shots. They aren't the guys who wrote the software, so they can't tell us what other hooks might be embedded in the OS. For all we know, she might have another team here on the station." He smacks his hand down on the desk. His coffee mug jumps.

"I don't think there are any other hooks in the OS," I say. "I ran some diagnostics this week after installing the loop and didn't find anything else."

He gives me a strange look. "I didn't think you could do that without my access."

Zark. I feel so comfortable with him that I forget to watch my tongue. I smile a little. "I might have a way to double check things."

His lips quirk up and he shakes his head. "I'm not surprised." His face changes, and he gives me a long stare. "We have a problem, though."

I wave my hands, unconcerned. "What, besides me losing my job? And that we're no closer to finding this creep than we were two weeks ago?"

"Actually, yes." He drums his fingers on the desk, then starts jabbing the screen. "Baker had something else embedded in her collar: a camera. Audio and video. And it was transmitting off-station."

"So now whoever is bankrolling the cover-up knows you're on their trail?"

He takes a deep breath. "Worse than that; they know *you're* involved."

"What?" I shake my head, thinking back to the arrest. "I was an innocent bystander. Just the poor schmuck who found the body. Twice. I wasn't there when you took her down; I was never in her line of sight." My voice tapers off; It doesn't sound convincing, even to me.

"Video and audio," he repeats. "They heard you." He taps the screen again and I hear my voice.

"You needed me. I got Smith to talk."

"Zark! What am I going to do?" I wail.

"We'll protect you. The good news is you can go back to work. Whoever is responsible knows about you, so I can talk to Patrick. When you're in the MCC, you're safe. I'll just have to make sure you get there and back safely."

"Don't be ridiculous, you can't babysit me. How will you find this guy if you're busy trailing me?"

He waves that aside. "I can work from anywhere. Maybe you can work twelve-hour shifts until this is over. That will give me more flexibility. And I'm putting a tracking loop on your holo-ring."

"Don't worry about it; I have one already written." He looks surprised. "I put one on Kara. She takes too many chances with men she doesn't know, and I'd never forgive myself if anything happened to her."

"What's the story with you and Kara?" he asks. "You two are so different. And she's what, a hairdresser? How did you two end up together?"

"How much time do you have?" I ask. "Just kidding. We met dirtside when I was going through the Techno-Inst. She gave me a good deal on a haircut because I had no money and an unstylish mop." I gesture to my head. "Some things never change."

"But why do you put up with her?" He gets up and fills his mug again. I hand him my mug, and he fills it, too. Coffee up here is almost as good as the pizza. "On Thursday when I arrived at the Multi-Grav, she came on to me stronger than anyone I've ever seen. Even after I told her I was there to see you, she didn't let up. I know you saw her. What kind of girl hits on the guy her friend is supposed to be dating?"

"She's my best friend. She's helped me out in some pretty tight times. It's just her way. But she would never hurt me." Not on purpose, at least.

"That's not the impression I got," he says.

"I know her better than you do," I say firmly.

He holds up his hands in surrender. "OK, you're right, I don't know her. Let's get some lunch."

I jump up from my seat. "Where are we eating today?"

O'Neill laughs and catches my arm. "I think you only love me for the food I can provide."

I make my eyes big and place a hand on his chest. "If you think I love you now, you should see what ice cream will get you."

"How charming. Love can be purchased with frozen treats. I wish I'd known that years ago," a cold voice says. I jump about a meter away from Ty.

Standing in the doorway, a tall, sophisticated woman examines us as if we were something unusual and perhaps noxious. Her lustrous brunette hair has subtle blue highlights, matching her ice-cold eyes. The soft, shoulder-length curls do nothing to soften her angular face, currently set in a disdainful expression. Her perfectly sculpted body is encased in a skin suit that leaves little to the imagination. She looks about my age, but modern science and buckets of money have made the age guessing game impossible. Something about her eyes screams of experience.

"Dame Morgan," says Ty, bowing low to the Chair of the Board of directors. I follow his lead, my knees knocking silently against each other. "How can I assist you?"

"I'm so sorry to interrupt your...." She waves her hand vaguely, sounding anything but sorry. "I need your input on an urgent matter." She ignores me completely. I'm okay with that.

"Yes, of course," Ty says, ushering her to a chair. Behind her back, he makes a face at me and points at his holo-ring. I take that as my signal to get the hell out of there, and I bolt for the door.

Out in the hallway, I stop. Where am I supposed to go? I've probably got a killer after me. The safest place would be the MCC, but I've been banned. I doubt Juan would turn me in, and O'Neill said he'd sort out Patrick, but I'm not holding my breath. He'll be busy with the Ice Dame for hours.

If our perp can put loops into the OS, he can also put trackers on an ID. Like mine. Rather than letting O'Neill track my holo-ring, maybe I would be safer to remove it from the system altogether. And that means I need direct, unrestricted computer access. But O'Neill's office is out of the question, and the MCC is probably off limits, too. I need another access point—and I know just the place.

SIXTEEN

Level 53 is way above my comfort level, but I don't have to stay in the public corridors for long. I slip across the concourse, trying to look purposeful. As usual, everyone ignores the woman in the coverall, and I soon duck down Radial 5. There are fewer people here, and when I turn right into E Ring, I'm alone. Throughout the station, the inner Rings are considered less prestigious, and up this high, they're reserved for necessary but unpleasant white-collar offices like lawyers, station middle management, and insurance agents. On a Saturday morning, they're deserted.

I slip into a bot-duct and zero in on the node's location. Although I made a mental note of this location, I didn't bother checking it on a station schematic. I reach the place—I know this is the right place—and I'm faced with a blank wall. I pull up a map of 53E5 and discover why. As I expected, the node is in a closet, but it's not accessible from this duct. It's in someone's office, on the other side of this blank wall. Zark.

I slide down against the wall and lean my head back against the cold metal. Since it's Saturday, there's not likely to be anyone around. As a station maintenance tech, (even currently suspended) I can access any location on the station, below 80 of course, with relative immunity. I'm supposed to have a maintenance reason, but I could come up with something pretty easily. Electrical circuit alarms chirp for no known reason, fire alarms go off if you burn the popcorn. Heck, if anyone has ever returned to this office in damp workout gear, I could probably make an air purity alert ping. I'm not worried about getting caught.

So why am I sitting here in a cold bot-duct, curled up in a fetal position? Now that I've stopped moving, my knees are jittering, and my stomach is queasy. The sad truth is, it has nothing to do with the killer potentially stalking me. I'm really rattled from that encounter with Dame Morgan.

It doesn't matter, I tell myself. A top-lev doesn't care if I've been talking to her security agent; she probably wouldn't care if I've been sleeping with him. I'm just a low-low-lev, and I'm happy to be. She has no reason to even think about me now that I'm out of sight. Right?

Here's the thing. Dame Morgan and I have some history. Let's just say our last encounter was not pleasant for either of us, and it's possible she may hold that against me. Let me rephrase that. It's *probable* she holds it against me. Don't let the fact that she didn't appear to recognize me fool you. She knows exactly who I am, and she knew ignoring me was the fastest way to set up camp in my psyche. I also have no doubt she can track me down if she wants. Heck, she can just ask Ty. He'd have no reason to hide me.

All the more reason to get off the grid. I shove myself up the wall and take a deep breath. Operation Illegal Entry is underway.

The office door in E Ring is covered with a list of names so long it looks like a shuttlecraft purchasing contract. I skip to the bottom, where the list ends with "Athletic Representatives." I think that means they help athletes get contracts; I saw an ancient vid once with a sports agent in it. Jerry something. I shake my head. Back to business.

I flick my holo-ring to life and enter the door override code. It obediently slides aside, and the automatic lights slowly brighten. I step into an open area lined with cracked plastek seats, a couple of cheap coffee tables with scratched vid screens and a reception desk. The walls are covered with pictures of sweaty people finishing races, making goals, and doing victory dances, with inspirational slogans printed in cheerful fonts over their heads. And, of course, a poster of a cat hanging from a tree. A dying tree sulks in a corner; I wonder if I can anonymously report it to agriculture for removal and rehabilitation.

I wind my way through the maze of connected offices filled with cheap simwood desks, worn couches and side tables, and functional but ugly shelving. My soft boots make no noise on the nappy carpet. The lights flick on as I enter each office, tracking my location via my holo-ring. In what turns out to be the last room in the suite, I find the location I'm looking for. On the back wall, two doors stand open. The one on the right leads to a private bathroom, the other is a closet.

The closet is only deep enough to hang a row of shirts and pants, but the left side extends another meter or so toward the bathroom. Boxes are stacked two-deep on the floor, under a set of shelves that holds hats emblazoned with sports team logos, rolled up posters and a stack of those foam "we're number one!" hands.

I know the node is here somewhere, so it must be on the shelves or behind the boxes. I grab the top box and heave it aside. Unfortunately, it weighs almost nothing and goes flying across the office. A jumble of cheap bobbleheads rains down all over the room, clattering on the furniture.

"Zark!" I scramble around the room, scooping up wiggly heads and bodies, some of them no longer attached to each other. I throw them into the box, and carefully set it just inside the closet. Behind the bottom box, which I move much more carefully, there's a pile of slippery, bright colored jerseys. I stick out a foot to scrape a few of the jerseys aside, and there's the node.

I shove the rest of shirts aside. As I duck under the shelves to sit next to the node, the door to the closet swings mostly shut behind me. It's dark in the closet, but my holo-ring provides enough light. I grab the direct connect cable and pull it from its self-retracting port in the node.

First things first: turn off my holo-ring ID. I've never done this before, but I've read several illegal blogs that detail the instructions. More importantly, I understand how the system works, so I know which of those instructions are accurate and which are red herrings posted by Ops security guys to catch people trying to do this. The actual process isn't difficult, but it's tedious and requires removing your ID from, well, I don't want to give you any ideas, so let's just say it's tedious.

It takes me a couple hours to remove all traces of my ID from the system. I've assigned myself a false ID number so anyone looking through the station rolls will still find my name but won't be able to locate my ring. Also, it will prevent the station admin system from assigning a new roommate to Kara, leaving me homeless. I also put in a relay, using this very node, and a couple others I've discovered since I started looking this week, to forward messages to my holo-ring. I want to be untraceable, not impossible to contact. Theoretically, this can't be done, but I do a lot of impossible things in the station OS. Finally, I open the access logs and delete the door override stamp that allowed me to enter this room, as well as the logs that tracked me through the offices, turning on the lights, so they won't know I've been here. I delete my virtual trail out to the concourse and up to Level 82, so it looks like I disappeared in Ty's office.

I've just made the final save when I hear a noise in the office outside the closet. Now that I'm not registering on the system, the lights have gone dark in the office. I reach an arm up and ease the closet door shut, trapping myself in the dark with the slippery jerseys and the illegal equipment. As quietly as I can, I scoot back into the corner of the closet, stacking the bobblehead boxes in front of me.

Under the door, a bar of light glows, making me squint. Someone has entered the office or moved close enough to trip the sensors. I unclip the direct connect cable and let it slide slowly through my fingers as it retracts into the box. The end pops back into the receptacle with a soft click. I freeze, pressing my ear to the wall, but hear nothing. I relax just a fraction. Maybe whoever it was didn't come all the way into this back room.

I sit in the dark, listening to my heartbeat as it slows to normal. Now that I'm not focused on my work, I realize how long I've been sitting here. My butt is numb, my legs are cramped and my head aches. I flex my shoulders and stretch my arms. There isn't room to stretch out my legs, so I try to ignore them. Rotating my head, I can hear popping and crackling in my neck. Pop, crack, BAM!

I freeze.

A loud but muffled voice rumbles through the wall, like someone on a voice-only holo-call. No one has ever figured out why voice-only calls prompt people to yell, but they do. I can't understand what he's saying, but he sounds put out. Probably got called into work on his day off. The voice also sounds familiar, in a vague, on-the-tip-of-your-tongue sort of way.

The closet door is flung open and a skinny arm reaches in to grab a couple hangers off the rack. I shrink back behind the boxes, praying he won't look down. The door remains open, light from the room seeming to spotlight me. All he has to do is glance over here, and he'll see me. I stay frozen behind my box and listen to the grunts of someone not really paying attention to a conversation.

"Yeah."

"Uh huh."

"Sure."

"What the—! Sorry, I wasn't talking to you. There's a stain on this shirt."

The hand reaches in again and grabs another hanger. I hold my breath. My heart is pounding so loud, I'm sure this guy could hear it if he wasn't on a call. Sweat breaks out all over my body.

"I'll grab a couple hats. There are stacks of them here in the closet. I hope we have the right team." My heart stops as he steps into the closet.

I freeze, waiting for the outburst of discovery. After what seems like hours, I look up.

The guy is standing, halfway into the closet, trying to wrestle a buttoned shirt over his head.

"What? He doesn't want them?" The headless guy bumbles out of the closet and my heart starts pounding again, like an entire track team on treadmills.

A couple wads of cloth come flying in the door, flopping gently onto my box. Finally, the door slams shut, trapping me again, but it feels like safety now. I suck in a deep breath and try to get my heart rate down to normal. After a while, the light under the door goes off. I sit in the dark, thankful I didn't wet myself.

Thirty minutes later, cold and shaky, I ease the door open just a crack. The office is dark and quiet. I slip through the narrow opening and shut the door behind me. The lights don't come on; with my holo-ring ID turned off, the OS doesn't know I'm in the room. I'm an always-prepared maintenance tech, though, so I have a flashlight. I turn it on.

A bobblehead, sans body, lays in the middle of the floor. I stare at it. How did I miss it when I cleaned up? And how did Shirt Guy miss it? Maybe he leaves bobbleheads around his office all the time? They did break pretty easily.

I scoop up the head and stash it in my pocket. As I straighten, I notice a picture frame on the floor near the desk. That must have been the crashing noise I heard when he entered the room. Curious, I carefully flip the picture over and my mind goes blank. Grinning up at me from the cracked glass is Errol Logan.

SEVENTEEN

I FLASH the light around the office, picking out personal items. Another picture sits on the desk: Errol with his arm around a girl on the beach. The girl looks uncomfortable—as if she was ambushed into getting her picture taken. On the wall behind the desk, hangs a certificate stating Errol Logan Hannity Wang Gutman e Vertol is a member of the Galactic Association of Athletic Representatives. A plaque on another wall shows Errol won the Rep of the Year award two years running.

How did I miss all this on the way in?

Panic floods through me and I bolt. I race through the offices, my flashlight beam swinging wildly over furniture and walls. I'm so rattled, I don't even check if the hallway is empty. I just dash out the door into E Ring and down the corridor. Miraculously, my luck holds; no one is in the area.

When I reach the concourse, I put my head down and stride to the float tubes, as if I'm on a mission. I don't want to draw attention to myself. Like always, no one seems to notice the station tech at all.

―――

I FIND MYSELF OUTSIDE SANCTUARY. Every station has one; it's a holo-room where religious ceremonies can be held. It's pretty busy on the weekends, but we're between the two scheduled Jewish Shabbat services. The access screen shows it's empty. Oddly, someone has set it to Cathedral, Gothic, which happens to be one of my favorites.

I push open the door; Sanctuary always has an old-fashioned door with hinges, which is a good thing since my holo-ring won't trigger any auto doors. As I enter the room, the holographic candle flames dance as if blown by the gust of air from the door. The ceiling appears to arch many meters overhead, and the digital walls radiate cold like real stone. I glide around the pews at the back and up the side aisle, stopping beside a small alcove between two confessionals.

Slumping down on the ground, I lean my head against the simulated stone, gazing up at the faux stained-glass windows. Sanctuary is one of my favorite places on the station, especially when I'm stressed or want to be alone. Although plenty of people attend services, very few come in the off hours. Plus, it has the added advantage of being a holo-free zone. Although the access screen outside shows how many people are inside, it doesn't track holo-rings and there are no records of who might come and go. Even the Station OS doesn't track Sanctuary visitors. I know; I've checked the files.

"Hey, God," I whisper. The Big Dude and I have an understanding, and I try to keep Him up to date on my life. "Things have gotten a little out of hand with this whole killer-trapping thing. I mean, I like you and all, but I'm not ready to come hang out permanently, ya know? Can you give a girl a hand?"

He doesn't answer, so I figure we're cool. Maybe if I just wait a while, He'll shove me in the right direction.

I close my eyes and try to let my mind clear. I'm not very Zen at the best of times, so this doesn't work. A whirlwind of thoughts and images surge through my brain like beer into a vacuum. (Kara and I tried that once — it's pretty cool when you vent it out the airlock, but a waste of good beer. Which is why we used the cheap stuff.)

Does Errol know Baker? Is he part of the cover-up team? Or is he the murderer? He was pretty peeved that Gonzeles and her partner continued on after we were disqualified. Maybe he's crazy enough to kill her in revenge? But who is funding Baker and her team? A sports rep doesn't make enough credits to pay for that level of support.

There's no guarantee Errol is just a sports rep, though. Maybe he's connected to someone more powerful. Most upper-levs prefer their life of leisure, but not all. Maybe he just loves sports and wants to work a real job.

Or maybe he isn't connected to this at all. Those bobblehead boxes were pretty dusty; they could have been there for months. I wonder how long Errol has been in that office. It's possible his predecessor had the node installed. Or someone broke in and installed it without anyone knowing. I just proved how easy it is to get in there.

Then why was Errol at the Multi-Grav? Was it just a coincidence that he and I both attended the same game? My brain spins.

I feel more than hear a staticky crackle, and my eyes pop open. The entire room shimmers and suddenly reconfigures itself. The cold stone wall I was leaning against becomes a slightly warmer plastered panel. The stained glass and statues fade into blank walls and the pews morph into modern chairs. At the front of the room, the crucifix fades out and a Star of David appears on the altar cloth. It's Saturday afternoon; time for Jewish services.

The door opens. Two women enter, whispering to each other. One stops short when she spots me. "Oh! The screen said it was empty!"

"Station Maintenance," I say, gesturing to my coverall. "We don't show up on the screen. Sorry about that. I'm finished here, so I'll get out of your way."

I scramble to my feet and stride toward the door, hoping the women won't notice I don't have any tools. They both narrow their eyes at me but continue to the front of the room. I hurry out the door.

I stand to one side of the doors, scanning the Level 40 concourse. Some people march purposefully across; others meander like they've got nowhere important to go. No obvious murderers staring at me with dagger eyes, so I drift around the edge of the open area and slip into Radial 4. There's a bot duct on B Ring that should be empty at this time of day. Obviously, our killer knows how to get into the ducts, since that's where bot 43H found the body, but I'm betting he doesn't hang out there.

As I tap the access panel beside the duct hatch, my holo-ring pings. O'Neill. I slip through the duct access door and wait until it slides shut before answering the call.

"Where the hell are you?!" He sounds almost panicked.

"I'm fine," I say, padding down the hallway to a cross duct. Around the corner, I lean back against the cool metal wall.

"I didn't ask *how* you are," he snarls. "*Where* are you? I tried to put a tracking loop on your holo-ring but there's no trace of you in the OS."

"I'm somewhere safe," I reply, sliding down the wall to sit on the hard floor. "If you can't find me, no one can, right?"

A grinding noise fills my ears. Probably his teeth. "Where. Are. You?" he asks very quietly, but each word sounds like a glass shard.

I take a deep breath. "I don't think broadcasting my location is a wise idea, do you?"

"Do you think someone is listening to this conversation?" he grits out.

"Not really, unless they've bugged your end." There's silence on the other end. Hadn't thought about that, had he?

"Look, just meet me somewhere. How about the place we first met? Don't say it."

I roll my eyes. "I wasn't going to say it. Now?"

"Yes, now."

EIGHTEEN

The Shuttle Dock, the bar on Level 4, is open but not too busy. I step out of the float tube and pause to look around the concourse. As usual, no one is paying any attention to me, so I skirt around the open floor toward the bar. About half-way there, an arm snaps out from behind a potted plant and yanks me back into the doorway of a closed shop.

"Hey! Oh, it's you." O'Neill shoves me behind him, into the corner of the doorway. He stands with his feet apart, facing outward, scanning the crowd.

"Aren't you going a little overboard?" I rub my arm.

He glances back at me. "Did I hurt you?" he asks, not sounding like he cares.

"No, I'm fine. Thanks for asking." Even to my own ears that sounds sulky. Better try again. I touch his arm. "Can we get something to eat? I never had lunch."

His head stops moving and then turns back over his shoulder to stare at me. "Do you ever think about anything besides food?"

"No."

He sighs and steps aside. "Come on." He nudges me in front of him toward the float tubes.

We get out on Level 27. O'Neill pushes me to the left and steps in front of me, scanning the crowded concourse. Apparently satisfied by what he did or didn't see, he steps aside. "Radial 10," he says. "Stay close to the wall."

Obediently, I walk along the wall, heading to the next cross corridor. O'Neill stays just behind me, to my right, his head constantly swiveling around to watch the crowd. He stops me at Radial 9, peering down the hallway before hustling me across it. "Don't you think we look a little suspicious?" I ask as I walk. "He isn't going to attack me in public."

"Probably not," he agrees as we turn down Radial 10. "But better safe than sorry. A Ring." It's early evening and there are plenty of people moving through the hallways. Some of them seem to know Ty; they nod and smile, but don't say anything.

We reach the end of Radial 10 and turn left into A Ring. We pass several doors marked with numbers, but no names. This is a residential area of the station. I glance over my shoulder at Ty. "Where are we going?"

He reaches around me and waves his holo-ring at the next door. "My place," he says. The door slides open onto a small living room and I catch my breath. The outer wall of the compartment is full-length windows. We're currently on the night side of the station; the glow from the sun lights up the right edge of the window. Before me, a huge blanket of stars spreads out to infinity. The view from the outer Ring always amazes me.

"Nice view," I breathe, staring at the stars. He laughs, and I tear my eyes away from the view.

"It's why I live here," he says. "So no one notices the cheap furniture."

I glance around the compartment. This room alone is twice the size of mine and Kara's but still tiny considering how much credit he makes. Of course, the outer Ring is three times as much rent as the inner Rings. And yes, I know how much he makes; I hacked his bank statements last week when I was poking through the OS. I told you we have a lot of free time in the MCC.

He has a couple comfortable looking chairs and a huge couch facing the windows. A table and four chairs that probably aren't real wood, but an expensive simulation, sit in the corner. Against the right wall, a sink and fridge flank a small panel boasting a subdued AutoKich'n logo. Two doors on the left likely lead to a bedroom and bath; standard mid-sized compartment layout. The decor is typical modern male, not fancy, but way nicer than mine.

I sink down into the corner of the Lether couch and wrap my arms around a tailored throw pillow. I feel strangely safe here. I don't know if it's because of Ty, or the view, or just the unfamiliarity of the space makes me feel like I'm in another world. Whatever the reason, my shoulders relax for the first time all day. I gaze out at the stars and let my mind drift.

"Errol Logan," I blurt out, jerking upright. Told you I'm not very good at the Zen thing.

Ty, over by the AutoKich'n, glances over his shoulder. "Your Multi-Grav Romeo?"

"What? Partner, you mean. He was only interested in my low-grav skills."

Ty rolls his eyes. "He was slobbering all over you. I hate to be the one to tell you this, but your low-grav skills weren't that impressive."

"We beat the pros!" I protest, stung.

"Did you see what happened to the pros?" Ty carries a couple glasses over and hands me one. I take a sip; it's a little bubbly, a little sweet and a lot alcoholic. "Johnson sprained an ankle in that wall-bounce stage, so they were moving slowly, for them. Wei has a bad shoulder that was acting up; that's why they were so slow in stage 3. You and Logan were lucky. And you were only in first place in stage 3. I'm afraid you were at the back of the pack for the first two stages."

I shake my head. "Whatever. He still wanted me to train with him."

Ty smiles. "If by 'train' you mean sleep with you. I don't think your athletic skills had anything to do with it. I said before you're attractive."

"In a lower-lev way!" I do air quotes.

"I meant that as a compliment!" Ty protests. "I told you I don't like upper-lev women. They're too artificially perfect."

"And I'm naturally imperfect." I glare at him.

"Exactly. Naturally attractive. Perfect is boring."

I narrow my eyes even more. What's his angle? He's probably just trying to flatter me, so I'll keep helping him. What is it with men and—oh! "The node on 53 is in Errol's office!"

"What?" O'Neill looks at me like I'm crazy.

I take a sip of my drink, mostly so I can avoid his eyes. Although it is tasty. "I used the node to remove my holo-ring from the OS. I thought it was in a storage room, but it's in the closet in Errol's office. What if he's our murderer?!"

"We interviewed him along with the rest of the athletes," he says slowly. "But we were mostly looking for witnesses at that point. We didn't have any reason to suspect him more than anyone else." Putting his drink down, he gets up and strides across the room, head down, his dark hair falling over his forehead.

I watch him as he paces, my mind strangely blank. It's as if I've turned the problem over to him, and now I don't need to worry about it anymore. What the hell has happened to me? I don't need a guy to take care of my problems! I give myself a shake.

"Don't you have enough evidence to question him again?" I ask.

Ty grins, more teeth-baring than smiling. "You watch too many *Ancient TēVē* shows," he says. "This station is corporate property. We can bring in and question anyone we want. But you're right, we do try to have some evidence. And yes, we have enough. The only problem is, I don't want to admit how we got that evidence. I don't want him to know you were in his closet."

"We-ell." I draw the word out as my mouth speeds ahead of my brain. "How about this? You could just say some routine maintenance required access to the closet, and the technician reported the node."

He shakes his head. "We don't want to admit to knowing about the node at all. As long as they don't know we know, they'll keep using it. And we can keep tracking its use. We'll just bring him in for routine follow-up questions."

I didn't realize he was tracking it, although I should have guessed. I've been using it for semi-legal stuff all week. "I guess I'd better log my own activity," I say with a sheepish shrug. "I don't want you thinking I'm part of the killer's cabal."

He rolls his eyes. "Please. You're so transparent. I don't think you could keep a secret of that caliber." He steps back over to the AutoKich'n and punches in a couple codes. "How's pasta sound?"

I stare at his back. He has no idea what caliber of secrets I can keep. A twinge of guilt spikes through me, but I quash it down. My secrets have nothing to do with this case, and he has no need to know them. I smile. "Pasta sounds great."

NINETEEN

AFTER DINNER, we head down to Level 1. Holding cells are located at the bottom of the station. I guess it's to keep any criminal elements as far as possible from the top-levs, although if anyone managed to escape they could use the float tubes like anyone else. Most of the time, the cells hold people for minor infractions: public intoxication, petty theft, etc. Real criminals are shuttled dirtside as quickly as possible to protect the station and personnel.

I've never been in the holding cells. They're located in the center of the station, where the concourse would be on any other Level. Here, the float tubes dump you out into a loud, narrow room. Hallways lead to maintenance areas that I've visited via bot camera many times, and a single thick portal labeled HOLDING. Access requires a specially coded holo-ring and a password issued by Security. O'Neill logs us through.

"Won't someone notice you didn't show up on the log?" he asks with a frown.

I shrug. "If someone audits the logs, and compares to the vids, they'll see that I didn't register. But I'm not worried. Unless there's a mass break out, no one is going to audit. They trust the system to work properly at all times. Otherwise, Baker and company would have been caught a long time ago."

He gives me a funny look. "How do you know that?"

I shrug again. "I worked in Auditing for a couple months."

He nods. "Right, I saw that on your records. Is there anywhere on station you haven't worked?"

"Pleasure Center," I reply promptly. Bringing up the Pleasure Center is a great conversation stopper. While officially there is no social stigma attached to working in or frequenting the Pleasure Center, unofficially it's a taboo subject. Let's face it, if you're going to have a virtual fantasy fulfilled, you really don't want to know who's programming it. Or who else might be there. It ruins the fantasy. So, when people hear those words, they change the subject. Always works.

"Why not?" He grins. OK, it usually works.

"I don't like to make people happy," I growl. "Are we there yet?"

O'Neill ushers me into a small oval room. The door at the narrow end of the oval is set into the only solid-looking wall. The rest of the room is lined with a standing height desk topped by one-way glass walls that look on a series of cells. The cells look surprisingly old-fashioned: dark, blank walls; hard, narrow bunks; utilitarian toilet and sink; bars on the far side with a heavily locked door in the center.

"What, no force fields?" I ask.

O'Neill rolls his eyes. "Bars are cheaper."

On the far end of the oval, the glass wall reveals a room with white walls and a couple chairs grouped around a metal table. There are no bars, just a closed door across from us. Sitting at the table, fingers drumming nervously, is Errol.

O'Neill draws up a couple tall stools and we sit at the desk facing the interrogation room. O'Neill speaks into his holo-ring, and after a short wait, the door opens.

"Errol Logan Hannity Wang Gutman e Vertol?" A tall, athletic woman with flowing blond hair strides into the room. Errol's head pops up, and his eyes widen a fraction. The woman's clothing is a standard Sec Agent uniform, but it's tight across the butt and the top three buttons gape open over her spectacular cleavage. Errol straightens up in his chair and smiles, revealing his braces. "I'm Agent Leeza Masterson Ugamba James. I'm sorry we had to bring you in on a weekend, but we have a few more questions."

"Of course, Agent Masterson," Errol gushes, his eyes drifting downward. "I'm happy to help."

She sits down at the table and launches a holo-file. After paging through a couple files too small for me to read, she fires off a series of questions about Errol's origin, job, and hobbies. Where he was Thursday night and every night before or since. Errol works all day, every day, and spends every evening at the

Multi-Grav gym. My eyes glaze over. How can Masterson stand such a boring conversation? And why? I could design an AI program that would ask all the right questions, monitor vital signs and facial changes during answers, and basically outsource this woman's job to a computer.

I'm in the middle of writing the seventh loop when Masterson produces a holo-pic.

"Do you know this woman?"

Errol's eyes widen and his mouth drops open. The holo shows Baker, before she drugged herself into a coma, of course.

"That's Agent Baker," Errol replies. He looks at Masterson, eyebrows creased. "I thought she was here undercover."

Masterson's eyes flicker. She wasn't expecting that answer. Neither were we. I exchange a glance with O'Neill.

Recovering quickly, Masterson says, "She is. I am her on-station contact. I take it she didn't tell you about me?"

Errol's head slowly shakes side to side. "She said she was working solo here."

Masterson smiles gently. "Standard protocol. Agent contacts are on a need-to-know basis. You didn't need to know. But, now you do. Agent Baker has run into a little, er, snag, and we need your help.

"But first, I need to confirm that you are, in fact, the person I need. Can you tell me the password Agent Baker gave you?"

A puzzled frown settles on Errol's pasty face. "Password? She didn't give me a password."

Masterson looks disappointed. "I guess you aren't the contact I needed after all." She flicks the holo closed and stands up.

"Wait!" Errol cries, looking like an anxious puppy. "I can help you! I'm sure I can. I've been undercover, too."

Masterson looks dubious but settles back into the chair. "I'm listening."

"Baker contacted me six months ago." Errol's wheezy voice squeaks a bit when he's excited. "She's head of a protection team for a top-lev who has received death threats. Board Security isn't up to the task, so she was sent in to provide covert protection."

Beside me, O'Neill twitches in irritation, his jaw clenching shut. I snicker. He glares at me for a second, then shakes his head with a rueful smile. Meanwhile, Masterson is nodding as if this is all old news to her.

"Baker asked me to house a node that would allow her to contact her dirtside

HQ without going through the system OS. Of course, I said yes! Anything to help the Board." His thin chest puffs up. "After I proved my loyalty, she asked me to shadow a possible suspect." He pauses importantly.

"And who was that?" Masterson asks, glancing up from her holo-notes.

"Triana Moore," he says.

TWENTY

Beside me, O'Neill bursts out laughing.

I ignore him. He keeps laughing, so I elbow him in the ribs. Hard.

"Hey!" He grabs the edge of the desk to keep from falling off his stool. "Assaulting a Sec Agent is a crime! There's a camera right there." He points at a panel above the door. While he's looking at the camera, I shove him off his stool.

"Shut up, I'm trying to hear this." I turn back toward the glass.

Spit flies out of Errol's mouth, he's so excited by his story. "So, I got Dmitri, the guy who runs the Multi-Grav center, to chat up Moore's roommate. He thinks I'm going to get him a sports contract." Errol laughs, a superior look on his face. He leans in closer to Masterson and whispers, "He's not that good."

Masterson nods, looking bored. Errol doesn't even blink. "He convinced her to bring Moore to the Thursday night qualifiers so I could work my magic." His eyebrows do some kind of spastic dance, which he obviously thinks is sexy, and O'Neill almost falls off his stool again.

"She was so into me! If I'd just had a little more time, she would have spilled all her secrets. Then that fraking Board Sec agent showed up! Baker was right; they're useless!"

O'Neill has his head down on his arms and his shoulders are shaking with muffled laughter. I blow out an exasperated huff. "He's right. You're useless."

"Did you notice anything suspicious about Moore?" Masterson asks.

Wait a minute! Whose side is she on? But Errol is clearly warming up to her, so maybe this is a good tactic. All part of her interrogation skill set.

"She picked up the low-grav stuff awfully fast," he says. "I think she's got experience in zero-G maneuvers. Probably military training. I can spot a professionally trained athlete." He puffs out his skinny chest to emphasize his point. O'Neill looks up just in time to catch it and covers his face again. My lips twitch.

"Anything else?" Masterson asks. She stifles a yawn, which even Errol can't miss. Disappointment crosses his face; he scrabbles for something to regain her interest.

"That Board Sec Agent!" he almost shouts. "Why's he dating a bot jockey? They must be working together to off one of the Board members!"

Ty wipes the tears off his face and shakes his head. "He's obviously just a pawn in this. She's not going to get any more real info out of him." He gestures toward the door. "We've got better things to do."

I slide off my stool and follow him across the room. Halfway there, a movement catches my eye; one of the cells has an occupant. Curious, I turn to look and stop cold. I've seen that face before. "Who is that?"

Ty glances at the guy. "That's Litovsky. Don't you recognize him?"

"Yes. No." I shake my head. "I never saw Litovsky, remember? He had his helmet blanked every time I was near him. But I've seen this guy. He was in the Shuttle Dock bar the night we met."

"What? Are you sure?" Ty flicks his holo-ring to life.

"Yeah, I'm sure. He was sitting right next to me. He almost choked on his drink when Kara, uh, smiled at him." I stare through the glass, thinking back to that night. He must have heard every word. Did we say anything important?

"Stay here." Ty pushes me back toward the stools and disappears out the door. I sink down onto the closest one. What the heck is going on?

A moment later, Litovsky's cell door opens and Ty strides in. Litovsky starts to get to his feet, moving slowly. He's a middle-aged guy, with the beginning of a bald spot in the back and wrinkles around his eyes. O'Neill waves him back down and sits on the opposite end of his bunk. I can't hear the conversation—we were getting audio through Ty's holo-ring before. I close my eyes, suddenly exhausted.

It feels like days since I've slept. Ty, Errol, Dame Morgan, Agent Masterson. They swirl through my brain. Do I need to worry about my safety? If I'm off the grid, I should be safe, right? But this guy, Litovsky, clearly knows about me. And if he knows about me, he knows where I live. Maybe Kara and I should clear out of our compartment until this guy is caught. I'm sure Kara can find somewhere else to sleep; she hasn't spent the night in our place in a couple days as it is. She's probably staying over at Dmitri's place.

My eyes snap open. Zark! Dmitri is part of this deal. I need to talk to Kara.

I surge to my feet just as the door swooshes open. O'Neill and I both start talking at the same time.

"I need to talk to Kara—"

"You were right, Lit—"

I fling up a hand, cutting him off. "I don't care about Litovsky. Kara is probably with Dmitri right now, and you heard what Errol said. He's part of this!"

"Calm down." O'Neill puts his hands on my shoulders. They're warm and strong and my heart rate jacks up a little at his touch. He lets go of one shoulder and slides his arm around me, guiding me to the door. I try to focus on what he's saying.

"I've run a background on Dmitri," O'Neill continues as we pace down the corridor toward the entry portal. "He's been on-station for ten years, has a solid work history. Before that, he was at the Junior Olympic training facility on Armstrong."

I give him a stony glare. "Work histories can be faked."

"That's why we're going to my office tomorrow so you can do your magic and make sure he's for real. But tonight," he holds up a finger as I open my mouth to interrupt, "we're going back to your compartment to talk to Kara."

I relax a fraction as O'Neill logs us out of the holding facility. "You know, she probably won't be there," I say as we step into the float tube. "It's Saturday night."

As we float up, O'Neill tells me about his conversation with Litovsky. "Chen screwed up when he dosed you with the Captio. Baker wasn't sure you'd really forget everything, so she assigned Litovsky to tail you for a while. After I came into the picture, she put Errol onto you, too. I still don't know if Dmitri is really in on this, or just a pawn recruited by Errol."

When we arrive on Level 3, O'Neill does his bodyguard routine, but this time it doesn't seem as amusing. Now that I know they've been watching me, I'm peeking behind every potted plant myself. The Level 3 concourse is mostly empty. This is working-class housing, and on Saturday night people are partying somewhere else or at home getting ready to party somewhere. We reach my compartment on C Ring, and the door stubbornly refuses to budge.

I slap my forehead. "I can't get in! My holo-ring isn't registering as an occupant."

Ty chokes back a laugh and waves his own ring at the door. The panel recognizes him as a guest and sends a message to the occupant—if there is one. We wait, then the door slides open.

Kara, sitting on the sofa, flicks her holo-ring to sleep. Her eyes are red, and she sounds stuffy. "Triana isn't here," she says by way of greeting, then notices me hovering behind Ty. "Or maybe she is. Why didn't you just come in?"

We step inside and the door shuts behind us. With three of us here, the place feels almost as claustrophobic as the MCC full of agents. Compared to Ty's place, it's really a tiny compartment; more of a sleeping room than a home. Even though the beds are folded away, the space is almost completely filled with our small sofa and two chairs. Even so, it's safe. Comfortable. Mine.

"Have you seen Dmitri today?" I ask, dropping down next to her on the couch. This is probably a stupid question; I think she spent the night at his place.

Tears fill Kara's eyes and spill down her smooth, caramel cheeks. Even when she's crying, Kara looks fabulous. "He dumped me!" she wails, flinging herself into my arms.

Ty gives me a panicked look and jerks his head at the door. Apparently, crying women are not his forte, either. I give him a little nod and he leaves. This conversation will go better without him.

The post-breakup flood is my least favorite phase of Kara's dating pattern. She finds a guy, goes out with him for a couple days, or sometimes as long as a month. While they're dating, she's always totally in love. She gushes about him constantly, sings and dances around, buys him gifts, spends all her free time with him. Then they break up. It doesn't matter who does the dumping, Kara seems to feel obligated to indulge in a crying jag afterward. I sometimes have the sneaking suspicion that she saves the tears for an audience, that is, me.

I push back my irritation. Kara is my best friend, and if she's a little dramatic sometimes, that's just part of the package. Fortunately, like the dating, the crying doesn't often last long. And her eyes were red when we came in; obviously, she was crying before, says the little voice in my head.

"He's a fraud anyway," I say, rubbing her back.

She pulls back a little. "What do you mean?" She sniffs adorably, rubbing her eyes like a little girl. Her professional grade makeup doesn't smear a bit.

I launch into an explanation of the last two weeks, starting with the dead body.

"Son of a bitch!" she hollers when I get to Dmitri's part in the story.

"Exactly," I reply.

Leaping to her feet, she announces, "I will cut off his balls and fry them up for breakfast!"

"You might be overreacting just a tad," I say.

Kara begins striding around the room like a general planning a very small battle. Three steps, turn at the door. Three more steps, turn at the couch. You get the picture.

"He will rue the day he spied on Kara Ortega Okilo! I will hunt him down and—"

"Yes, I know, balls, frying, breakfast. Look, Kara, you can't sauté any testicles right now. We don't want him to know that we know." I grab her arm as she makes another swing past the couch. She deflates suddenly and drops back down beside me.

"But he was so cute!" Her eyes start filling again.

"Stop!" I grab both her shoulders and shake her gently. "Focus, please. There is a murderer loose on the station, and he may think you and I are a threat. We need to move out of the compartment for a few days, to somewhere safer."

Kara takes a deep breath. "You're right. We need to focus on ourselves. He's not worth my time." She squares her shoulders. "We can stay with Stacia."

Stacia is another aesthetician from her salon. She's a nice girl, but she *never* stops talking. She also has a husband who thinks he's a guitar virtuoso and two small children in a two-bedroom compartment. "You can stay with her, I'll find somewhere else. It will be too crowded at Stacia's."

She gives me a sly look from under her lashes. "Maybe you can stay with Ty."

I give her the stink eye. "Our relationship is purely business, I told you that."

"That's not the impression I got," she replies. "He is clearly into you. I think this whole investigation thing is just a ploy to keep you close."

"Right. He staged a couple murders because he knew I'd refuse to date him if he just asked." I get up from the couch. "Wherever we stay, we need to pack some stuff." I open the closet door and grab a messenger bag from the top shelf.

"Is Ty waiting outside? I'm going to let him back in," Kara says, stepping over to the door. "But I will wait until you pack your underwear because if he sees your nasty granny panties he will run away, and you'll never see him again. I could loan you some lingerie."

"Ew! I'm not wearing a used thong!" I wad up a pair of my maligned undies and throw it at her just as the door slides open. "No!" I yell, but it's too late.

Kara ducks, and Ty reaches out a hand to catch them before they hit him in the face. His lips twitch as he shakes them out and holds them up. "Panty fight!" he says with a grin. "My kind of party!"

Hot blood surges up my face. I step into the closet and pull the door shut. "I'll just stay in here until you catch the murderer."

TWENTY-ONE

BEFORE WE LEAVE THE COMPARTMENT, Kara insists I shower and change out of my uniform. She shoos O'Neill back out and picks out a flowy, flowery tank top and leggings. She shoves me and the clothes into the bathroom. When I emerge, she pushes me down in a chair to do my hair. Normally I just run a comb through it and go.

"What are you dressing me up for?" I ask as she yanks another device through my brown mop.

"Whether you choose to believe it or not," she says, "that man is very interested in you. So, take a few minutes and make yourself look nice."

"We're working together, not going on a date," I grump. "Besides, I'm not staying with him; I have other places I can go to hide."

"Right. Where?"

I glare back at her. She grabs my head and turns it back around so she can continue working. I smell hot metal and flowery stuff. "I know this whole station. I have some places picked out."

"You rather bunk down in a cleaning duct than spend a night with an attractive man?" she asks. "You are crazy and stubborn."

"He hasn't offered me a place to stay, anyway."

"He will." She drops the comb and points to the mirror on the closet door. "I've always said you could look fantastic with just a little work."

I look in the mirror. She's right. Whatever she's done to my hair made it look smooth and full instead of wispy and tangled. She's applied a little makeup, too, that makes my eyes sparkle and gives my cheeks a little flush. She hands me a delicate, flowered chain that looks perfect with the floral top. Maybe I should let her dress me up more often. The transformation is astounding.

Behind me, the door swishes open and I turn. O'Neill steps across the threshold and stops with a grunt of surprise. "Wow," is all he says, but he looks stunned. I grin.

O'Neill and I walk Kara up to Stacia's compartment in Slice 7. Stacia invites me to stay, but the child screaming from behind one bedroom door and the guitar moaning from behind the other convince me I've made the right decision. O'Neill and I head back to the concourse in beautiful silence.

Before we step into the bounce tubes, he turns to me. "You're coming back to 27 with me." This doesn't sound like a question.

"To your place?" I ask, my voice squeaking a bit. "You only have one bedroom."

"We can share," he whispers, his deep voice sending a shiver up my spine.

I take a shaky breath. "I can find somewhere else to stay. Since I'm off the grid I can pretty much stay anywhere."

"You're staying where I can keep an eye on you," he says in a firm voice.

When we reach his apartment, he directs me to the bedroom door. "You can stay in here. I just changed the sheets this morning. I'll sleep on the couch. It's actually pretty comfortable."

"I – thank you," I reply. I put my bag down on the bed and look around. The huge bed takes up most of the room, covered in a soft, deep blue blanket. A small bedside table stands on either side of the bed, and the wall to my right is a series of cabinets and drawers. The outside wall shows the same amazing view as the living room.

"Sunrise comes at 2 am on this side of the station. You can opaque the window with this." Ty steps past me and picks up a slim card from the bedside table. He presses one edge and the stars dim until the window is black. "The lights are here at the bottom." He presses the card again and the lights fade out. Then he brings the stars back.

Standing there in the dark, staring out at the stars, I can *feel* him beside me, even though he's a meter away. His breath is slow and even, but heat radiates from his body. My heart stumbles into a gallop and my lungs tighten. A tingly warmth floods through my chest and down into my stomach. Then his fingers skim my upper arm and I gasp.

He steps closer, behind me, and slowly slides his hand around my waist. I take another shaky breath. Slowly, slowly, his head lowers. His warm breath brushes through my hair, on my cheek, against my neck. Blood pounds in my ears. I sway back against him and gasp again when his lips touch my neck.

His lips leave a trail of fire against my flesh from my neck to my ear. I arch back against him and close my eyes. One hand strokes lightly up and down my side while the other rests flat against my stomach. The heat of his fingers presses through my shirt and a matching heat builds inside me. When the edge of his hand grazes my breast, I moan.

His hand clenches against my belly then starts tracing patterns, his fingers hot and light against the silky fabric. They slide a little lower and a sharp vibration against my belly button makes me jump. He freezes for a second, then starts his magic again. His holo-ring buzzes again.

With a groan, he pulls back a little and looks down at his hand. "I have to take this," he whispers. His voice is rough and he's breathing fast. He bites gently on my earlobe and steps away. "I'll be back."

As he steps through the door, the lights come up in the living room. There's enough light for me to find the remote. I drop down on the edge of the bed and turn up the lights until I can see myself in the mirror hanging near the door. My hair still looks fabulous, and my makeup is perfect. Kara is a genius at her job. Apparently, she's made me irresistible.

What was that? OK, I know what it was, and it felt amazing, but now I'm hot, hollow, frustrated. And confused. Ty has flirted with me since we met, but he was just joking around. This sudden intense physical connection has totally thrown me. I can't even seem to come up with a coherent, well, anything. The only thing I can think is I want him to come back and pick up where he left off.

But do I? I don't engage in flash romances like Kara. In fact, watching Kara go through guy after guy kind of makes me nauseous. I'm the kind of girl who likes to have a good solid relationship before moving to the physical stuff. Usually, I'm friends with a guy for months before we even have a date. This sudden heat is way outside my comfort zone and my experience. And as much as I want him to come back, part of me is afraid of what I'll do if he does.

I'm also a tiny bit curious. Who was so important that he would interrupt, well, that? Or is this just a way of passing time for him? Maybe when he's bored he makes out with the closest girl he can find? And then drops her when something more interesting comes along? I can't answer most of these questions, but there is one I can answer.

I get up and creep over to the door. I listen for a minute, but just hear Ty making those "I agree" noises we all use with people who talk too fast or too much. I ease my head into the living room.

Ty is sitting on the couch, with a pillow in his lap. My lips twitch. I guess he was getting hot and bothered, too. He's looking up at the window, the upper half of which has transformed into a vid screen. A woman with curly black hair and chocolate brown eyes gazes down at him. She has wrinkles around her eyes and a little grey in her hair. I guess she hasn't followed the usual schedule of aesthetic corrections. Although I can't hear her, she's clearly excited about something and her hands are flying around as she talks.

Then she smiles. This woman has Ty's smile. I look from her to Ty and back. Same facial structure, too. He confirms my guess when he says, "That's great, Mom." I duck back into the bedroom, hoping she didn't see me.

Now I don't know what to think. What kind of guy interrupts a make-out session to talk to his mother? I also don't know what to do. I can't go out there, and I can't just sit in here. Although suddenly, I'm exhausted. I move my bag to the floor, pull off my sandals and lay down on the bed. I'll just close my eyes for a few minutes while I wait for Ty to come back. Then we'll need to talk.

TWENTY-TWO

I STRETCH, the sheets silky smooth against my arms. This bed is so warm and comfortable, I don't want to get up. The pillow is cool and the perfect firmness, too. I roll over and my leg collides with something. Someone? I freeze, and my eyes fly open.

Propped up on one elbow, Ty smiles at me. His shoulders are bare, his chin has a dark shadow, and even in the dim light, the blue blanket makes his eyes look like bottomless pools. He looks so sexy my heart starts racing. I realize my leg is draped over one of his and I quickly yank it free. Dragging my eyes away from him, I glance down at myself. I'm still wearing my flowered tank top. I relax a fraction.

"Good morning," he says, his voice deep and rough. "How did you sleep?"

I gulp. "Fine. Great, I don't, I mean, I uh, must look terrible."

"I think you look great. All sleepy and mussed. Very sexy."

I blink. "Sexy? I think you need eye surgery. Look, I don't know what happened last night. The last thing I remember was lying down to wait for you to finish your call." Going for a less intimate position, I scoot back and sit up against the headboard. I suddenly remember what we were doing before the call, and I flush.

He sits up too. The blanket slides down and reveals a well-defined, muscular chest with just a sprinkling of dark hair, strong biceps, and hard abs. I suck in air. I knew he was fit, but he doesn't look this, um, chiseled in his daytime clothes. I gulp again and try to tear my eyes away from his stomach.

"Hey, my eyes are up here," he says with a laugh. "But you can admire if you want." He strikes a ridiculous pose.

I smile—a tight, nervous smile. He gives me a long stare, then reaches over to the bedside table and snags a collared shirt. As he pulls it on over his head, I get one last look at those glorious muscles. He pulls the shirt down then shakes his head, and his sexy bed head settles into its usual casual style. Shiny.

Ty climbs out of bed. He's wearing grey plaid boxers, which he promptly covers with a pair of jeans. "When I finished my call, you were asleep. I tucked you under the covers and went to sleep. Out there." He points out the door. "I prefer a woman be awake when I crawl into bed with her."

"I wasn't awake when you got here," I say, gesturing to his pillow.

He shrugs. "You were mostly awake. When I saw you waking up, I climbed in just to tease you." He smiles, a warm sexy smile and stops buttoning his jeans. "Now that you're awake, I could crawl back in, if you like."

"I, no, no, I'm getting up," I say, shooting out of bed as if launched. I grab my bag and scramble to the door. "I'm going to use the bathroom," I say, not looking at him. Instead, I look in the mirror and am surprised that my hair and makeup both survived the night with very little damage. I will never doubt Kara's expertise—and professional grade products—again.

When I return from the bathroom, where I've scrubbed off the makeup, the bedroom is empty. I'm wearing a fitted, blue blouse and a straight black skirt. My hair, after a quick comb, still looks fabulous. I definitely need to learn how Kara did that. I fiddle with my things a bit but finally venture into the living room.

Ty is getting coffee from the AutoKich'n. A blanket and sheet lay, neatly folded, over the back of the couch. The station has rotated us to the sunward side, but the auto filters in the windows block the harmful radiation and the too-bright light. Ty hands me a coffee and gestures toward the table.

"You look great," he says. "I have nothing against makeup, but I think I like you better this way. Seems more natural for you."

"It *is* natural." That came out kind of harsh, so I soften my tone. "But thanks."

"That outfit is nice, too." He smiles.

I growl. "Kara repacked my bag while I was showering. It's full of frilly girl clothes and lacy lingerie."

Ty's lips twitch. "I hope those are for my benefit. Can't wait to see them." He takes a sip of his coffee, and a faint wash of pink crosses his cheeks. Is O'Neill blushing? "About last night. I hope you didn't think I was trying to, I don't know, extract payment for giving you a place to stay. I didn't plan that. Although I've been wanting to do it for a while now." He grins, kind of sheepishly.

I wonder if he knows what effect that smile has on me. Probably. A wave of heat creeps up my cheeks. "I didn't think that," I mutter into my coffee. "I wasn't really thinking at all. I don't usually let my hormones run the show. Look, I like you, really. But I don't bunk hop. I know a lot of people treat sex like any other two-person sport—find a willing partner and play! But as far as I'm concerned, it's special and not something I'll just jump into. I know you're probably surprised to hear that, considering what you know about Kara, but there it is." That's my story, and I'm sticking to it.

He smiles, a blinding flash of teeth and eyes. "Don't worry," he says in low bedroom drawl. "I won't rush you. We can work our way up to it and have a lot of fun along the way."

My face gets hotter, but I give him a tight smile. I've spent enough time with him to know he's very good at telling people what they want to hear. He probably even believes it. But I also know how this works. We'll finish the job, and he'll be back to his upper-levs, and I'll be back in the MCC and Level 4 bars, hoping to meet someone half as shiny as Ty. I'm generally content with my life, but for the first time in years, I wish my social standing was different.

Ty jumps up and slides his finger gently along my jaw as he heads back to the AutoKich'n. "Eggs, pancakes, and bacon, right? I can't get blintzes and Cynn'mon Rolls, but I can get the rest."

"I'll stick with coffee," I say. "I'm not really hungry."

He comes back to the table with a plate and sets it down. Frowning, he presses a hand to my forehead and lifts my wrist to check my pulse. I bat him away. "Very funny."

"Seriously, the only time I've seen you refuse food was when you were poisoned. Are you sure you're ok?"

"Yeah, I'm fine. I'm watching my diet today. Gotta keep my girlish figure."

He stares at me for a minute, then shrugs and digs into his breakfast. "What shall we do today? You are my only priority."

"I'm going to church," I say. "You can join me if you want."

"Really?" He looks startled. "Why?"

"Well, one, because it's what I do on Sunday mornings, and two because it seems like a good plan to seek divine intervention when you've got a homicidal maniac after you." I sip my coffee, pretending his response means nothing. That I don't care what he thinks about me.

"That sounds reasonable," he replies with a nod. "I haven't been in a while; do you think you can put in a good word for me?"

I relax, hiding my relief. "Sure. The Big Guy and I are like that." I cross my fingers and hold them up.

Ty laughs and cleans his plate.

After church, I'm starved. "Of course, you are," says Ty. "Let's go to Belle76."

"Wow, you really frequent the haunts of the rich and famous, don't you?" As we step into the float tube, I enjoy the feeling of his warm hand on the small of my back. At Level 76 he urges me out and then slides his arm around my waist. It's a casual gesture—as if we've been dating for years.

"I've never been there before," he says. "But my coworkers tell me I'm not taking advantage of all the perks of this job if I don't use my position to get into snobbish, overrated restaurants once in a while."

Belle76 is in the A Ring, of course. The entrance, at the end of Radial 1, is a standard grey door with the word Belle engraved in the metal. Ty waves his holo-ring at the door, and it slides open.

Inside, we find a small room, tastefully decorated with a couple brocade sofas and a small desk. One sofa is currently occupied by an upper-lev couple who are so busy making out they don't even pause as we walk by. The other holds a scandalized looking man and woman whose clothing identifies them as wealthy, dirt-side tourists. Seated behind the desk is a woman dressed in top-lev business attire, with her zebra striped hair smoothed back into a perfect French roll. She looks up at Ty with just the hint of a professional smile.

"Welcome, Ser O'Neill y Mendoza bin Tariq e Reynolds." She reels it off as if Ty comes here every week. "We are honored that you are joining us. Will there be any more in your party today?"

Ty blinks then smiles. "No, just the two of us."

"Of course, Ser, right this way." She stands and gestures toward a blank wall beside her desk. A section of the wall dissolves to form a doorway. The dirt-siders gasp. As we step through the door, I hear the man demanding to know why they must wait when we did not. The door re-materializes behind us, and his voice is cut off.

"Phase shifter," I say with an impressed nod. "I didn't realize that technology was commercially available."

"I don't think it technically is," Ty says. "It's also not very cost-effective, I'm sure. But impressive." He presses his hand against my back again to urge me forward. The contact makes my spine tingle.

The short corridor is wide enough for us to walk side by side and painted a pale grey above an old-fashioned chair-rail, with silver and black vertical striped wallpaper below. At the end, it opens out into a huge room filled with white linen-draped tables surrounded by men and women in designer clothing. Beyond them, a wall of glass reveals the same stunning view as Ty's apartment. The chink of silver against china and low conversations drifts down the hall along with an amazing scent.

"What is that smell?" I ask. "Never mind, whatever it is, that's what I'm having."

We reach the end of the hall, and a man appears. His suit looks like it was taken from a vid about 19th century Earth, except it's done in multiple shades of red. Pale green hair is combed back from his face and flows down to his shoulders in rolling waves. He bows. "Welcome, Ser O'Neill y Mendoza bin Tariq e Reynolds, to Belle76. Please, follow me."

"I thought you said you've never been here before," I whisper to Ty. "They all know your name! The whole thing!"

"I haven't," he whispers back. "I'm sure they got it from my ID."

I shake my head. "They're really good at memorizing names, then. I still can't remember it all."

The green haired host seats us at a table next to the window, carefully sliding the chair in under my rear end. He whips my napkin off the table, flicks it open like a magician producing a dove, and drapes it across my lap. Then he turns and does the same for O'Neill. He flicks his fingers and a couple of clones appear, one with pink hair and a green suit, and another with yellow hair and a blue suit. They remove some dishes and cutlery from the table and add more, then all three disappear.

"How do they decide what to take and what to bring?" I ask. "They don't even know what we're going to order."

"I don't think we order anything," Ty says. "I'm pretty sure this is a set menu."

"Well then, that made even less sense." I've seen vids where the characters eat in a fancy restaurant and the waiters remove chargers, but this was just random stuff. "Why do you need two more forks than me?"

"Gotta do something to impress the jaded elite." Ty laughs and jerks his head. "Watch how they react."

The dirt-siders from the lobby are being seated near the inner wall. The woman takes her seat and yelps when the chair catches her in the back of the knees. The man, however, grabs the host by the shoulder. I can't hear what he's saying, but his arms are waving toward the windows. The host stares blankly until the dirt-sider flicks at his holo-ring, and then he smoothly ushers them to a table in the front corner.

"Good thing bribery isn't illegal here," Ty murmurs.

"Bribery runs this station," I reply.

He gives me a strange look. "You say that like you've seen it in action. A lot."

I ignore him, focusing on the couple. "You were right," I say slowly. "She's oohing and ahhing up a storm. Very impressed."

Silence falls and stretches out into awkwardness. I look around the room for something to comment on but don't come up with a thing. Ty opens his mouth and closes it again. This is so weird; we've always had plenty to talk about.

Finally, a waiter approaches. He's wearing the same suit as the host and his two friends, but this one is pale yellow. He's not carrying anything but does a complicated little bow and backs out of the way. Two girls appear, each wearing a long rainbow striped caftan thing, and carrying a tray balanced on her head. Each tray holds one tall stemmed glass. The first girl kneels beside the table and the waiter whisks the glass to our table. And repeat.

I bite my lip until the waiter and his minions disappear into the kitchen, then burst out laughing. I clap a hand over my mouth. Ty rolls his eyes at me, his lips quirking. Behind him, Ms. Dirt-side gives me a disapproving glare. This just makes me laugh more.

"That was spectacular," Ty says. "Not a single drop spilled."

"I wonder how long they had to practice to keep from stepping on their robes when they stood up? Is this a restaurant or a circus? And are you sure you can afford this place? Hiring all these people can't be cheap."

"If we talk about work I can expense it," Ty replies with a smile. "But if you'd rather go home and order pizza, I'm ok with that, too. I'm afraid it will scandalize the dirt-siders if we leave now, though."

"That makes it an even better idea," I say, throwing my napkin on the table. "Do you think we should drink these? I'm sure you'll be charged."

We look down at the glasses on the table. Mine is a swirl of brown and white fluid; Ty's is a greyish green. He picks his up and raises an eyebrow at me. I raise mine and sniff. It smells sweet and almost fruity. I raise both my eyebrows—I so wish I could do just one. We clink our glasses together and take a gulp.

"Ah! Water!" Ty chokes out. "Hot! Hot! HOT!"

I shove my glass into his hand; it was kind of creamy so it should kill the heat. "Maybe we were supposed to share these," I say. "Drink the green one first, then the brown?"

Ty gulps down the brown drink. Tears are pouring down his face, and his cheeks and neck are brilliant pink. Sweat springs out on his forehead and rolls down his face. He finishes the brown drink and flails around blindly until I hand him a glass of water. Behind him, Ms. Dirt-side's eyes are bulging out of her face. Her partner has twisted around in his chair, and they're both staring as if we're a strange stage show. I'm sure the people behind me are watching, too.

The green haired host materializes by our table. A minion behind him bears a tray with a glass of what appears to be milk. Green Dude offers it to Ty, who grabs it and pours the contents down his throat.

"Ser O'Neill y Mendoza bin Tariq e Reynolds, I am so sorry! That drink was intended for another patron! A million apologies! The waiters will be punished! I am so sorry!" Greeny bows with each emphatic apology. Behind him, the minion bows in exact opposite timing. They look like a strange mechanical toy. I bite my lips to keep from laughing.

O'Neill holds up his hand and the host stops talking at once. Ty uses his napkin to wipe the sweat and tears from his face; the fuchsia is finally fading from his cheeks. He takes a couple deep breaths, then looks at me. I smile a little.

"I think we're done here," Ty says, the words coming out in a rough whisper.

"Ser O'Neill y Men—" Ty cuts him off with another gesture. "Ser O'Neill," he tries again. "We are so sorry. There will be no charge, of course. Please accept our invitation to return at another time, our compliments."

"I'm not sure I'd survive another visit," Ty says. He staggers to his feet, and I jump up, too. The host and his minion direct us across the room, continuing to bow in turns. We leave the restaurant through a different door which dumps us out at the next Radial corridor. As we're leaving, I hear Mr. Dirt-side holler, "Check, please!"

"I wonder if the exit is here so new customers can't see departing customers' reactions," I muse as the door slides shut behind us.

Ty snorts. "Should I put a review on WhaDa?"

The door opens again, and a cloud of Virile cologne envelopes us. We turn; a blond man stands on the threshold. He's obviously top-lev, or pretty close; they all look kind of manufactured—as if they've been given standard parts: straight nose, firm cleft chin, long lashes, full, but not too full, lips, bronzed caramel skin. Most of them have had aesthetic surgery to look like the perfect specimen, and there doesn't seem to be a lot of room for diversity. It's kind of creepy. The blond stares at us, and after a moment I realize he was the male half of the couple trying to copulate in the lobby.

"What's the matter, O'Neil, can't handle the hot stuff?" He lifts a glass of the grey-green drink in mock salute.

O'Neill dips his chin. "Ser Bezos. If I'd know that was your drink, I would never have tasted it. You're certainly known for, uh, inflammatory selections."

Bezos grins, apparently taking the comment as a compliment. He takes a gulp from his glass, smacks his lips and gives a big, "Aaahhh. That hits the spot. For a real man." Ty nods pleasantly again, and Bezos shifts his attention to me. I drop my chin and turn my face slightly away, allowing my hair to fall forward. I don't need any attention from a top-lev brat.

"Who's your little chica?" he asks, leering at me. "Didn't realize you were into girls, O'Neill! Gloria Huateng said you're gay, but maybe you swing both ways?" He waves his hand back and forth like a gate. Ty's face continues to express nothing but polite interest. I would punch this guy in the nuts and drag Ty away right now, but I know this rat's mother is on the Board. Bezos takes another swig. I can smell the alcohol and a hot peppery aroma as he leans forward. "Hey, I know you, don't I?"

"I doubt you've had the opportunity to meet Ms. Moore," Ty says. "Have a pleasant afternoon Ser Bezos, we must be going."

Bezos grabs my arm. I freeze. "No, I'm sure I know you. Just let me think a little." He scrunches up his face and I imagine a little man inside his head, trying to crank-start his brain.

"I was at the Multi-Grav competition on Thursday," I say quickly. "You walked right by me."

His face relaxes, and he finishes off the drink. "Sure, that makes sense."

Behind him, the blonde from the lobby wails from their table half-way across the room, "Nicky!! I'm lonely!"

Without another word to us, Bezos wheels around, almost losing his balance, and staggers back to his date. O'Neill and I escape up the corridor.

"Well, that was fun," I say as we take the float tube down to Level 9.

Ty barks out a short laugh. "You didn't burn out your throat and one of your lungs like I did. Or get insulted by one of your bosses' sons."

"I can't believe you have to put up with that little dweeb," I say. "If you didn't work for the board, I would have poured that drink down his pants."

"And been on the next shuttle dirt-side," Ty finishes. "You know top-lev kids are untouchable. Besides, his pants looked too tight to pour anything into them."

I smirk. "You noticed his tight pants? Maybe Gloria was right about you."

He wraps an arm around me and drags me out of the float tube. "Believe me," he growls in my ear, "I'm much more interested in your pants than his."

I push away, but he holds me loosely. "I'm wearing a skirt."

"Even better," he whispers, reaching down and running a finger along the back of my thigh, just under the hem of my skirt.

I suck in a breath. "This top-lev behavior is not very becoming," I say primly.

O'Neill laughs and lets me go. "Where's this deli you were raving about? Do they have milkshakes? I need something to cool my throat,"

"And your jets," I mutter, although I'm kind of disappointed he let go so easily. My hormones seem to be winning this weekend.

Ty laughs again and grabs my hand. "And my jets," he agrees. "Lead on!"

TWENTY-THREE

WE ORDER lunch at my favorite deli. I get Pastram'n'rye, fries, and a soda. Ty has his milkshake - chocolate - a meatball sub, and carrots. What kind of person gets carrots at a deli? And I hate to tell him but adding carrots does not make that meal healthy. When the order arrives, I grab the bag and drag Ty back to the float tubes. He tries to do his bodyguard thing, but the whole homicidal whack job idea has gotten old.

"Where are we going?" Ty asks.

I smile. "Wait and see."

We step out on Level 20 and I lead the way to the greenhouses on A Ring. The outer Ring of every fifth level is used to cultivate plants. Some of them are open to the public, but Level 20 is closed. Station management doesn't want random people to have access to the station's food source.

As a maintenance tech, I have access to everything. I wave my holo-ring at the door, then swear under my breath. After yesterday's software surgery, it doesn't work, of course. I really didn't think that through.

"Can you open this door?" I ask Ty. Board security probably has access, too.

"Yeah," he replies slowly. "Why? This is just a Farm, right?"

"Just open it."

He waves his ring at the panel and enters a code on the screen. The door slides open. Warm, moist air pours out around us, bringing scents of flowers, herbs, soil, and even water. I hand Ty the lunch bag. "Come on."

We pass between rows of low hydroponic tables, overflowing with plants I have no interest in identifying. They're green, they smell good, they probably grow food. That's good enough for me. As we move deeper into the compartment, the plants get bigger and the spaces between them get smaller. Although the tables are laid out in a neat grid, the large plants hang out into the aisles, making the room look like a jungle. I pull a large frond of some kind out of the way and push on through, with Ty right behind me.

After about ten minutes, I veer to the right and lead the way to the windows. We duck under another heavy plant and enter a small clearing. A tiny patch of real grass covers a gentle hill. A sim-wood bench sits at the top of the rise, facing the windows. Large tree-like fronds arch over it. Trailing vines and flowers spill down a wall behind the bench and fill the area with a heavenly smell.

Ty stares around the glade. "What *is* this place?"

I shrug, pretending it's no big deal. "If you look at the station schematics, this is the break room for the Farm Techs. But as you can see, they've made a few minor modifications. I discovered it a few weeks after I started at the MCC; they had modified the bot routes to avoid this area, and I was curious. They let me come here as long as I don't report it to anyone." I gaze at him, enjoying his amazement. "I'm trusting you to keep this secret."

He smiles, settles down on the bench and pats the seat next to him. "This is beautiful. I won't tell a soul."

We pull out our lunch and start eating.

"So, was that your mom last night?" I ask after a few minutes of munching.

"Yeah. My sister got engaged. They're all very excited," he replies. "We don't talk that often; dirt-side calls are expensive."

"But you're a rich Board Security Agent," I say.

"Right, have you seen my pay stub?" He pauses and gives me a weary but amused look. "Never mind, you probably have."

My face gets hot, so I redirect the conversation. "Younger or older sister?"

"Lillien is a couple years younger than me." He steals one of my fries. "She's the one getting married. Aretha is a year older than me; she's single. Akiko is the baby, but she's married with three kids already. My brothers, Roberto and Yuri are twins. They're between me and Lili."

"Your mother has six children?"

"My parents have six children," he corrects me and steals another fry, dipping it in his milkshake. "Lili just moved out last year, but they all live nearby, except me."

I stare at him. "Let me get this straight. Your parents are still contracted. The same two people, together for, what, thirty years? And SIX children?"

He nods, chews and swallows. "My parents aren't contracted, they're married. Till death do us part and all that. I know it isn't common anymore, but surely you've seen a wedding ceremony on one of your *Ancient TēVē* vids."

I sit back. "I thought that was fiction. Why would anyone sign a contract with no exit clause?"

Ty shrugs. "They wanted to spend their lives together, not just a few years. They wanted to be an 'us'; really be a couple instead of two people who sleep together and maybe have children together but then split up. They wanted their kids to have a permanent family. I guess you can ask them when they're here."

"Your parents are coming here? And you want me to meet them?" My head reels. We've only known each other a couple weeks, we're not even in a relationship, and he's talking about introducing me to both his mother and his father!

He laughs. "You should see your face! Don't panic, they aren't coming until next year. Besides, I introduce all my friends to them if I get a chance. They're great people." He reaches for my plate again.

I smack his fingers. "Get your own fries, rabbit boy. Those are mine."

Friends? Is that what we are? I thought we were coworkers with a little sexual tension thrown in. I had even entertained brief fantasies of contracting with him for a year or two—a non-procreational contract, of course. But now, I don't know. Although he said it in a kind of off-hand manner, I can tell he thinks getting married is the ultimate goal. He might not consider a short-term domestic contract in the meantime.

I try to imagine growing up in a family with both parents and five siblings. I can't. My mother changed partners every couple of years, and I've never met my biological father. My two half-sibs spent a lot of their childhoods with their own fathers, a circumstance which still arouses some jealousy in me today. We were never very close since they would be gone for six to nine months at a time. We definitely weren't what I'd call a family, and their stays on-station rarely overlapped, so they barely knew each other. To me, they were just those annoying kids who showed up once in a while.

"What about you? Ty asks. "Any siblings?"

"Just two," I answer. "My half-sister is three years older, and my half-brother is three years younger. Mother read an article that indicated three years is the perfect spacing. She's big into planning."

"Are they here on the station?" he asks.

"My family is boring," I say airily. "Is your sister doing a short-term contract, or is she actually getting married like your folks?"

"Lili and Jie had a two-year contract," he replies as he gets to his feet. He wanders down the little hill and stretches out on the grass. "It ended last month, and I guess they decided to make it permanent. This hill is at a perfect angle for looking out the window," he marvels. "Come and see."

I pile the empty containers into the bag and leave it on the bench. Sliding out of my sandals, I pad down to Ty and stare down at him. He smiles and reaches up a hand. "Watch the sunrise with me," he suggests, tugging gently on my arm.

I let him pull me down, but instead of sinking gracefully beside him like an actress in a RomCom, my knees crash into the ground. "Ow!" I holler, losing my balance. I tip forward and my elbow jams into Ty's gut.

"Oof!" He curls away from me into a fetal position, and I drop onto my back, rubbing my knees.

"Are you OK?" I ask a few seconds later, rolling onto my side.

He stretches carefully and turns back to me. "I'm glad you didn't hit any lower," he says, still rubbing his stomach. "Come here." He slides the arm that isn't clutching his belly under my head and pulls me close. "I think it's safer to keep you close. Look, dawn."

As the station rotates toward our primary, we lay on the grass watching the sun appear. The auto filters cut the harshest light, allowing us to see the edge of the solar disk as it appears in the window. I lay with my head pillowed on Ty's shoulder, snuggled against his side as if I belong here. His fingers brush gently up and down my bare arm, tracing unidentifiable patterns on my skin, igniting little sparks that gather in my stomach.

The heat travels up to my chest and spreads into my breasts, and I turn to look at him. He isn't watching the sunrise; he's staring at me, his eyes fixed on my lips. At my movement, he rolls up onto his side, his other hand sliding across my stomach. My breath catches in my throat and I lick my dry lips.

He leans in close, his lips just millimeters from mine. "I'm going to start working on that project we discussed."

I swallow. "Project?" I ask. What the hell is he talking about? And why is he talking? Just kiss me already!

"You know," he says, his breath hot against my lips. "Working slowly toward sex." His lips touch mine just as his holo-ring vibrates.

"Zark it!" we mutter in unison, and then we both laugh. He rolls onto his back. "It's my boss; I have to take it."

The top-levs call, and we snap to attention. I sigh and sit up, pulling my shirt down into place. Not wanting to listen in to his conversation, I jump up and pace around the edge of the glade, trying to get my brain to start working again.

"I have to go; some kind of emergency. Probably nothing, but that's how the board is," he says, grabbing the lunch bag off the bench. He comes toward me, his eyes warm. "I'll take you back to my apartment; you'll be safe there. When I get back, maybe we can get back to that project." He slides an arm around me and steers me to the door.

TWENTY-FOUR

Ty leaves me at his apartment, telling me not to open the door for anyone. So, when the door chimes less than five minutes later, I'm a bit flustered, but I'm not stupid enough to answer. Fortunately, O'Neill has state of the art tech, so I tap the panel by the door. A vid feed from the corridor outside springs up; it's a man I don't recognize dressed in a Sec Agent uniform.

I click the intercom button. "Yes?"

"I have a message for Ms. Moore from Dame Morgan," he says.

See, I told you she would track me down. My eyes narrow. "Send it via the OS," I reply.

"Dame Morgan wished it to be hand-delivered," he says waving an envelope.

I think for a moment. Top-levs sometimes use antiquated means like paper messages. It's usually some kind of power play: look, I'm rich enough to have minions to deliver my commands. And, I have to admit that after my brilliant software hack, she might not be able to send me a message via holo-ring. But our resourceful killer could easily know this. No way I'm opening this door with him out there. "Leave it on the mat," I say.

He places the note on the ground, bows toward the door and walks away. I use the control panel to swivel the camera around. No one is within ten meters. To the right, the messenger strides briskly away, and a family has just emerged from an apartment to the left. Now, while there are witnesses, I should be safe. I open the door, snatch the envelope and smack my hand on the panel, closing it again.

The thick paper is a little rough and blemished as if it were handmade. Of course, faux hand-made everything is very popular right now. A glob of red wax, imprinted with an elaborate cursive M, seals the flap. I slide a fingernail under the wax and pop it off.

A single folded page slides out. Inside, hand-written, it says:

4 pm, 83A.

A summons to the top-lev. I check the clock—it's 3:30.

After changing into my uniform, (which, fortunately, Kara didn't remove from my bag,) I take the float tube up to Level 40. I check the schedule on the Sanctuary screen. I have twenty minutes before the next service. After all that's happened today, it's hard to remember it's still Sunday.

Although there are people inside Sanctuary, I ignore them and stride to the small alcove I sat in yesterday. A few folks look up, but as usual, they see the Maintenance Tech uniform, and their eyes just slide right over me. I crouch down on the floor, by an air vent. A quick twist of a tool and the vent is open. I glance around, but I can't see anyone over the tops of the pews. I slide my arm into the vent and grab a small cube attached magnetically to the top of the air duct, about twenty centimeters in. A quick yank and it comes loose in my hand.

I snap the vent cover back on, give it a few quick turns with my screwdriver and scramble to my feet. Another quick glance around the room assures me no one is paying me any attention, so I glide out of the room.

It's now ten minutes to four, and one doesn't keep the Ice Dame waiting. As I ride the float tube up to Level 82, I open the tiny box I pulled from Sanctuary. Inside is a holo-ring. Not a standard issue, but one encased in a delicate gold filigree of flowers and leaves. I take a deep breath, remove my own untraceable holo-ring and slide the new one onto my finger. I put my off-grid ring into the box and stuff it into my pocket.

You can't just pop up to Level 83. The regular float tubes top out on Level 82. In the center of the concourse, there is a blank door. Behind the door, a guard sits behind a tall, sleek desk and a single float tube goes up to the penthouses. I hand my summons over to the guard and wait while he calls upstairs. A few minutes later, he jerks his chin toward the archway behind him and I step into the private tube.

The Level 83 concourse is smaller than the other Levels. It's more of a circular lobby, about 15 meters across. There are trendy couches and plush chairs grouped around low tables, with large potted plants offering some privacy between groups. A highly polished grand piano sits silent in the middle —the pianist must be on break. Twelve real wood doors are spaced evenly around the outer wall, each one flanked by two tall tables holding huge identical flower arrangements in cut glass vases. The scent of real lilies wafts over me, making my nose twitch. I step out of the float tube and move toward the door marked with a small A.

As I approach the Morgan suite, the door whooshes open. I step into the marble tiled foyer. A vast, antique sideboard stands along the right wall under a mirror in an ornately carved frame. A tall vase against the opposite wall holds ornamental curling Wafti branches from Armstrong Forest. The two-meter-tall, tightly curled branches appear to be dusted in gold. They actually grow that way, but they're very fragile, making them difficult to transport and fabulously expensive. I've always loved them; I have a smaller, synth version in my compartment. Next to these, mine would look tacky and cheap.

Dame Morgan steps through the archway across from me. "Annabelle," she says, her cultured voice hard and disapproving. "Did you have to dress like a," she pauses, her lips pinching together and nostrils flaring as if the words smell bad, "space janitor?"

I look down at my clean coverall. "Yes, I do. I *am* a space janitor, Mother."

TWENTY-FIVE

Yeah, Dame Morgan is my mother. I told you we had a history.

Now don't get all pissy with me for not telling you sooner. This is my deepest, darkest secret, buried below the crush I had at age eleven on my mother's fifty-year-old yoga instructor and that incident the first week at the Techno-Inst when I—never mind, that's another story. Even Kara doesn't know. Partly because I don't want to be the poor little rich girl, but also to make sure my mother couldn't find me. When she walked in on us in O'Neill's office, my cover was blown.

So, here's the deal. I was the result of a procreational contract between my mother and a carefully selected, exhaustively tested, highly rated, and as yet publicly unidentified sperm-provider, whom I refer to as Dear Old Dad or "DOD" for short. I've never met DOD; I'm not even sure Mother has met him. She may have picked him out of a catalog. I was carried by a surrogate, so as not to interfere with Mother's busy schedule. Running a galactic empire is a 24/7 job.

I grew up here on SKK-142, right in this penthouse suite. My mother wasn't Chair at that time, but she was on the Board. I seem to remember our address was 83G, but I know we didn't move after she was elected. I think they just change the addresses so the Chair always lives in Compartment A. The penthouse compartments are all identical in structure, so no one really wants to move.

I went to school with the other top-lev children, including the obnoxious Nicolai Bezos, sexual predator Gloria Huateng, and their whole entourage. I was not the most popular of the group, as you can imagine. Often, I was privately tutored as I trailed along with Mother on her business trips. She tried to train me to be her successor, but I was always more interested in coding than managing. As soon as I reached legal age, I escaped. A sympathetic employee of the SK2 Corporation helped me falsify my identification, hide away some funds, and apply to the Techno-Inst. Then I got my education, met Kara and moved back up here.

With all the places in the galaxy to live, why did I move back up to SK2? I guess because it's home. And with thousands of employees on station, I figured my chances of coming to Mother's attention had to be pretty low. One more minor grievance to lay at the murderer's feet. Although, without him (or her) I wouldn't have met Ty. I'm not sure that's a good enough trade-off for getting pulled back into my mother's web, but….

Zark. I'm going to have to figure out how to tell Ty about all this. He won't be pleased when he finds out I'm an undercover top-lev brat. You've heard what he says about us.

My old bedroom hasn't changed. I would have expected her to throw out all my stuff and convert it to a yoga studio (although she already has one of those) or a guest room (ditto) or even a closet. But everything I left behind is still here, sealed in the hermetic closet, dressers, and shelves. (When you jet set around the galaxy for months at a time, you don't want your stuff getting dusty.)

The massive bed is made up in shades of blue; the same duvet I used as a teen. It's clean; the staff changes all the beds weekly, whether they've been used or not. Blank white walls hide the closet and dresser drawers; they're opened remotely and don't require handles. A couple generic pictures hang on the wall. I was allowed to select the subject matter (one is a space scene, the other pastoral) but the actual pictures were chosen by our decorator. The bedroom has no window, but a skylight looks out the top of the station. Right now, it's blanked.

Using the gold filigree encased holo-ring I'd hidden in Sanctuary all those years ago, I break the seal on the closet door. Mother sent me up here to put on something more presentable, so I pull out a flowered knee-length dress and sandals. Thanks to Kara's magic, my hair is still fabulous. I hang my coverall in the closet but pick up the box holding my off-grid holo-ring. I don't want to leave this; I might need it later. I rummage around in the dressing table drawer and find a long gold chain. Stashing the ring inside the locket hanging from it, I sling the whole thing over my head and tuck it inside my dress. Then I head back downstairs to face the Ice Dame.

TWENTY-SIX

I DRAG my feet down the grand staircase that wraps around the vaulted living room in my mother's penthouse. The twelve penthouses assigned to the Board of Directors take up the entire Level, and each has an internal second story. Like Ty's living room, they all have an external glass wall, but that's where the similarity ends. The room is two stories high, and at least four times as wide as his. It is filled with wildly uncomfortable antique furniture, a grand piano (although no one in the family plays) and a realistic looking fireplace.

The staircase curves down from the bedroom level, with a carved wood railing and clear plasglas stairs. They're one-way plasglas, of course; my Mother would never allow anyone to look up her skirt. As I tromp down the steps, I can hear her voice coming down the hall from her office. She must have some underling working on Sunday afternoon, poor slob.

"And of course, you know my daughter, Annabelle." My mother gestures toward me as she leads someone into the room. "I hope she has been helpful in your investigation, Agent O'Neill."

I turn to stone on the bottom step. Ty glances in my direction. "I don't believe I've had the honor," He gets to the first half of "honor" before he, too, freezes, in mid-bow. Surprise, shock, horror, and anger chase each other across his face before it smooths into the emotionless mask I've seen him use when speaking to top-levs. It takes about 2 seconds, total. He smoothly completes the bow. "My mistake. How nice to see you again, Sera Morgan."

"Annabelle, see the agent out, then meet me in the office. We have business to discuss." Her tone is cordial, but underneath I hear the steel. She waves a graceful hand in my direction and exits, stage right.

"Ty," I start, but he cuts me off.

"Sera Morgan, you'll have to excuse me. I have work to do." He stresses "work" as if I don't know what that means. He's already across the foyer, waving the door open.

"Let me explain," I plead.

He smiles pleasantly, but I can feel his sense of betrayal bubbling under the surface. "No explanation is necessary. I hope you enjoyed your little adventure, but I don't have time to babysit you right now. I still have a killer to catch."

"But what if he comes after me?" I whine. This morning he was so worried about my safety that he wouldn't let me out of his sight. "Aren't I still your best chance of catching him?"

His lips thin, and a thread of anger colors his even voice. "I'm sure I can catch him without your help. And you'll be fine if you stay here with your mama."

I run after him but stop on the threshold. Gloria Huateng lounges on a green plush chair in the lobby, as if she's been waiting for someone. She catapults to her feet when Ty appears. He smiles and says something to her and gestures toward the float tube. I step back and let the door slide shut between us.

"But I don't want to stay here with Mother," I whisper. He knows my mother; surely, he would understand if he'd just let me explain. I choke down the suffocating lump in my throat and square my shoulders. Tonight, after Mother's precious dinner, I'll go down to his apartment. He'll have to listen, if only because he wouldn't dare ignore a top-lev.

DINNER IS every bit as horrible as I'd expected. The guest list reads like a Who's Who of station residents. I cringe when Nicolai Bezos stumbles in the door with his amorous girlfriend. He's dressed appropriately in an evening suit, but she's wearing a dress that looks like a threadbare, tie-dyed t-shirt. It probably cost a fortune. Based on their bloodshot eyes and overly careful movements, they've been imbibing all afternoon, without bothering to make use of any BuzzKill. Of course, my mother's parties are probably much better if you're buzzed.

In an effort to avoid Bezos, I step behind Don Putin and come face to face with Dame Zuckerberg. Like everyone who has walked in the door, she stares at me for several seconds before extending a limp hand. I touch my knuckles to hers and give a regal nod, just as I learned years ago, in my deportment classes. Strange how easily it all comes back to me.

I've changed into the new evening gown that was laid out on my bed. It has clearly been made to my exact measurements and the many shades of blue complement my eyes. It's fitted to my hips, then flares out to a full, floor-length skirt. As I move around the room, I say a silent prayer that I won't trip over the hem. Silla, one of the few household staff who has been here long enough to remember me, helped me put up my hair into an elegant but slightly untidy roll. She assured me this hairstyle is all the rage, and since I've recently seen Kara wearing hers in a similar fashion, I believe her. I try not to touch it to see if it's stayed up.

My mother, dressed in severe black that makes her look fragile and elegant, glides down the staircase, somehow drawing the attention of every person in the room. This is one of the many things I *didn't* learn in Deportment classes; maybe it can't be learned. She smiles graciously and reaches out a hand to me. Tonight's grand entrance was part of the "important business" we discussed this afternoon. I take a deep breath, curve my lips into the much rehearsed "so happy to be here" smile that is barely a smile at all, and step up onto the bottom tread.

"Thank you all for joining us today." Mother's husky voice travels easily through the room, simultaneously projecting both welcome and superiority. Another skill I didn't, or wouldn't, learn in the dreaded D class. "As you know, SK'Corp finished the quarter with record profits, once again." She pauses while a cheer goes up and glasses are raised. "I am also pleased to take this opportunity to welcome my daughter, Annabelle, back on station after her recent training and internship." She leans down from the step above to kiss my cheek, her cool lips almost brushing my skin.

"Welcome home, Annabelle," Dame Zuckerberg booms out, ever my mother's staunch supporter. She raises her glass. I smile and wave, like a good little puppet. Glasses are raised again to toast my "return."

As my mother leads the way into the dining room, Nicolai Bezos lurches up beside me, his equally unsteady date hanging from his arm. I can smell the alcohol on him and nearly pass out when he leans into my face to whisper. "Ha! Knew you looked familiar! Ms. Moore my ass! Slummin' with the help, eh?" He leers and winks, whacking his elbow into the door frame as we step through into the dining room.

Unfortunately, the blonde was hanging on that arm, and she slams right into the wall. She drops to the floor like a jelly donut in double gravity. Blood gushes from her nose onto Mother's white carpet. The crowd of guests pushes me forward. Bezos stays beside me, his date's disappearance not even registering. From the corner of my eye, I see one of the staff rush over to the girl. I glance back, knowing my mother would kill me if I "made a scene" by trying to help. Everyone else ignores her, carefully skirting the growing puddle of blood.

"I have been helping Agent O'Neill with a case since, er, I returned," I say, moving toward my seat at the end of the table. (Another of the important business matters my mother needed to discuss today: seating charts. Ugh.) Bezos stumbles after me. "I believe you're seated here," I say, sliding my hand along the top of a mahogany chair back. Much as I despise my mother's life of constant acquisition and consumption, I must admit there's something about real wood. It just begs to be touched.

Bezos leans over and squints at the hand-lettered place card. He reaches for it but misses, and swings around from the momentum. I grab his arm before he ends up on his butt. Bad enough that his girlfriend ended up on the floor; Mother prefers only two casualties per party, and we have a long way to go before this is over.

"I'll jus' sit down there by you," Bezos announces, finally capturing the card and brandishing it wildly. "Whoever's next to you won't mind. We have a lot of catchin' up to do!"

He staggers away from the chair and rams into a sharply dressed, dark-haired man. The newcomer must be built like a rock; he doesn't even flinch. "You can talk to Annabelle after dinner," he says, snagging the chair and somehow dropping Bezos into it.

Bezos grins up at the other guy. "Bobby, my old frien', where the heck did you come from?" His head swivels around the room. "And where's Candice?" His glazed eyes zero in on his wine glass and Candice is forgotten again. "Waiter!"

Bobby Putin bows to me, the dark plum silk of his beautifully tailored suit glimmering in the candlelight. "Annabelle, how nice to see you again. I'm sorry I missed your Multi-Grav performance the other day. I'm told your execution of Stage 3 was masterful."

I smile faintly. "I didn't think you recognized me."

Putin escorts me to the end of the table and pulls out my chair. "I didn't, then. But when I saw you tonight, it clicked." He reaches out a hand and touches a wisp of straight brown hair that has escaped my updo. "What did you do to your beautiful red curls?"

"Just trying something new." I glance at him as I sit down. His brilliant green eyes are focused on me, and it gives me a little thrill. One of Bobby Putin's most devastating tricks is his ability to make you feel like you're the only person in the room worth talking to.

"I admire your use of a pseudonym in the Multi-Grav gym," Bobby says, dropping elegantly into the chair next to me. "I've always suspected we top-levs get treated differently in these supposedly democratic arenas, but I haven't been selfless enough to put it to the test myself, yet." He smiles in a self-deprecating way. "Besides, Bezos would refuse to give up any advantage. He believes he's earned it."

"Why do you compete with him, then?" I ask.

He shrugs and gets to his feet. "We've been friends forever. I can't abandon him." He turns smoothly away, bowing to the man who has just stopped beside me. "I believe this is your chair, Don Huateng. I was just warming it up for you." With one more smile at me, he's gone.

Don Huateng is nine million years old. He's old enough that he's had every cosmetic and corrective surgery in the database, and he still looks like a week-old baked potato. His face is seamed with wrinkles, his eyes are cloudy, his back is stooped. His family insists he is sharp as a tack, but tonight he's a mumbling, drooling old geezer. Two smartly uniformed young men lower him into his chair, slide the chair up to the table without visible effort, and step back against the wall.

Knowing my mother will review the surveillance vids later, I smile at the old man and offer him my hand. He coughs on me then settles back in his chair and closes his eyes. I look directly at the camera that I know is hidden in the corner of the room and raise my eyebrows. As I'm wiping my hand on my napkin, Huateng starts snoring. I give myself a mental shake and turn to my other side.

The chair to my right is empty; someone is running late. I wouldn't care to be in his shoes later. Mother might never say anything, but she always remembers a slight, and exacts revenge when you least expect it. I lean over casually and look at the name tag, but don't recognize the long string of names. Probably some off-station business connection who got lost on his way here. If he isn't local, he might just get off this one time.

Everyone has finally settled down when the door is flung open. Gloria Huateng poses in the opening, waving at the assembled guests. She's wearing a sheer, skin-tight dress that plunges to her navel, narrow strips of fabric stretched tight across her superhuman breasts. The color of the material exactly matches her skin, so she almost appears to be naked from the hips up. The bottom half of the dress fades from golden tan to a deep green and the hem is embellished with sparkles. From about knee height, the skirt flares out into a wide swirl. Today her hair is a bronze mass falling in waves to her hips. She looks like an over-sexed mermaid.

"So sorry we're late! We were," she giggles suggestively, "busy. I think you've all met my date, Tiberius O'Neill y Mendoza bin Tariq e Reynolds." She smiles wider and drags O'Neill through the door. He's in dark grey evening wear and looks fantastic. My stomach drops. Why does he keep appearing?

"Hey, Annabelle!" Bezos' drunken bellow rings through the room. "Your boyfrien' is here!"

I will my face not to turn red, and stare Bezos down until he loses focus and reaches for his drink. Ty ignores everyone in the room but the hostess.

"My deepest apologies, Dame Morgan," he says, bowing to my mother. She waves them toward the empty seats on the far side of the table. Instead of just walking around Mother's end of the table, Gloria drags Ty in my direction. Another latecomer arrives and makes apologies to my mother, but I'm too busy staring at Ty to even hear his name.

When they reach me, Gloria drops O'Neill's hand and throws her arms around Don Huateng. "Grandfather!" she coos. The old man opens his eyes, glares at her, then me. He smacks his lips together and goes back to sleep. Gloria smiles at me. "Aren't you lucky! My grandfather is so entertaining. Enjoy your dinner, Annabelle."

Bitch.

Ty bows stiffly with a murmured, "Sera Morgan," as Gloria drags him back up the other side to their empty seats.

The chair next to me is drawn out, bringing my attention back to my end of the table. The other late arrival. Seated, he's taller than me, with a crooked nose that makes me think he hasn't had any cosmetic surgery. If that's the case, he's probably in his mid-fifties, although there is no grey in his auburn hair. He's dressed in an odd robe-like thing, with a cowl. It's draped over a standard collared shirt, and expensive, highly polished shoes peek out beneath. The robe looks like high-quality silk. He smiles at me, offering his hand.

"R'ger Chaturvedi," he says. "You must be our host's charming daughter, Annabelle."

"I'm not sure about the charming part," I reply, making Chaturvedi laugh. Nearby diners turn to look, but he ignores them. "Where are you from, Ser Chaturvedi?"

"I'm visiting from Station Aldrin," he replies. That explains the odd clothing, although not what he's doing here. SA-09 is the oldest station still habitable, orbiting the farthest star in our quadrant. Although transports go there, of course, and to Armstrong, the planet in that system, people who live there rarely venture this far. They're known to be a rather hermit-like civilization.

"What brings you to Kelly-Kornienko?" I only half listen to his answer as I try to catch O'Neill's eye. Although seeing him here with Gloria makes my blood boil – I've never liked that sleazy wench – I desperately want to explain my situation to him. As Chaturvedi rambles on about touring the galaxy and business opportunities, I gaze down the table at Ty. He's seated on this side of Gloria and has his back half turned toward me, focused completely on his date. I grind my teeth.

"And then I decided to open a brothel on ST-29." Chaturvedi sits back and takes a sip from his water glass.

"That's nice," I say. "Wait. What?"

He laughs. "You seemed to be drifting a bit."

"I'm sorry. I'm just back from, er, my internship, and I'm still adjusting to the time difference," I lie.

He laughs again. "I can see you're distracted, but I'm not buying your reasoning." He looks pointedly down the table just as Gloria's nerve-grating titter rings through the room. "Did she steal your boyfriend?"

I stare at Chaturvedi.

"I heard the young gentleman," he gestures toward Bezos with his napkin, "as I arrived."

I flush. "Ser O'Neill and I do not have any established personal relationship," I answer primly. "We have worked together recently on a project, and I need to discuss some new developments." I wince mentally; I sound like I'm channeling my mother.

"I see," he says. I'm not sure I like what he sees. "Perhaps you'd be best advised to wait until Monday morning to discuss these developments. He looks busy."

I gaze down the table for a few seconds, but Ty still has his back to me. Maybe Chaturvedi is right. Monday morning is the time for business. And our relationship has always been about business. If I tell myself that enough times, maybe I'll believe it. I shake my head and focus on Chaturvedi. "Please, tell me more about your plans for galaxy domination via prostitution."

R'ger is surprisingly good company. He tells me about growing up on Armstrong, one of the first planets our ancestors inhabited after leaving Earth. He is one of those people who can make scraping gum off the deck sound like an amazing adventure, and soon he has me laughing about a story involving his sister, a goat and fourteen bicycles.

"So, you can imagine what the sheriff said about the helmet." He finishes in a deadpan tone that has me holding my sides in an effort to stifle my giggles.

"Sell!" Don Huateng bolts upright and yells. "Sell TXHEK! Twenty thousand shares!" He slams a hand on the table and collapses back into his chair, snoring again. Behind him, one of the uniformed guys flicks his holo-ring to life and starts texting.

Chaturvedi stares. "Is that young man actually selling the old guy's stocks?" he whispers to me.

I nod. "Don Huateng is considered an oracle. Look." I gesture down the table. Every person there, including my mother, is either texting or whispering into their holo-device. Ty looks around, catches my eye and grins. I smile back, but his face goes blank—as if he's just remembered he's mad at me—and he turns away.

I sigh and turn back to Chaturvedi. "Are you going to get in on the action?"

He shakes his head. "I don't own much stock. My holdings are primarily real estate."

"Like that brothel on ST-29?"

He shakes his head. "That was a lease. And it didn't pan out. The sexbots unionized, and I couldn't afford to hire them." His eyes twinkle and I chuckle. "Listen, I'm here on my own, and my meeting isn't until Wednesday. Would you be available to show me around the station tomorrow or Tuesday?"

My eyes start to narrow, but remembering Mother is watching—or will be later— I smile. "It's a pretty standard station layout," I say. "Probably just like ST-29."

The faint lines around his eyes crinkle as he smiles. "Yeah, I know. But it's always better to see a place with a local. You know all the quirks and secrets. Plus, I like having a smart, pretty girl to laugh at my jokes."

He's a guest in Mother's penthouse, so his background has been thoroughly checked. And he arrived last week, which means he hasn't been here long enough to be the murderer. In fact, Ser Chaturvedi is probably the safest companion I could have, barring Ty. But I need to talk to O'Neill tomorrow. And check if I'm back on the schedule in the MCC. If I'm not, I'll have lots of time to kill and I certainly don't want to be at Mother's disposal.

"I have a couple appointments I must keep in the morning," I say. "And one of them may extend into the afternoon. How about if I call you when I know my schedule?"

R'ger flicks his holo-ring, sending his contact ID to mine. Then he lifts his glass. "I look forward to it."

TWENTY-SEVEN

The next morning, I'm up early. I put on my station coverall, which I locked into a fingerprint coded safe drawer yesterday. I wouldn't put it past Mother to have the staff dispose of it. Of course, she probably has override authority on my safe drawer, but I added a few lines of code to the loop to secure it.

I run down the stairs, through the dining room and slide into the kitchen. The pastry chef, Dav, pulls fresh croissants from the oven as I walk in. He's a middle-aged man with laugh lines around his eyes and wavy brown hair. Looking up when the door opens, he smiles and slides two hot croissants onto a plate.

"Welcome home, Sera Annabelle!" he says, handing me the plate. The buttery scent makes my mouth water. "One chocolate and one plain, right?" He grabs a mug off the shelf and slides it into the coffee machine. "And a cappuccino coming up!"

I put the plate down on a counter and give him a hug. He holds me for a second, then swings away to grab the coffee mug. I dust the flour off my uniform.

"It's good to see you Dav," I say before taking a bite of the pastry. Ecstasy! "And good to taste these again! How's Celia?"

Dav smiles and waves a hand. "I made extras when I heard you were home." He slides the rest of the batch onto a wire rack to cool. "Celia is good. Tino's spouse had a baby last year, so she spends too much money spoiling the granddaughter." Dav doesn't look like he minds. He's well paid here; much better paid than a bot programmer, I can tell you.

I eat my breakfast, getting caught up on the staff gossip, while Dav completes his cleanup. When I finish my coffee, I grab another chocolate croissant and have him put a few more into a bag. It can't hurt to butter up O'Neill. Saying goodbye to Dav, with a promise to stop by and visit Celia later in the week, I slip out the back door and down the steps to the service duct.

Up here on 83, the service duct is used by people, not bots. It runs beneath the penthouses, allowing servants to access their work areas without using the front door. It's slightly wider than the bot ducts, and it's two meters tall rather than the usual one and a half. It's also brightly lighted, well ventilated and painted a pleasant shade of green instead of bare metal. I trek down the long corridor, past the stairs to the Said penthouse and later past the Gates's. Finally, I reach one of the four sloping radials that connect the ducts to the lobby and jog up it to the float tube.

Down on 82, the guard pays no attention to me; his job is to keep the undesirables out, not stop the top-levs from leaving. I recall a mental map of this Level and make my way to grid 126.9: O'Neill's office.

The office door whooshes open when I reach it. I rock back in surprise, but then remember I'm wearing a top-lev holo-ring. Mother must have upgraded it to adult status while I was away; I didn't get this level of access before. I think of the havoc Nicolai or Gloria must cause with top-lev access and wince.

Ty looks up with his professional mask on but scowls when he sees me. A second later, the mask is firmly back in place. He rises and indicates a chair. "How may I help you, Sera Morgan."

"You can stop calling me that, for one thing," I snap. I throw myself down into the chair. Wait, I'm supposed to be buttering him up, not making him angry. I sit forward and place the bag on his desk. "I brought you some fresh croissants baked by our pastry chef this morning." I smile hesitantly.

"Thank you, Sera," he says, moving the bag to one side. His lips quirk for a second. "Would you like one?"

"No, those are for you. I already ate."

"I'll have these with my coffee later." He folds his hands on the desk. "I really am quite busy this morning, so please tell me how I can assist you."

Zark, I was planning on talking while he had his mouth full. No one can be angry while eating Dav's croissants. OK, plan B. "Look, I know you're angry. I'm sorry I didn't tell you who I really am, but I knew you'd have to report me to my mother. She didn't even know I was here until Saturday morning when she saw me in your office. I've been AWOL for six years."

I stand up and wander across the room. "I don't want to be a top-lev. It's all about buying and owning and controlling. No one up here cares about anyone but themselves. My generation just party like over aged frat boys or manage some part of the family empire. I didn't want any of that. So, I left."

I pick up a picture on the bar; it's of a younger Ty with a girl who looks very much like him. "Is this Lillien?"

He crosses the room and takes the picture from me. "It's Akiko," he says shortly, putting it back on the bar. "I'm really very busy. Does this sad story have a point?" He crosses his arms.

"I just want you to know that I didn't deceive you on purpose. And this isn't just some top-lev lark. I *am* Triana Moore much more than Annabelle Morgan. And I can still help you. I'm still a Maint Tech with magic programming skills." I smile hopefully, wiggling my fingers at him.

He walks back to his desk and sits down. "Thank you for your interest, Sera Morgan, but I no longer require your assistance. And I don't care to work with people whom I cannot trust. Please see yourself out." He waves a hand toward the door and turns his attention back to his screen.

"Did you at least have time to talk to Patrick?" I ask. "I'd like to get reinstated in the MCC."

He looks up at that. "You're really planning on going back to work there?"

"Yes!" I practically shout at him. "I told you, this is who I am. I don't want to be Sera Morgan. I just want to get back to being Technician Moore."

He stares at me, hard. After a moment, he relents. Barely. "You can tell her you were assisting me with an investigation. Tell her to call me if she has any questions. That's all I can do for you."

My shoulders slump and I trudge to the door. A quick glance back shows me nothing but the top of his head as he focuses on his work. I step out into the hall and wave the door closed. I will not cry. Blinking furiously to clear my vision, I stump back out to the concourse and take the float tubes down to the Ops Center. I have to see a lady about my job.

THE OPS CENTER is on Level 10. It might seem like the nerve center for the station should be closer to the center, but since it's all monitored through the

OS, it doesn't matter where they're located. Station Security is on 40, because they have to physically deploy to any Level when needed, but the rest of us are kept downstairs.

I use my Morgan holo-ring to open the door. Before I visited Ty, I was a little worried about how I'd get in, since I jacked up my own holo-ring. Maybe I can plug in up in the penthouse and fix my programming errors. But right now, I need to patch things up with Ms. Patrick.

"Sera Morgan?" A man seated near the entrance looks up in shock. His expression changes to confusion. "Triana? What the heck? The system registered Annabelle Morgan."

I make shushing motions at him. I've known Leon Page since I started working in the MCC. He's the Ops Center Comm Tech; he makes sure the station can communicate with everyone in the system and monitors the long-haul signals. He's also a stickler for following the book. I could tell him the name must be a system error, but then he would feel compelled to investigate how such an error could occur. And once Leon starts investigating something, he doesn't stop until he finds the answer. Maybe he should work with O'Neill.

I can't tell him I am Annabelle; I don't want the whole station to know. I still have some slim hopes of being able to go back to being just Triana. Fortunately, Leon is also a total celebrity hound. So, I give him a conspiratorial look. "Sera Morgan asked me to hold her holo-ring while she meets someone her mother doesn't approve of," I say. This is illegal, but it happens often enough, or so I've heard. I pat an empty pocket. "I'll be giving it back to her later today. Please don't mention it to anyone."

"You know Annabelle Morgan?!" he whispers, incredulous. "What's she like? How did you meet her? Can you get me an autograph?" Leon is so star-struck, he doesn't realize that while Annabelle showed up on his screen, Triana didn't.

"Ms. Moore!" Patrick's voice rings out across the room. "Front and center!"

I lean toward Leon and whisper, "I'll see what I can do," then straighten my back and march over to the command station in the center of the room. The Ops Commander's desk is a step up from the rest of the room, but even with this advantage, I'm looking down at Inspector Patrick. She doesn't look pleased, although I'm not sure if that's because of my height, or my poor performance last week.

"I did not invite you into my Ops Center, Technician." Patrick's pinched mouth looks like she just binged on lemon Sow'rPops. She sits down in her chair which immediately rises so she's at eye level with me. It's a neat bit of programming; I wrote a similar loop in school. But to actually use it? This woman has a major Napoleon complex. Just what I need.

"I wanted to explain what happened last week," I say.

"I'll tell you what happened," she snaps. "An egotistical technician decided she didn't need to bother with protocol. I've read your reports, Moore. You think you're smarter than everyone, and you don't need to follow the rules."

I stare at her, my mouth open. I've seen all of my personnel reviews; even the classified ones. I can get anywhere in the OS, remember? None of them say anything about me having an ego or overstepping the rules. Deleting video or too casual on the comms, yes, but never anything about an ego. "I'm sorry, Inspector Patrick, I don't know what reports you're referring to," I say.

She smiles, her mouth a cruel curve. "I'm sure you don't," she says with feigned disbelief. "You are hereby suspended without pay. A remedial training schedule will be set up for you within a month. Do not bother me again."

"A month without pay?!" I cry. "But I was helping Board Security. Ask Agent O'Neill. He'll tell you what happened."

"Board Security?" she asks, her pale face getting even more pallid. "What do they have to do with this situation?"

"Agent O'Neill is investigating the murders. *Multiple* murders. I was helping him when I made that call. If you just contact him, he can explain. There's no need to suspend me." I don't have enough saved to make a month's rent without my paycheck, and I refuse to take any money from my Mother.

"Murder?" she laughs. "There has never been a murder on this or any other station. Security is too tight." Is she crazy? Doesn't she remember me calling…Oh. Baker's team must have gotten here before they were arrested. Even so, this is a blatant lie; everyone knows about the Sterling case over on PD-49.

"Yes, there has." I say it slowly as if to a spoiled child. "I called in a dead body on Friday morning, remember? That's what started this whole remedial training thing."

"I don't care for your attitude, Moore." Patrick spits the words out as if they burn her mouth. She pulls up the log from last week. "You will speak to me with more respect. And there is no record of any murder call. None." She waves the holo in her hand at me. "I have noted your call to me in which you totally disregarded protocol. You were irrational and incoherent, and I relieved you of your duties. That is all that happened on Friday, and your pathetic attempts to sensationalize and rationalize your behavior are childish and unprofessional."

"Please," I beg. "Just call Agent O'Neill. Board Security. He'll explain it all."

Patrick glares at me, and her chair rises a little higher so she's looking down at me. "I will contact Agent O'Neill, if and when I see fit. Don't hold your breath. Farquad! See Technician Moore out." A huge dark-skinned man wearing an aide's patch steps forward, and she turns her chair away from me, clearly dismissing me. I give up.

"Don't worry, Triana," Farquad whispers as we walk to the door. "Her inspection should be done in a week or so. Rash will bring you back online. I'll make sure he calls this O'Neill guy even if Patrick won't."

"Do you remember the dead body call?" I ask. That's what I got reprimanded for, after all: blurting out sensitive information when the whole Ops Center could hear.

He shakes his head. "I wasn't here on Friday. But no one else has mentioned it either, which is really strange." He gives me a baffled look.

Not so strange if you know about the Captio. I try to smile but have no luck. I know Rash will bring me back if he can, but now that Patrick's gone on record listing me as a remedial and who knows what else, he may not find it easy. He'll for sure need to get a statement from O'Neill for the files. Of course, once Patrick leaves, I can always doctor the files. Stepping through the door, I turn. "Thanks, Farq, you're a good friend."

"I know," he smirks, stepping back to allow the door to shut between us.

TWENTY-EIGHT

STARING at the Ops Center door will do me no good, so I turn and retrace my steps to the main concourse. I have a whole day, no, a whole month! stretching out in front of me. I guess I could call Chaturvedi, but it's early yet, and I'm not really sure I want to spend the day playing tour guide. On the other hand, maybe I could make some credit under the table by giving behind-the-scenes tours of the station. If I fix my doctored holo-ring, I'll be able to access everything without anyone tracking me. I definitely need to do something to pay the rent if Patrick really has cut off my pay.

Maybe I *should* just give up and go back to being a top-lev. At least I wouldn't have to worry about making ends meet. Suddenly, I wonder if Mother put Patrick up to this. Maybe she was trying to get me fired! No, Patrick's anger feels personal. I don't know why she is so vindictive, but there must be something. Unless she somehow figured out who I am, and she has a grudge against my family? That doesn't seem reasonable, either. Maybe she just hates me because I'm so tall. I do what I always do when I'm feeling depressed; I head down to see Kara.

I step out of the float tube on 5 and head toward the far side of the concourse. You-nique You is located right on the center concourse; one of the most prestigious locations on any Level for a commercial venture. The shop belongs to the very flamboyant Shaniqua, who goes by just one name. Shaniqua is well over two meters tall, and everything else changes on a weekly basis. Today Shaniqua is dressed in a flowing violent green caftan, with a silver crew cut, long, long lashes, sparkling pink eyeshadow, and a green Fu Man Chu mustache.

"Kara's in the back." The deep voice is heavy with a dirt-side drawl. "Go on through." Shaniqua turns back to the client who shifts nervously. First-time customers always look nervous, but Shaniqua is so talented they always come back.

I push aside the vintage beaded curtain that covers a standard station door. It swooshes open and closes again behind me. This room is filled with stacks of towels, shelves of bottles, boxes and bags and the pungent chemical smell of the trade. In the back corner, Kara stacks a couple trays into the sanitizer. She squeaks when she sees me and almost drops the trays.

"Where have you been! You didn't call me yesterday! What happened with the delicious Ty?" She slams the sanitizer shut and launches herself at me, wrapping me in a bear hug.

I hug her back, and I must have held on too long because she pulls away and fixes me with a narrow-eyed stare. "What?" Kara's hair is curly lavender today, and her skin is a dark brown, almost black. With her (still) violet eyes, she looks fantastic. Her usual skin-tight camisole and short skirt are covered by a loose white lab coat with the You-nique You logo over the left breast.

"Things are not going well. Do you have time for a chat?" I say, looking around for somewhere we can sit.

Kara grabs my hand and drags me out to the front. "My first client isn't due for an hour. Come out to my station. I need to touch up your roots, anyway."

I drop into the chair and lean back. "Actually, could you reverse my hair?"

She goes still. "You want to go back to natural? What happened? Aren't you worried about being recognized?"

"Too late for that," I say. "I've been caught."

While Kara goes to work on my hair, I tell her about Mother finding me in O'Neill's office. Kara has always known that I'm hiding from my upper-lev family, but I never told her how high up they are. When I reveal Mother's identity, Kara makes the appropriate shocked face, but it just doesn't look right.

I grab her wrist as she lowers the hood over my head. "You don't seem very surprised," I say, my eyes narrowing.

She stares back at me then heaves a sigh. Gently unwrapping my fingers from her wrist, she checks the settings on the hood and sits down on the stool tucked into the corner of her station. She takes her sweet time flicking the controls on her holo-ring and engages the hood. As it hums to life, she finally meets my eyes.

"I'm not," she confesses. "I knew who you were before we met."

"What?!"

She sighs again. "Remember the first week of school? When I sat with you in the cafeteria and we decided to be roommates?" I nod. "Didn't it seem odd to you that I didn't already have a roommate?"

It had seemed odd; Kara is the kind of person who always has a flotilla of friends hovering around. In fact, that day she's talking about, it wasn't just her who sat with me; her entire entourage took over the blissfully empty table I'd commandeered. "I thought maybe you had too many friends to choose from and didn't want to hurt anyone's feelings."

Kara shakes her head. "Actually, Varla and I were planning on rooming together. But the week before school started, I was visited by an upper-lev named Hy-Mi."

I groan. Hy-Mi is my mother's private secretary and personal aide. He does everything for her. Hy-Mi took me to my dance recitals, music lessons, doctor appointments. In many ways, he was a more stable parental presence in my life than she was.

"He never mentioned any other names, but if you google Hy-Mi, every hit leads back to Dame Morgan's private aide. Anyway, he said a young woman would be coming to the Techno-Inst, and he would pay me handsomely to ensure she had a place to live." Kara looks a little sick. "He also said he'd continue to pay if I would report back to him regularly."

It's a good thing I have this hood on because, if I didn't, I think my head would explode. Blood pounds in my ears, and I can't see. She's been spying on me! For YEARS!! My hands curl up into fists, and I just want to punch something. Or someone.

"Triana?" Kara leans in close to me. Tears well up in her stupid purple eyes. "I'm really, really sorry. But it was so much money! And I didn't tell her anything important, really, I didn't. Just that you were still alive and doing well in school. Things mothers like to hear, but nothing personal."

I close my eyes and concentrate on taking deep breaths. A shudder runs through me, and I force my hands to uncurl. A glass presses against my fingers, and I take a sip of water. More breathing and more water. Finally, I open my eyes.

"How much did she pay you?" I grit out.

Kara's head drops. "Enough to cover tuition and half our rent. You know," her head pops back up at this point. "I'm really surprised you didn't figure it out a long time ago. There's no way we should have been able to afford that apartment." I must have given her a dirty look because she blanches. "I split the remaining rent fifty-fifty with you. She really helped both of us."

I rub my eyes. "I thought I was making it on my own," I moan. "That was the whole point; I had escaped! I was independent! I thought I didn't need the Morgan wealth. But I'm just as much of a freeloader as those other top-lev brats!" I stare at her. "And it's your fault!"

"Now wait a minute!" Kara yells. "I *helped* you! And who cares if your mother paid for our rent?"

"And your tuition," I mutter.

"Exactly. She paid *my* tuition, not yours. And I *earned* that money fair and square by spying on you."

A laugh forces its way out of me. Kara smiles hopefully. "Is she still paying you?" I ask softly.

Kara shakes her head, her lavender corkscrews bouncing wildly. "After we graduated, Hy-Mi dropped by again. Did you know he was at graduation?" I did not. "He gave me a big chunk of change for 'services rendered,'" she makes air quotes with her fingers, "and told me our business relationship was concluded. Then he hit on me."

"Hy-Mi hit on you?" I almost shriek. "He's, like, ninety years old! And has a bucket load of kids! Grandkids! Probably great grandkids!"

She shrugs. "What can I say? I'm hot."

I laugh. I can't stay angry at Kara. "You didn't hit that, did you?"

Kara rolls her eyes but doesn't answer. I'm not sure what that means. I'm also not sure I want to know. "He gave you money?" I ask. "How much? Is that how you were able to afford the buy-in here on-station?"

She nods again. Kara is a junior partner in You-nique You—apparently thanks to my mother. I always did wonder where she got the funds, but I don't like to pry. I figure everyone has secrets, and it's best if we respect that. "Are we ok?" she asks.

I rub my eyes. "I don't know. I just can't think about this right now. Was that really the last time you talked to Hy-Mi? After graduation?"

"Yeah, that was it. No money or contact since. Which is kind of a shame," she continues, tapping her sparkling violet nails against her lips. "I could use a pile of credits right now. Any chance you want to disappear again?"

Peering out from the hood, I can see she's joking, but I'm not laughing. "I might just do that," I say slowly. "But it won't be here."

"Oh, honey, don't leave!" Kara throws her arms around me, hood and all. "I need you! Besides, what about the delectable Ty?"

I close my eyes again. "He's out. He seems to think I was slumming for kicks. That I enjoyed tricking him. I don't know!" I wail. "He's so mad he won't even talk to me."

Kara rubs my shoulders. "You've got it bad! But don't worry, he'll come around. He was really into you; this won't keep him away forever."

"You think?" I'm not so sure, but she nods violently, her curls bouncing like a bobblehead. I sigh.

I spend the next few hours under the hood while it does its molecular magic. Kara takes her scheduled clients: a haircut, a skin tint, two redefines. Just before lunch, she comes back and whisks the hood off with a flourish. Staring in the mirror, I wonder what I was thinking. The stick-straight, mud-brown hair I've had for the last six years wasn't glamorous; I'd chosen it to be unnoticeable. But these frizzy red curls sticking out all directions? Why did I want them back? I look like a clown who's done overtime in a steam room.

Kara sees my expression and laughs. "Don't panic!" she says, spinning my chair away from the mirror. "Let me style it! Your current cut doesn't work for curls." That's an understatement.

She combs and snips, sprays and smooths, all the while keeping up a flow of gossip I have no need to respond to or even hear. Finally, she spins me back to the mirror.

"What do you think? Isn't it cute?" she gushes.

I stare at myself in amazement. "My hair has never looked this good," I say. "What did you do to it?" The frizz is gone; smooth auburn curls flow in beautiful spirals, framing my high cheekbones and blue eyes, just brushing my shoulders. "I'm never going to get it to look like this again, am I?"

"Incentive to stay here as my roomie," she says. "Only I know the secret! You'll have to stay. But promise me you'll put on some nicer clothes. That station coverall doesn't deserve hair like this."

She loads me up with hair products, which I pay for using Annabelle's allowance account.

Even with my hair back to normal, I can't think of myself as Annabelle. The allowance account, the clothes, the bedroom, even the filigreed holo-ring on my finger, belong to that other girl—the one I feel like I'm impersonating. Knowing

I was never really free of the Morgan money or influence doesn't change that feeling.

It does change my attitude, though.

If my mother wants me to come home and play top-lev, she's going to have to pay for the privilege. Not that an exorbitant hair treatment like this will even dent the pile of money in that account. It appears my Mother continued to deposit an allowance for the last six years, including step increases on every birthday. So, I'm going to use Annabelle's money. I insist on paying Kara the full rate for the treatment and put an extravagant tip on top.

She protests, but I insist. "For all those years you did it at cost. I owe you."

"Even knowing I was spying on you?" she asks, her usually confident voice a meek whisper.

I laugh, without humor. "I should have realized I got away too easily. If I'd thought about it, I would have realized someone was watching. I also should have realized a popular girl like Kara Ortega Okilo didn't need to room with a nerdy loner. I guess I was wearing rich girl blinders."

She smiles, and hugs me, hard. "Let me know when it's safe to go home, ok? I hope it's soon. It's noisy at Stacia's."

I smile in agreement, and an idea occurs to me. "Why don't you come stay with me? I have a huge room and lots of quiet."

"Stay with the Ice Dame?!" she squeaks. "Are you crazy? I don't know if that's terrific or terrifying. Would I have to talk to her?"

"Only if you want to. You could probably pretend to be one of the domestics, and she'd never even know you were there. She doesn't have a clue who works for her." That's a lie. My mother is extremely observant. She knows the name and background of every person who enters her home. And if she's known where I was all these years, I'm sure she knows exactly who I've been living with. I suspect Kara's complete record is on her personal watch list.

"I think I'll stay with Stacia a while longer," she says. "But maybe I can come up sometime when she's out and see the penthouse?"

"Sure, I'll give you a holler next time she's off-station," I reply, gathering up the enormous bag of hair products. "She's funding some new dirtside startup, so it could be soon." We hug, and I'm off to the float tube.

I stop at my favorite noodle stand on the way up and bring the steaming container up to Level 82. The guard does a double take when I walk up, then blanks the surprise from his face. "Nice to see you, Sera Morgan," he says. "The new look is very becoming." Brown-noser.

I make it to my room without running into the Ice Dame. After lining up the bottles and jars on my bathroom vanity, (how am I ever going to remember what to do with all this stuff?) I sit down on the little settee in the corner with my comfort food. Tucking my legs up under myself, I wrap a blanket around my shoulders and slurp up some noodles.

What the heck am I supposed to do now? I'm suspended from my job. I don't want to work for my mother. I can't go home. Ty isn't talking to me. I don't want to hang out with Gloria, Nicolai and that bunch. Oh, and don't forget, there's a killer possibly after me. I suppose I should just lay around and enjoy the luxury, but I'm restless. On days like today, the station seems way too small.

I'm starting to really feel sorry for myself when my holo-ring vibrates.

TWENTY-NINE

"The new hairstyle is very becoming; I almost didn't recognize you," R'ger Chaturvedi greets me in the lobby of his hotel. "I'm so glad you were available, my dear."

I smile politely. "I'm between projects right now, so I'm happy to entertain any friend of my mother's."

He grimaces. "I wouldn't say your mother and I are friends, exactly," he says slowly. "More like business acquaintances."

"Even better." I wonder if he can hear the sarcasm in my voice. "I can claim our visit on my tax return."

He gives me a strange look. "Is this a bad time?"

I shake my head. "Sorry, I had a bad morning. But I'm ready for something fun. What would you like to see?" Showing a middle-aged stranger around the station is hardly my idea of fun, but it's better than sitting around in Mother's penthouse. Besides, if she sees me, she'll give me a job. Something exciting like archiving files.

"Well," he looks around the room as if he's afraid someone will overhear him. "I've heard there's an illegal BunG jump on Level 54."

"Really?" I ask, my eyes widening. "You want to BunG out the airlock?"

"Good heavens, no," he says gently, as if that's what he thinks I expect him to say. "I wouldn't mind seeing it, though. Can we watch?"

Down on 55, I lead him through the greenhouse in A Ring. On this Level, the area is an open, park-like setting. Trees, grass, flowers, a little stream meandering through. We cut across a meadow and join a small group of people leaning their heads against the glass wall.

"This is perfect timing," I tell R'ger. "The sun is at the right angle to illuminate the launch zone, but not high enough to blind us." I point out the huge docking arms that stick out on Level 42. "Unless you came to the station in an executive shuttle, or a cargo drone, your ship docked there. That cruise liner is from Sally Ride; see the nose art? All the S'Ride ships are decorated like that."

R'ger smirks at me. "I know. I may be a rube from Armstrong, but I've traveled a fair bit."

"Sorry!" I reply. "I was just trying to be a good tour guide." I lapse into silence.

"I thought spacewalks required training and certification?" Chaturvedi says. He smiles, encouraging me to resume my lecture.

"We call them ESA: Extra Station Activities. And, as you pointed out earlier, it's an illegal jump," I reply. "Actually, semi-legal is probably a better definition. The station management knows about it, and taxes the income, but doesn't acknowledge its existence. A lot of activities on this station are like that."

"What kind of person would risk his life on an illegal," I raise my eyebrows and he corrects himself, "semi-legal ESA?"

"It's actually extremely safe. The jump was started by Budarendi Rakotondrandria." He looks blank. "Also known as Bud Tondra? The father of the recyclable space suit?"

R'ger stares. "Bud Tondra was from SK2?"

"Yeah, he's a local folk hero. Lower-lev inventor makes good," I say, dragging a hand through the air in front of me as if pasting up a title. "He perfected it here and then sold the design to AstroTech for billions. They still have the original forming booth down there; you step in and a suit forms around you. It snaps on an oxygen tank, and you're good to jump. Completely automated, so there's no possibility of human error. Of course, the suits are fairly crude. Big mitts over your hands, baggy suit, misshapen bubble head. But they work, and the material is completely recyclable.

"Look! There goes one!"

We stare through the glass at the open space below us. A figure karooms out of the airlock and away from the station, a translucent suit loose around his form. He spins and twists around, only a narrow rope keeping him from flying out into the galaxy. Or more likely, I squint at the angle, into the side of that S'Ride liner.

The figure flings his arms and legs out. "That guy must parachute dirt-side," I mutter to R'ger, under the loud exclamations from the rest of the tourists grouped around us. "He thinks that will slow him down. There's no friction in space."

The human projectile reaches the end of its tether and zooms back toward the station. "He's going to splat into the side!" a woman's voice shouts.

R'ger raises an eyebrow at me, and I smile. "The smart BunGs they use will stop him before he splats against the wall," I say. "You ready to try it?"

He laughs and shakes his head. "Watching is enough excitement for me," he says. "What else have you got?"

We spend the afternoon doing the full-bore tourist bit. I take him to the rainforest on Level 75, we poke through a black-market bazaar on Level 7, then stroll through the glittering shops on 46. After coffee and pastries at Dolce Amour, where I charge the huge bill to my mother's client entertainment account, we float down to Level 8 and watch a round of zero-grav basketball in the sports center.

Transparent aluminum separates the observation deck from the zero-grav floor. The players leap and bounce off walls, ceiling and floor as they hurl the ball around the room. One player scores, and I realize it's Bobby Putin, looking sexy in his sweat-dampened skin suit. When he lands in a deep squat on the window and then shoves off again, the four girls sharing the deck with us all sigh. The guy with them starts fanning himself. I must admit, his athletic skill is amazing. When they take a time-out, he notices me and waves. I'm embarrassed to say my heart speeds up when he smiles at me, but I try to look cool when I wave back. The rest of the spectators give me the evil eye.

"OK, that's enough sports," R'ger laughs, ushering me out of the observation deck. So, we bounce back up to the low oxygen chambers on 43, where we stare through similar windows at visitors from Klimuk who stare back at us.

"I'm not sure if we're the zoo animals, or they are," says R'ger.

"Kelly-Kornienko is one of the few stations that has dual oxygen environments," I say, sounding like a bad travel-vid narration. "This chamber is meant to allow natural interaction."

"Still looks like a zoo to me," he replies. "We can't go in there, and they can't come out here. Weird to think we're all descended from the same ancestors."

"Acclimatization to low oxygen doesn't take too many generations," I say. "And I've read that most of the settlers on Klimuk were from high altitude locations on Earth. No one else could survive there." As we watch, a Klimukan suddenly points through the barrier at a gaudily dressed woman on our side. She grabs the arm of the man next to her, arms waving, mouth going non-stop. Although the audio channels aren't active, it's obvious she is talking about the woman's clothing. The man flicks his holo-ring to life and takes a picture of the woman.

"He's probably ordering a copy of her robe for his wife," I tell R'ger. "This section was built for all kinds of lofty, idealistic reasons, but mostly the Klimukans come here to shop."

We visit the museums of art and history, then wander down to one of my favorite restaurants on Level 11 for dinner. "It isn't expensive," I tell R'ger as we take our seats, "but the pierogis are to die for."

The Happy Poel is not what you'd call upscale. Well, obviously, since it's down on Level 11, you knew that. It looks like every other eatery in the lower half of the station, except for a dense display of stickers and magnets on the front of the counter separating the kitchen from the small dining area. Shabby, mismatched stools wait along the counter, the dishes and flatware are all recyclable, and greasy stains mar the floor. A scattering of lower levs occupy a few of the other plastek covered tables. The owner claims his recipes are all family secrets, but the food is just standard fare. Except for the pierogis.

My holo-ring vibrates to indicate the menu has been downloaded, and R'ger opens his palm to flick his to life, but I wave a hand. "Don't bother looking," I say. His brows draw down in surprise, but he sits back and folds his hands in his lap. I wave to catch the attention of the burly man behind the counter and say, "We'll have the Happy Platter, Ye'an."

While we wait for the food, R'ger spins some space dust about growing up in the wilds of Armstrong. "I'm the sixth of nine children," he says. "My parents needed that many kids to care for all the livestock. The re-kows have to be milked three times a day, so you need enough hands to manage that."

I nod wisely. "I've heard they give twenty-five liters a day," I say. I have no idea; I've never heard of a re-kow before today.

"No, you're lucky to get a pint. But they bite if you don't keep them milked. I fell asleep in the hay barn one day and woke up with a huge bite taken out of my shoulder." He rotates his arm carefully. "Still gets stiff at 2 pm every day."

I roll my eyes. "I'll bet if I searched you right now, it would say you were a single child, raised in the city."

He smiles. "No, I have a sister. Remember, I told you about the goat the other night. Her son is about your age. Arun. You'd like him." He flicks his holo-ring and a pic pops up on his palm. A young man with dark olive skin and thick black hair smiles at me from the deck of some kind of boat. "I took this last year when we sailed through the Tivu Islands. He's a pilot based out of Sally Ride, but he loves the water, too."

"No wonder you thought I was an idiot for telling you about the S'Ride nose art," I say.

He looks affronted. "I never said you were an idiot."

"No, you're too polite for that." I laugh. "What does he fly?"

"Small trader," R'ger replies, serious for once. "It's an interesting story. He left home when he graduated from secondary school. Said he wanted to make it on his own, not on family ties. He moved to S'Ride, worked as a cargo handler for a few years until he earned a scholarship to flight school. Then he worked his way up in a small transport company. When the owner retired, he sold out to Arun." R'ger smooths the crumpled napkin lying next to his plate and looks up at me from under his bushy eyebrows.

I return his gaze, keeping my face neutral. What is he getting at? Does he somehow know my background? "How enterprising of him," I say after a long pause.

Ye'an appears beside us, his hand wrapped in a fold of his apron, carrying a large platter. Steam from the freshly cooked pierogis wafts toward us, making my tummy growl. R'ger laughs and rubs his own stomach. "I'm glad I'm not the only one."

The Happy Platter contains a dozen different types of pierogis, both savory and sweet, some fried, some steamed, some baked. Small bowls of sauces are tucked in among the pastries. Ye'an hands us each a pair of "traditional chopsticks" and offers a "bone appeteet."

R'ger picks up the sticks. "Traditional chopsticks? I'm no historian," he says, "but I don't think the Poels on ancient Earth used chopsticks."

"Shh!" I hush him. "The *Księżna* will hear you." I give my head a slight jerk at the back corner of the restaurant. An ancient woman sits in a throne-like chair, a thick, dark blanket over her lap and tucked around her. Her eyes are closed, and her head nods slightly, the wispy gray hair drifting around her face. She's wearing a lumpy, black sweater over a glaring pink t-shirt that appears to have a grumpy cat on the front, although it's hard to see with the blanket partially covering it. She looks like a sweet old woman—if you don't know any better.

"What's a 'chesna'?" R'ger asks, staring at the tiny crone.

"*Księżna*," I correct him. "Ye'an says it means 'Duchess' in ancient Earth Poelish. She's his grandmother or great-grandmother, and she pretty much runs this Level. You don't want to piss her off. She also believes herself to be an authority on all things Poelish, so questioning her knowledge of pierogis, and how they're meant to be eaten, would really annoy her. People disappear when they upset the *Księżna*." I use my chopsticks to pick up a steamed pierogi and take a bite, sighing in contentment. I love good food.

R'ger drags his eyes away from the Duchess. "Why did you bring me to the lair of a mafia queen?" he whispers, the chopsticks hanging limply from his fingers.

I tap on his hand and show him how to hold the sticks. "The *Sprzężaj*, not mafia. And they don't kill anyone; they just make them disappear."

He looks at me, his face a mask of disbelief. "They just make people disappear. You do know that's a euphemism for killing them, right?"

"Actually, it isn't. The *Sprzężaj* have made a name for themselves by deporting undesirables. Everyone who disappears from here turns up somewhere else, completely alive. Trust me, I've done the research. But forget about that." I pick up a pierogi. "I brought you here because the pierogis are delicious! Try one of these fried ones."

We eat in companionable silence for a long while, commenting occasionally on the amazing flavors. R'ger eats almost as much as I do, and we stage a mock sword fight with the chopsticks in a duel over the last cinnamon, brown sugar pierogi. I finally hold up my stick in surrender.

"You've fought valiantly," R'ger says, "and if I were a gentleman, I would allow you this prize. But since I'm leaving in two days and you can come here whenever you want..." His voice trails off as he takes a bite of the pastry and sighs.

We order espresso and sit back. "How did you happen to find this place?" R'ger asks. "I've been to SK2 several times over the years, and no one has ever mentioned it. Folks on the upper Levels don't usually come down this far, do they? But somehow, I don't think you're a normal upper-lev, are you?"

I eye him for a moment. Maybe I should tell him my story. After hearing about his nephew, I think he'd understand, and maybe have a new perspective on my situation or even some advice on how to handle my mother. I don't think handing him knowledge of my alternate identity could put her at any kind of disadvantage. Although I hardly know this man, for some reason, I know I can trust him. Maybe I need to just trust my instincts like Ty did with me. Of course, look how that turned out. I take a sip of my coffee, blow out a breath, and launch into my story.

He listens silently through the whole thing. I tell him about moving dirtside, and working my way through the Techno-Inst. I relay Kara's revelations about her agreement with Hy-Mi, although I leave out my feelings of betrayal. I talk about my job in the MCC, and kind of lump together the discovery of the body, Patrick and losing my job.

R'ger glances away and asks casually, "How does the Board Agent fit into all this?"

I wrinkle my nose, expecting the question, but not enjoying it. "He's investigating the body," I say shortly, "so he questioned me. My mother walked into the office while we were talking." I scratch my head. "At the time, I thought that was how she knew I was on-station, but now that I've heard Kara's story...she obviously knew I was here." My voice trails off.

"Why do you think she waited until now to invite you back home?" he asks, his hazel eyes now fixed on my face. His eyes drill into me, and I drag mine away.

"Invite? Ha." I think about it for a minute. "She wants to keep tabs on me, and it's easier when I don't know she's watching. But once we'd come face to face, she couldn't exactly pretend ignorance anymore, right?"

"Could be. Maybe she's worried about you." He sips his drink and avoids my eye.

"Right." I snap. "I think it's more about control than concern. Whatever. I don't want to talk about it." I fling my napkin onto the table. "Shall we go?"

R'ger puts a hand on my wrist. "What about her?" he says, nodding toward the ancient woman in the corner.

"What about her?" I repeat. "Do you think she's reporting to my mother, too?"

He starts to shake his head but stops and looks considering. "Maybe. No, I was wondering if you've talked to her about the murder. I'm no expert in the underworld, but it seems like she might be a good source of information."

I can't believe I hadn't thought of that myself. The *Księżna* knows everything that happens in the lower part of the station. She must have heard *something* about Gonzeles, who was killed on Level 8. She won't talk to Sec Agents, but maybe she'll talk to me.

"I need a gift," I mutter, patting my pockets. If I'd thought of this before, I could have lifted something from Mother's house. Maybe a vase or small painting. Or some of Dav's croissants.

"Will this work?" R'ger asks. He's holding a small, flat rock in his palm. The rock has been carved and painted, depicting a pastoral scene in minute detail. "It's a regional art form," he says. "The rock comes from the Vistula River on Armstrong. Smooth but very lightweight." He hands me the rock. "It's a family craft, passed on by parents to their children. Some of the artists are tenth or eleventh generation."

I gaze down, taking in a meadow with grazing cows, (re-kows?) flowers, and a hill with a castle on top, then look speculatively at R'ger. This is exactly the type of gift the *Księżna* favors. I wonder how he knew. Clearly, R'ger is much more than a rube from Armstrong. Since he's a business associate of my mother's I should have realized that from the start, but his aw-shucks charm has distracted me from the truth. I make a mental note to be more cautious about what I tell him.

"If you use a magnifier, you can see people in the windows of the castle, and individual leaves on the trees," he says, apparently oblivious to my suspicions. "Vistula River rocks are naturally magnetized, so it should fit in nicely with the current decor." He gestures toward the kitsch-encrusted counter.

"This is beautiful," I breathe, reluctantly handing it back to him. "But I can't ask you to part with such a treasure."

He smiles and folds my fingers around the cool stone. "I always bring a half-dozen of these with me on every journey. You never know when you'll need a unique bribe."

"Seriously? But they must cost a fortune!" I stare at it again, entranced by the detail.

"Sadly, they do not. At least not at the source. Now, if you were to try to buy one off-planet, they would be fabulously expensive. Fortunately, they don't take up much mass or space in my luggage, and I've found they are well worth the trouble. Take it."

With a muttered, "Stay here," I set my napkin on the table and approach the crone in the corner. She appears to be deeply asleep, but a glance at Ye'an tells me she's receiving guests. He wouldn't let me get within three meters if she didn't wish to be disturbed.

I sit down on the low stool next to her throne and place the painted stone on her blanket shrouded knee. Then I sit back and wait. Around me, the patrons of the restaurant ignore me and the old woman as if we don't even exist. Many of them probably think she's just the owner's old mother. The rest know better than to approach, or even look at the *Księżna*. Drawing the *Księżna*'s attention to oneself can be a risky proposition.

As I discovered many years ago. When I formulated my plan to escape the station, a long-time station acquaintance introduced me to the *Księżna*. The *Sprzężaj* doesn't do charity work. But if you can provide a trade or a profit, they can make a person disappear. I'd paid an enormous amount for the disappearance and promised favors at a later date as well. Those favors have been called in over the last two years since I returned to SK2, but that's another story.

In light of Kara's recent revelations, it suddenly occurs to me that my relationship with the *Księżna* was probably not exactly as I remember it. When the old woman opens her eyes, I throw caution to void and ignore protocol.

"What happened to Yavula?" I ask. The Tereshkovan woman had been a custom clothier on SK2 for decades before I was born. When I was trying to run away, a series of careful conversations had led me to her. Although she'd made most of my clothes for years, until then I hadn't realized she had connections to the seedier side of SK2. "She introduced me to you, and then 'retired' while I was off-station. Where did she go?"

The *Księżna* picks up the miniature and tucks it away somewhere. "Is zat really vat you came here to ask me, malutka?" she croaks.

I stare into her cold grey eyes. "No, but you're going to tell me anyway. You owe me."

Her dead gaze hardens on me. "Ze ledger is even. Demanding answers ven none are owed you iz not a vize course."

"Six years ago," I say, "I paid you a large number of credits and promised several favors in exchange for your assistance in 'relocating'. Now I find you were paid by someone else for that same relocation," I bluff. I have no proof, but suddenly, I'm convinced my mother pulled all the strings behind my escape. From this vantage, the whole thing was way too easy.

Is that a slight flush on the *Księżna*'s cheeks? She looks away for a long time —as if deciding what to tell me. Finally, she sighs and pinches her lips together. "Ve must speak in private," she says, pressing the touchscreen on the arm of her chair. With a slight lurch, the throne and stool begin to rotate into the wall, like the entrance to a secret passageway in an ancient vid. R'ger lurches to his feet, but I wave him back to his seat. I send a quick text.

All ok. Wait.

When the platform stops rotating, we're in a small, well-lighted room with a comfortable couch, a kitchenette and a half-open door leading to a tiny bathroom. One-way glass offers a view of the restaurant. R'ger is seated again, looking relaxed, except his eyes, which are fixed on this corner. Ye'an continues to cook as if the *Księżna*'s sudden departure is normal. Maybe it is. No one else seems to have noticed.

The *Księżna* throws off the blanket and gets to her feet. Bright orange fitness leggings encase tiny but muscular legs and a surprisingly firm butt. Without the huge throne and blanket, she looks completely different. Still ancient, but more like one of those ninety-year-old marathon runners than a crippled old babushka. She strides across the room and takes a beer from the small fridge. Popping the top, she turns to lean against the counter, staring at me as she takes a swig.

The *Księżna* puts the beer down on the counter and folds her arms across her chest. When she speaks, her accent is gone, replaced with crisp, station-standard diction. "Yavula retired to Tereshkova, as you know. Her relocation was funded by SK'Corp, as was yours. The payment you provided me was deducted from the full cost charged to SK2. I can't believe you thought that paltry amount was enough for a first-class relocation." She laughs dryly.

"What about the favors you called in?" The pierogis sit like lead in my stomach. My mother controls SK'Corp; she funded everything!

The *Księżna* waves a hand. "Those were minor tasks. Hardly worth counting."

"They counted to me," I say, my voice surprisingly firm.

She gives me hard look and a short nod. "You're right." With obvious reluctance, she hands the painted stone back to me. "What did you really come here to ask?"

"What do you know about the body that was found on Level 6?" I pocket the rock before she changes her mind. If she thinks she owes me these answers, I'm not going to argue.

Her dark eyes follow the rock until it disappears into my pocket, then she jerks her eyes back to my face. "Rumors say a top-lev is involved. Someone at the highest level is funding the cover-up, so someone at the highest level must be committing the murders."

Nothing new there. "How many are you aware of?" I ask.

"The Gonzeles girl was the fifth," she says. "Three female, two male. All lower-levs, except the first one. She was staying on Level 68."

Only one more than Ty suspected. "You know the identities of the victims?" I ask.

The old woman nods. "We specialize in making people disappear, so when someone else starts manipulating the system, we notice." She rummages in a drawer and pulls out a small square of paper and an old-fashioned pencil. She scribbles, then turns back to me, holding the scrap in her hand. "The girl from 68 was visiting. The official logs show she departed on an S'Ride cruise ship, but she did not. The next three were lower-levs who now appear to have *officially* transferred off-station the day before their bodies were reported but then forgotten."

She taps the sheet against her lips, thinking, then hands it to me. "There are the names."

"Why are you giving this to me?" I ask. I glance at the paper, but only Gonzeles' name is familiar.

The woman grimaces. "As you pointed out, we owe you. Besides, having a top-lev running around killing people isn't good for any of us. Since you're one of them, maybe you can get this psychopath sent away for treatment."

"I think you overestimate my influence," I reply, sliding the paper into my pocket.

She waves away my comment. "Talk to your mother. I'm sure she can take care of everything."

I narrow my eyes at her. "How do you know my mother isn't involved in the cover-up?"

The *Księżna* laughs, and it sounds genuinely amused. "The Ice Dame wouldn't be involved in anything so disorganized as murder. Too hard to control a psychopath. And mayhem is bad for business. No, Dame Morgan is smart enough to know covering up is not a long-term solution."

"So, all I need to do is figure out who's doing the killing, and I can let my mama take care of it?" I ask sarcastically.

"Exactly."

THIRTY

As we stroll back to the concourse, I hold the stone magnet out to R'ger. "I didn't need a bribe," I say. "Turns out she still owed me one."

Again, he folds my fingers around the cool rock. "Keep it. You might find it useful later. Why did she owe you?"

I look away. "Old story," I say. I slide the stone into my pocket and the scrap of paper crinkles. "But she did give me some information that may help with the investigation."

R'ger smiles. "Good. But don't tell me. I think the less I know, the better."

When we step through the door to the penthouse float tube lobby on Level 82, the small vestibule is deserted.

R'ger raises an eyebrow at me. "Is this normal?"

"No," I reply. "This desk is *never* left unattended. Whoever is on duty today is going to find he's been reassigned to guard a dirtside gas mine. Let's see what's going on upstairs."

I flick my holo-ring to life and sign in to the station surveillance system. Apparently, the Annabelle holo-ring really does have full access; the page loads immediately. I bring up the cameras in the Level 83 lobby.

R'ger peers at me through the holo. Maybe it's just an effect created by the ring, but his eyes seem to be sparkling. "Looks safe enough," he says without inflection. "Shall we go up?"

"Sure," I reply slowly. "But let me make a call, first." I flick a speed dial, and my call goes to message. "Ty, if you're monitoring this, come out to the penthouse vestibule. The Sec Agent on duty is missing."

I wait for a few seconds, peering out to the busy Level 82 concourse, but Ty doesn't come charging out. "OK, let's go," I tell R'ger. We go back into the vestibule and float up to the penthouse lobby. I step out trying to look casual, but ready for anything. R'ger rolls across the floor, like a vid hero, coming to a crouch behind a large overstuffed chair. Or at least he tries. About halfway there, his robe gets tangled around his head, and he ends up on his back like a dead bug, legs flailing. Fortunately, for his dignity and my sanity, he's wearing shorts beneath the robe. He struggles upright, pulls the robe down over his knobby knees and grins. His eyes dance. I roll mine.

The lobby is still empty. It's also still perfectly arranged, with every chair, vase and table in place. "The guy down at the desk probably went to take a leak," R'ger says, slowly rising.

I snort. "Take a leak?" I ask. "What the heck does that mean?"

"I thought you were some kind of ancient slang guru?" He retorts, rubbing his shoulder. "It means exactly what it sounds like."

"Ew." I circle around the perimeter of the room. "Did you hurt yourself with your dramatic entry?"

"Go ahead and laugh," he says. "But when the laser blasters are singeing your curls, you'll wish you had my ninja skills."

He continues jabbering on about his lightning reflexes, but I don't hear the rest because I've just discovered another body.

"R'ger!" I screech. "Call emergency services! She's still breathing!" I drop to my knees and check for a pulse. Thank heaven for all those old medical dramas I've seen. I yank one of the froofy quilted arm-covers off the couch and clamp it over the huge bloody gash in her side. The cloth soaks through in seconds, and red oozes out around my fingers. As I kneel there, my vision tunnels until there's only my fingers, the sticky cloth and crimson puddle spreading around me. Please God, please God, please God…

Time telescopes and what feels like hours later, strong hands grasp my shoulders and pull me away from the woman. A Med Tech in a pristine white coverall slides into my place without releasing pressure on the wound. I stumble to my feet and stand swaying in a corner.

"Triana, are you ok?" O'Neill's face swims briefly into focus before my stomach heaves, and I whirl to vomit into one of the potted plants. Just like old times.

THE VACUUM OF SPACE

I'M SITTING in a plush brown velvet sofa in the penthouse lobby. One of the top-lev maintenance staff has cleaned my hands and spread plas sheets over the furniture to protect it from my blood-soaked clothing. Sec Agents swarm over the room, taking holos and fiber samples and who knows what else. R'ger perches on the arm of my couch, absently rubbing my shoulder while we sit. He looks as shell-shocked as I am.

Med Techs spray-foamed the girl into a cocoon and carted her away on a float bed almost before I realized what had happened. And then it took a little longer to realize I know her. Camille. Carina? No, Candice, Nicolai's drunken girlfriend. She was pretty messed up. The black eye was probably from running into the wall at Mother's place the other night, but the other injuries were newer. While I'd tried to stop the bleeding from that huge gash, R'ger had called for help. It didn't take the Med Techs long to respond; as you can imagine, calls to the top-Level are answered immediately.

"Would you like to do the interview here, Sera Morgan, or move down to my office?" Ty asks when the Sec Agents have finished, and the maintenance staff has moved in to erase the evidence. "Or perhaps, your compartment?" He waves toward Mother's door.

"No!" I say, a little too loudly. I shake my head and try again. "Here is fine. Have you looked at the vids yet?"

"I want to hear your story first." The way he says "story" makes me a little uncomfortable. He flicks his holo-ring. "I'll be recording, of course."

"The guard downstairs was missing—did you get my message?" He shakes his head. "I called you as soon as I noticed he was missing. Then I checked the live vid and couldn't see anything, so we came up."

"We?" Ty's voice is sharp.

I gesture to R'ger, who had moved away when O'Neill approached me. He's talking to another Board Sec Agent on the other side of the room. "R'ger and I. We came up, and when I came around that couch, I saw her. Camille. No, Candice."

"You know the victim?"

"Kind of. So do you. She's Nicolai Bezos' girlfriend." He gives me a blank stare. "Remember, we saw them at Belle76? And she was at Mother's dinner party on Sunday, until she walked into a wall and gave herself a concussion or something. That was before you arrived. I'm pretty sure that's where she got the black eye. I don't know who hacked at her. She was in bad shape; he might have beaten her up a little first." I'm babbling now, and my hands are shaking.

Ty sits down beside me and takes my hands. "Breathe," he says. I do a few deep breaths and get a grip on myself.

"Really, that's it. I found her. I tried to stop the bleeding while R'ger called it in, and then the Med Techs arrived." I pull on his hands. "Whoever did it has to be on the vid, they can't have erased it already. Pull it up, quickly!"

"It won't do any good," he says, as he flicks his holo-ring.

"What do you mean? Oh." The holo in his hand is a grainy, pixelated mess. "Someone messed with the cameras before the murder?"

"It's not a murder," Ty says, his voice grim. "She's still alive. Maybe she'll be able to tell us more once she's stabilized. But yes, this means either the creep has a new set of technicians, or he has some skills himself. And now he's not just randomly killing people; he's planning ahead." He slams his hand down on the arm of the sofa.

"And you!" He turns on me. "You're running around the station with some middle-aged gigolo! Who the hell is 'R'ger' if that's his real name? I know how you are about pseudonyms."

"That's a low blow." I glare at him. "And R'ger is a business associate of my mother's. That means he's been more thoroughly vetted than a Sec Agent. Or a Maint Tech."

I leap to my feet, sick of his high-handed moral superiority. "I am not as stupid as you think! R'ger arrived on-station *after* the first four murders happened. There's no way he's the culprit! And that's right, I said four! There have been five total, which you might know if you'd spend more time doing your job and less time sniffing around hyper-sexed top-levs with breasts the size of small moons!"

I rip the scrap of paper out of my pocket and fling it at him. "Here are the names of the victims!" I shout.

He catches the paper and stares down at it, before stuffing it into his own pocket. Then he grabs my arm. "Just because he passed a security check doesn't mean he's clean," he hisses. "And he could still be involved. There were half a dozen people on this psychopath's payroll and that's only the ones we know about! Your 'R'ger' could be Baker's replacement!"

"Why don't you go ask your precious boss about R'ger?" I fling a venomous look at my mother's compartment door. Someone from every compartment has at least poked their head out to see what's going on, but Mother's door has remained closed. I'm pretty sure she's home, but clearly, she doesn't care to get involved with the riff-raff. "I'm going home!"

I fling around toward the float tube, but Ty's iron grip is still locked around my arm. "You aren't going anywhere! You can either go into that compartment, where I know you will be safe, or you can go to a cell on Level 1."

We glare at each other, but I can see he really means it. Fine. I wrench my arm away from him and stalk to the door marked A. It slides silently open and closed again behind me. I kick the wall, wishing desperately for a door that can be slammed.

THIRTY-ONE

CAMILLE. No, Candice. I know nothing about this girl. I've called down to the hospital where they refused to tell me anything until I flashed my ID. Once the Morgan name popped up on screen, the comm tech couldn't wait to pass me off to the top administrator on duty. He assured me that Candice is in critical but stable condition, whatever that means. Her family is with her.

I didn't even know if she had a family.

To be fair, I only met her twice, if you can even call it that. And she was drunk both times. But her boyfriend is a friend of mine, or at least he's a colleague who isn't a business rival, which is what passes for friendship among the top levs.

I hate it here.

I'm sitting on the bottom step when Mother sweeps into the living room. "Are you hurt?" she asks, almost sounding gentle.

"I'm fine," I say tonelessly. "A girl I hardly know was almost killed outside our front door, I can't live in my own place because there's a psychopath on the loose, and I got blood on the Sierna tile." I gesture to the bloody footprints across the foyer, tears spilling down my face. I wrap my arms around myself and rock back and forth.

After a slight hesitation, Mother sits down beside me. She awkwardly pats me on the shoulder and I fling myself into her arms. Just once, maybe she'll be a real mother. I cry for what feels like hours. At some point, Hy-Mi arrives and takes me off the Ice Dame's hands. I don't really know how it happened, but suddenly I'm being helped up the stairs by the old man.

I brush tears away with my sleeve, but Hy-Mi hands me a soft white handkerchief. I wipe my eyes, blow my nose and tuck the cloth into my pocket. Hy-Mi taught me years ago that a lady always has a handkerchief laundered before returning it. I almost smile at the thought. The old guy has always been here for me. When we reach my bedroom, I drop down onto the bed and look up at him with bleary eyes. He looks old and tired, and gray, in a way he never did before.

"Are you ok?" I ask him. I know he's well over eighty, but mother provides stellar benefits for her employees. Rejuvenation surgery is part of the deal. Life expectancy is close to 130 these days if you live in the right financial demographic.

"I am well." He bows slightly.

"No, you aren't." I bow back, mocking him.

"I've missed you, these last six years." He smiles, a little sadly. "You're right, I'm not in the best of health. You know, Victoriana passed away last fall. It's been, difficult."

Victoriana was Hy-Mi's first spousal contract. They'd remained friends for decades after the contract ended. In fact, I believe she was the reason several of his later contracts fizzled out before their expiration date. Well, her and my mother. Hy-Mi's attention was always devoted to the two of them, and there wasn't room for another woman, no matter how hard he tried. Clearly, Victoriana had his heart. Mother, on the other hand, pays him well for that devotion, but he has a sense of loyalty to her that boggles my mind.

"I'm sorry to hear that," I say. "I didn't realize."

He bows again. "With Victoriana gone, my children off-station, and you absent, life is a little bleaker. Plus, I'm just old."

I smile a little. "You don't seem any older than when I left," I say, but it's a lie.

"You never were any good at bluffing," he says to me. "Don't worry, I may be a bit faded, but I have a lot of good years ahead of me. Now, what are we going to do about you?"

"What do you mean?"

"You won't be happy here," he replies. "That's why I convinced Dame Morgan to let you leave all those years ago. I knew you needed something different. She hopes you will decide to stay, but I don't see that happening. We need to figure out how to let you live your life while still satisfying some part of your mother's desire for…" he trails off.

"Desire for what?" I ask. "A cookie cutter version of herself? She should have gotten a clone instead of a daughter."

Hy-Mi makes a superstitious hand gesture. I've seen him do it many times, but he's never been willing to explain it, or even show it to me. He does it so quickly, you'd only notice if you're paying strict attention. I think he's embarrassed to admit that a sophisticated, well-educated man like himself has superstitions. *I* think there's lots out there bigger than any of us know and if making hand signs comforts him, then I'm all for it. Of course, I also believe there's a big invisible dude watching over the universe, remember? Who am I to judge?

"Don't speak of clones," he says. "I've read they're attempting human cloning over on Cernan 2. Again. History is doomed to repeat." He shudders.

"It was just a figure of speech," I say. "Look, I don't want to live here. I'm happy being a Maintenance Tech down on 2. If she'll just let me be Triana, I'll come visit once in a while. If she wants an heir, she can get my brother. He should be done with Universitat soon, right?"

Hy-Mi nods absently. "Maybe that would be enough. You must convince her."

My eyes widen. "Me? Convince *her*? Yeah, that's going to happen. Can't you talk to her?"

"You must do this yourself," he replies. "Helping you leave six years ago almost cost me my job. Besides, you aren't a child anymore. You must learn to stand up for yourself." He looks me up and down. "Being on your own has been good for you. You are stronger than you think."

"Except I was never really on my own, was I? You and Mother were pulling the strings the whole time! Besides, I got fired, you know," I say. Hy-Mi gives me an inscrutable look, so I continue. "Well, suspended for a month. There's an auditor named Patrick, and I made a colossal error on the comm. She remanded me for retraining. When I tried to talk to her, she suspended me. The retraining was fair enough, although I only made the error because I was helping O'Neill. But when I tried to get her to contact him, she got really testy. It feels like some kind of personal grudge, but I have no idea why." I flick my holo-ring and start a search.

"She couldn't know about your connection to Dame Morgan?"

I glance at him. "How could she?"

The search results pop up, and I make the connection. "How pathetic is this? Her son was in my class at the Techno-Inst. Different last name, of course, but now that I think about it, she does resemble him. He was pretty smart, but I beat him out for an internship."

"The Ahari Corp internship?" Hy-Mi asks.

I look at him in surprise. "You really did keep tabs on me, didn't you?"

"It was my job," he says. "That wasn't just any internship; that was the most prestigious position available to a student. Perhaps Patrick believes you took that from her son."

"Would she really be that vindictive over something that happened years ago, to her son? It's not like I stole his lunch money or ruined his life prospects. He got another perfectly good internship and last I heard he's working in the Ops Center in PK-35. That's way better than being a Maint Tech."

"People do not always behave rationally when their children's welfare is involved," Hy-Mi answers, and I'm not sure if he's talking about Patrick or my mother. Or maybe himself. "Perhaps something can be done about this Patrick." He turns toward the door, but I stop him.

"Do you know anything about R'ger Chaturvedi?" I ask.

The old man goes still for a second, then turns back to me. "Why do you ask?"

I shrug. "I met him here the other day and spent today showing him the station. Agent O'Neill suggested I was unwise to spend time with someone I don't know when there's a deranged killer on the loose, but I know you must have done a background on him before he was invited here."

He relaxes a fraction. "I think you're safe with Ser Chaturvedi. Agent O'Neill can contact me if he has specific concerns." Hy-Mi nods to me and leaves.

LATE THE NEXT MORNING, R'ger and I meet for breakfast at Sweetcide. It's a bakery on Level 34 that is famous for nothing. I'm not sure how he even knew about it; I've never heard of it. The bakery is tucked away on B Ring, between an appliance store and a travel agency. I arrive a few minutes early, order coffee, and squeeze into one of the four tiny tables jammed between the pastry counter and the wall.

As I wait for R'ger, other patrons flow through, ordering bagels, muffins, and scones. None of them get a beverage. I start to wonder if I've made a mistake. How bad can the coffee be?

It's bad. The surly girl behind the counter slams a plastek cup down on the counter, slopping grey liquid over the side, grounds floating in the puddle. I fill the cup to the top with cream, sprinkle two packets of Shug'r on top, and plunk it down on the stained plastek tablecloth, making another grainy puddle.

After a while, R'ger trudges in. His greying reddish curls stick out every direction, and his eyes are bloodshot. He orders something at the counter, waiting until the girl hands him a sludgy, green drink. Then he shuffles over to me, setting his drink on the table and hanging a canvas messenger bag on the back of his chair.

I give the drink a dubious look and ask, "How did you select this particular venue for our breakfast meeting?"

R'ger takes a swig of his swamp water. His cheeks balloon, his eyes bug out, and I start looking for cover. After an ominous pause, he swallows with obvious effort and offers a small grimace. "It was suggested by a business associate. I'm thinking she's soon to be a *former* business associate. She may be trying to poison me." He picks up the glass and contemplates its contents.

"Please tell me you aren't going to drink the rest of that?" I beg. "You can have my coffee instead."

He gives my cup a stern look as he sets his beaker down. "Thanks, I'll pass. How are you feeling today?"

"I'm OK," I say. "As OK as I can be, I guess. You don't look so good."

He laughs and raises his glass in salute. "Flattery will get you everything." He sets the green stuff down without drinking. "I didn't sleep well. I was hoping this 'Eye-Opener' would give me some energy, but… Maybe food would be better. Do you want to try the donuts?"

I look around at the steady stream of people buying pastries but decline. "Uh, no. I think I'm going to cut my losses here. What do you say we go get something from Dav?"

"Dav?" he asks as we get to our feet. I grab our two beverages and set them into the dish bin by the door. The surly girl gives me a poisonous look and mutters something.

Waving cheerfully at her, I call out, "Have a great day!" then duck in case she hurls something at me. She looks like she wants to, but she just keeps muttering and selling muffins.

"Dav is Mother's pastry chef," I tell R'ger, leading the way back to the concourse. "Breakfast from Dav tops anything this place could produce, trust me. Hey, you forgot your bag." I stop, looking at him, then turn back toward B Ring.

R'ger grabs my arm and swings me back toward the concourse. "I didn't have a bag," he says, walking faster.

"Yes, you did," I say. "It was a tan messenger bag, and you hung it on your chair."

"No, I didn't," he repeats and gives me a hard look.

"Are you using me as a cover for some kind of black-market drop?" I ask, laughing.

He walks a little faster and doesn't answer.

I stop cold. "Seriously?" I ask him, catching up as he almost races across the concourse. "Slow down! You're supposed to be inconspicuous."

He slows his pace. "Like you're some kind of expert smuggler?"

Shaking my head, I laugh. "No, but I've seen lots of vids. What was in the bag? Wait, I don't think I want to know."

He smiles reluctantly. "It was just a bunch of those painted rocks. The *Księżna* sent me a message last night; she wanted to buy them."

"I hope you got the money up front," I say as we step out on 82. "I wouldn't trust her any farther than I could throw her."

He shrugs. "It wouldn't be a huge loss. And I'd consider it money well spent. It allowed me to cross 'black-market smuggler' off my bucket list."

Twenty minutes later, we're sitting in the top-lev lobby, eating Dav's croissants. I snuck in through the back entrance and pilfered a plate of them while Dav was consulting with the chef. I guess Mother is planning another big dinner for next week. She's always got some kind of entertainment in the planning stages, and I'm sure she'll let me know if my presence is required. I'm just glad I was able to get in and out without attracting her attention.

"They cleaned up the crime scene pretty fast," R'ger says, his gesture encompassing the pristine area.

I wrinkled my nose. "Can't inconvenience the residents," I reply. A creeped-out shiver runs down my spine, and I turn in my chair, so my back is to the area where we found Candice.

"So, is this a permanent move?" R'ger asks me, jerking his chin at compartment A. He hands me a cup of coffee he purchased on Level 82 while I was on my pastry liberation run. "Did you give up on the job downstairs?"

"No!" I shake my head, flakes of pastry flying in all directions. R'ger hands me a napkin. "I told you about Patrick, the investigator, right? Turns out her son was in my class, dirt-side. Could she be holding a grudge against me because I won an internship her son wanted?"

As R'ger considers, the door to Suite F opens and Bobby Putin strolls out. He's wearing a shiny red athletic skin suit, and he looks fantastic. Every muscle and, er, bulge is outlined in mind-shattering detail. My brain reminds me that his perfection is thanks to lots of money and medical know-how, but my libido doesn't care: he's hot. When he notices me, he waves and saunters our direction. Down girl!

"I don't know her, obviously, but I suppose it's possible," R'ger replies. It takes me a second to remember what he's referring to. "I know some people who hold grudges like that, although personally, I think it's childish. But if she thinks not getting that internship killed her son's chance at something bigger, she might hold it against you."

"Whose reputation are we shredding?" Bobby asks, dropping a gym bag on the floor, throwing himself into a chair, and scooping up a pastry. I can't decide if his obvious conviction that he is welcome anywhere is attractive or irritating. His ability to eat Dav's pastries and still look like a Greek statue is definitely irritating. I suck in my gut.

R'ger gives me a questioning look, and I shrug. "Annabelle's boss suspended her, and we're discussing whether it might be a personal grudge."

"Your boss?" Bobby's eyes dart back and forth between me and R'ger. His dark hair falls into his face, and he gives a practiced flick of his head to throw it out of the way. "You mean the Ice Dame?"

R'ger lets out a short laugh. "Are they still calling her that?"

I shake my head. "No, I've been working down on one of the lower-levs."

Bobby's green eyes widen. "The pseudonym wasn't just for the Multi-Grav games?" he asks in amazement. How did he figure that out so fast? "The Ice Dame kept saying you were away on an internship, but she never said where. You've been slumming!" He points at me, laughing.

"I have not been 'slumming'!" I cry. "You said it yourself; top-levs are treated differently. I didn't want that, so I changed my name and took a real job in the MCC."

"MCC?" he asks. "Maintenance? You're a space janitor?"

While I glare at Bobby, R'ger explains about Patrick suspending me. Somehow, he manages to keep O'Neill and the dead bodies out of the picture.

"And you really want this job back?" Bobby asks, looking thoughtful. "Why?"

Looking away, I sigh. "I like being independent," I finally answer. "I like living with people who aren't consumed by how much money they can make or spend; who don't view every encounter as a possible business transaction.

They're just more real down there." I look at R'ger and Bobby, silently begging them to understand.

Bobby meets my gaze for a long moment, his head nodding slightly. Then his eyes snap to the float tube. I half-turn in my seat, and Nicolai staggers out. Bobby jumps up and meets him halfway across the room, steadying his friend before he plows into a small table.

"Is he ever not drunk?" I whisper to R'ger.

With Bobby holding him up, Nicolai staggers over and collapses into the chair Bobby just vacated. Up close, Nicolai looks even worse, and his smell is indescribable. My eyes water when he breathes out, so I scoot as far back as my chair will allow. R'ger offers the bag of pastries to Nicolai, who pushes them away in favor of a swig from the flask he produces. When he waves it at us, we both decline.

"Didn't mean to hurt her," Nicolai mutters. My eyes snap to his face.

"I'm sure he means the other day at your Mother's party," Bobby says, doubtfully. "She looked pretty bad after her encounter with the wall." He turns to Nicolai and takes the flask, flipping the lid back on. As he stashes it in his bag, Nicolai makes a grab for it. Bobby fixes him with an icy stare. "I thought you were going to sleep it off last night? Here, take some of these." He hands Nicolai a bottle of BuzzKill.

"You carry those all the time?" R'ger asks.

Bobby shrugs. "No, but I thought Nic might need some. We were supposed to train this morning. Multi-Grav." He answers R'ger's unasked question.

"Wha's tha point?" Nicolai wails, the bottle still unopened. Bobby takes it back, shakes out two tablets and drops them into Nicolai's hand.

"The point is, you need to get your mind off Candice and training is a great way to do that. Once you get the alcohol burned out of your system and get your blood flowing, you'll feel better." He pulls a water pac out of his bag and hands it to his friend. "Swallow those and go change into your workout gear. I'll wait here for you." Nicolai gives him a dull look but gulps down the pills and staggers to his feet.

After the door to Suite D closes behind Nicolai, Bobby relaxes again. "He's really broken up about that girl," he says. "Her family won't let him see her; they say it's his fault she was hurt. That she wouldn't have been up here on 83 if she hadn't been dating Nic. Which is true. She works in a boutique down on 27. Nic and I stopped in there one day on our way home from the Multi-Grav, and he got her contact. He's hardly left her side since. She isn't good for him, though; they're always wasted."

He looks around the room carefully and leans in close to us. "I heard this attack on Candice isn't the first one. That there's a murderer running loose on the station. If this guy is attacking people up here, no one is safe." He winks at me. "Maybe you should convince your boss to hang out in dark corridors, Annabelle."

THIRTY-TWO

"They've done a good job of covering things up, haven't they?" R'ger says after Nicolai and Bobby take the float tube down. He takes a sip of coffee and leans back in his chair.

"Yeah, but it isn't going to last." I contemplate the last croissant. With a sigh, I leave it for R'ger. I can always get more. "Someone must have paid Candice's family to hush it up. I'm sure the board is worried about a panic. An enclosed station is a bad place for a riot."

He scratches his jaw. "Maybe I'll cancel my meeting and head out today," he says. "Better safe than sorry."

"It's a little late to make that decision." O'Neill and two guys in Board Agent uniforms step out of the float tube. A few minutes ago, I was panting over Bobby Putin, but he has nothing on Ty O'Neill. I mean, Bobby is spectacular. He's as physically perfect as money and medical science can make him. But I'm drawn to Ty in a way I've never been attracted to anyone. Even today, with his bloodshot eyes, heavy scruff of beard, and rumpled shirt, I want to throw myself at him. I sternly remind myself that he's a colossal jackass and we aren't friends right now.

Unaware of my mental drooling, Ty continues, "Ser Chaturvedi, you need to come with us. We have some questions for you."

R'ger eyes him curiously. "Can't I answer your questions here?" He gestures to the chair across from me. "Have a seat."

O'Neill glances at me, then looks away. "No, thank you, we need to go down. I'm sure Sera Morgan will excuse you."

"What's going on, Ty?" I ask.

He stares at me, then looks over my head, as if I'm not even there. "We've found another body and have some questions about Ser Chaturvedi's whereabouts."

I narrow my eyes at O'Neill. "He's been with me most of the morning," I say. "And you know as well as I do that he wasn't on-station when the first deaths happened."

O'Neill angles his body away from me and focuses on R'ger. "Where were you at 3:15 this morning?"

"I was in my hotel room, of course." R'ger doesn't appear to be at all worried. "Feel free to check my holo-ring records. "

"We have checked the station records, Ser." Ty's face is tight, but his voice is bland. "There is no record of your holo-ring *anywhere on-station* last night. Did you by chance spend the night on one of the cruise liners docked here?" His face gives away nothing, but the tone of voice indicates he doesn't believe R'ger was on a cruiser. I'm sure he's already checked docking records.

"No," R'ger says, getting to his feet. He's starting to look a little concerned. "I spent the night in my room at the Hilltonne on Level 76. I'm sure the desk staff can provide you with my room access records."

"You would think," Ty agrees. "But they can't. They show no record of you ever returning to your room after you left yesterday morning with Sera Morgan."

"Your Agent escorted me down to the lobby last night! Have you talked to him? And what about the Hilltonne staff?" R'ger demands, his voice a little higher. "That lobby is always staffed; I spoke to the desk personnel when I arrived last night!"

"Agent Tariq confirms he left you in the lobby of the Hilltonne last night. That doesn't mean you stayed there. But, by all means, let's go down and speak with the staff, Ser." O'Neill gestures toward the float tube.

I get up to follow, but both men turn and stare me down.

"You stay here, Annabelle," R'ger says. "I'm sure this is some kind of misunderstanding. I'll call you when I'm done with them. In the meantime, could you contact my lawyer?" He flicks a contact code to my holo-ring.

O'Neill holds up a hand as if to stop him, but I glare at him. "I'll take care of it," I tell R'ger.

As the other two agents lead R'ger away, O'Neill leans in close. "He's going to need that lawyer, *Annabelle*."

―――

THE ON-STATION REPRESENTATIVE of R'ger's law firm promised to send their best agent to Ty's office immediately. R'ger must be a lucrative client to get that kind of response. After I've filled them in as much as I can, I pace around my bedroom.

The rest of the day passes like shuttle fuel at absolute zero. I check in with Kara, but she's busy at work. I leave a message on Ty's account, demanding information. I call R'ger's lawyer again, but they won't tell me anything. I pester Hy-Mi, and he puts me to work hand-lettering place cards for Mother's next event. This is ridiculous, because I have the worst handwriting in the history of paper, but it keeps me busy for a few hours.

Mother's office is a large room on the main floor of her compartment. She has an executive suite down on 82, of course, for business purposes, but this is her personal office. Rows of real books line the walls, and a faux fire burns on an ornamental hearth. It's very realistic; uneven warmth wafts out as it crackles away. Until I saw a real fire dirt-side, I was convinced this was a flawless copy. But it's just a copy; if you watch long enough, the pattern of the flames repeats, and the artificial wood smoke smell is just a little wrong. When I'm not analyzing the tech, it's pleasant enough. I stretch my cramped fingers toward the heat and flick on the vid screen above it.

The volume is muted, and some serial drama takes up the top portion of the screen. Beneath the melodramatic actors in expensive clothing, massive mansions, and cutting-edge land vehicles, text streams of news and financial information tick along the bottom edge. TXHEK, the stock Don Huateng prophesied about over dinner on Sunday, is down 27%. I wonder if Mother sold in time.

A pink banner proclaiming "private message" flashes across the top of the screen. Automatically, I flick the retrieval command on my holo-ring before realizing this message is not for me. This is Mother's private office; the screen is keyed to her holo-ring, so I'll get an error message.

To my surprise, the message downloads anyway. Maybe it *is* for me. Or maybe the sender doesn't realize I have the family access. To be fair, *I* didn't realize I had the family access codes loaded on my ring. I flick it open.

The message is from Hy-Mi and addressed to my mother. I'm about to close it when I spot the word "Patrick." Mother could have any number of contacts named Patrick, but this is too weird a coincidence. I read the message.

Contacted Patrick. Situation resolved.

What the heck?

THIRTY-THREE

I've left a dozen messages for Ty, and a similar number for R'ger, and heard nothing. Mother is still out somewhere, but I'm not calling her. Hy-Mi has checked in looking for her. I'm amazed he doesn't have a tracking loop on her holo-ring, but maybe his dedication to her isn't as strong as I'd thought. Or maybe she forbade it. But when he tells me he doesn't know where she is, I use it as an excuse to hack into the station OS.

From Mother's office, I can connect directly just as I did in Errol's closet, except this time I'm sitting at a desk, in a well-lighted room, in front of a roaring fire. I turned up the intensity and now blue and orange flames are licking the roof of the fireplace. I had to crank down the volume because it sounded like the whole place was ablaze.

First things first. I pull up Mother's ID and find her location: Level 23. Wait, what?! What is she doing on Level 23? I call Hy-Mi. A holo of his head and shoulders appears in my palm.

"Hey, Hime, what's Mother doing down on Level 23?"

"As always, Sera, I'd prefer you not call me that." His stern voice and impassive face make me grin, thinking back to my teen years. "How do you know she's on Level 23?"

"Hmm, you probably don't want me to answer that," I say. "But she's there, in C Ring, Slice 5."

"Ah, yes, she has a business relationship that requires her occasional attendance at that location," he replies. "Don't roll your eyes."

I do it anyway. I can almost feel him twitch in response. "That's not a real answer, but if you tell me she's safe there, I'll drop it. There's a psycho loose on the station, you know." Although I didn't tell him about the murders, I'm sure he knows. Hy-Mi knows everything that happens on SK2. In fact, now that I think about it, I was crazy to ever think he *didn't* know about me working down on 2. And of course, anything Hy-Mi knows, Mother knows.

Hy-Mi is silent, then he frowns. "She's safe enough," he finally says. "She always takes security with her these days."

"Okey-dokey. Just thought you should know." It's my turn to be silent for a while. "I, uh, saw your message to Mother on the office screen. For some reason, it downloaded to my holo-ring. What did you mean that the Patrick situation was resolved?"

Hy-Mi stares. For a moment, I think the vid has frozen, but then he glances away. This silence thing is getting old. "Hy-Mi, is that the Patrick down in Ops? Did you talk to her?"

"My discussion with Patrick is of no concern to you," he says, slowly.

"Did you pay her off?" I demand. "You were just talking about how I need to stand on my own, and now you're bribing people to, to, OH! I'm hanging up now!" I flick my ring and banish his image.

I sit there, shaking with anger. And a little guilt, caused by the corner of my brain that shouted "Hooyah!" when I realized Hy-Mi had taken care of my problem. Just like he always did when I was little. I drag my hands through my hair, rubbing at the headache building in the back of my neck. In the now-dark screen over the fireplace, my reflection stares back at me. My crazy red curls point in all directions. I shake my head, and my hair doesn't fall back into place like Ty's. I hesitate to think this, but he might have a better aesthetician than Kara. No, that can't be true; it must just be his natural shiny-ness.

I roll my shoulders and pull the OS back up on my holo-ring. *Focus, Triana.*

I search for R'ger and find he is being held in the cells down on Level 1. I break into the Hilltonne surveillance system. Feeds from room 324 are missing, just twelve hours between noon yesterday and today. O'Neill might have deleted them when he got copies, but why would he? Someone else may have deleted them to implicate R'ger. Or, a little voice says, R'ger might have destroyed the vids because they showed him doing something illegal.

Ugh! If I'd wanted to be an investigator, I would have stayed in Internal Audits instead of quitting after three weeks. And I would have been able to pass this off to someone else due to a potential conflict of interest, right?

Mother strides into the room. I quickly log out and disconnect my holo-ring. "Mother? Is everything ok?"

She shoos me out of the desk chair and sits down. "I've posted a second guard in the lobby on 82," she says. "You are not to leave the suite until this killer is apprehended."

I roll my eyes. "Mother! I'm an adult, I've been living on my own for six years! I'm smart enough to stay in well-occupied areas where I'll be highly visible."

She fixes me with an iron glare. "You may use the lobby here on 83, but you are not to leave this Level without an armed guard."

I look away. "Yes, ma'am." I hate that I'm so quick to cave, but she's scary. She owns this station and everyone on it. Why do you think I ran away? I wonder again why I came back. Maybe I should apply for a job on S'Ride, where R'ger's nephew lives. If he really has a nephew.

I wait to see if Mother is going to say anything else, and when she doesn't, I slink out of the room.

———

This has been the longest two days of my life! I've spent longer than that without leaving this compartment before, but I always had something to do. Now I'm stuck here without a job or school work or anything. I slept, watched vids, read books, even worked out in Mother's athletic sim. It's strange. I could happily spend a couple days alone in my tiny compartment down on 2, but since I'm forbidden to leave this huge suite on 83, it is a prison.

I spent some time trolling through the OS—still nothing new on R'ger. Poor guy is locked up in a much smaller space. I really should stop whining. I try cracking into O'Neill's files and get a message saying my intrusion is being tracked and reported back to him. That is new. If I wanted to, I could probably disable the tracker, delete the report and get into his files, but I've lost interest. His impersonal message makes it clear he knew I would try to break in, and that he doesn't want my help.

I jump up from my couch and stalk across the room. I flick my holo-ring, and the huge space scene on the wall disappears and is replaced by the station news feed. As I pace, stories about the current stock market correction flow into editorials on education and political reports. I let the audio wash over me, catching occasional phrases here and there. The ticker across the bottom scrolls along, almost mesmerizing if I don't try to read it.

What was that? I flick the controls and scroll the ticker back to the previous bullet. Holy zark!

*Services for Chief Inspector Rhinalda Patrick Inaldin Wang von Krieken will be held Thursday at noon in Sanctuary. *

Services? I click on the link and find a brief news article: the inspector was found dead in her quarters yesterday evening. Cause of death was not listed.

Heart pounding, I drop back onto my couch. Inspector Patrick is dead. Less than two days after Hy-Mi's message saying the Patrick situation had been resolved. I mentally review what I know of the other victims on-station. Except for Patrick, and Candice, I can't even begin to imagine what their connection to Mother could be. Maybe it's a coincidence. Surely Mother isn't ordering murders to solve problems?

On the upside, this means Rash should be back and I can go back to work. There's no safer place on this station than the MCC, so Mother can't object to me getting reinstated. I ignore the little voice that tells me otherwise and change into my uniform.

Out in the lobby, a crowd of young top-levs loiters. Apparently, my mother isn't the only one forbidding her offspring to leave the nest. Gloria holds court near the Huateng suite; Nicolai, Bobby and a couple other young men are playing a card and drinking game across the room. I guess Bobby's disgust at Nicolai's drinking didn't survive the boredom. They look up when I approach.

"Nice costume," Con Said says between gulps of some nasty smelling beverage. "You here to clean up after Gates barfs?" The rest of the group laughs as though this is the funniest thing they've heard all day. Ming-tu Gates turns an even nastier shade of green.

"Bobby, can I have a word with you?" I ask, wondering how much he's imbibed. He tosses a vapor tube to Said and stands.

I drag Bobby into the foyer of our suite and turn. "How stoned are you?"

Bobby smiles. "Not at all. That stuff really doesn't do anything for me. I require real-world stimulation." He leers at me but his eyes are clear and his hands, steady.

"Give me a break," I mutter. "I need to go down to Ops. Will you help me?"

His eyes light up. "I'm not sure what instructions the guards have been given," he says. "I've come and gone a couple times in the last few days, but some of the others can't get out. Nicolai's holo-ring blares an alarm if he goes within 5 meters of the float tube."

I roll my eyes. "Dame Bezos is in my mother's pocket," I say. "Mother commanded me to stay, so Dame B is probably trying to do the same. Why doesn't he just take his ring off?"

"Take it off?" Bobby's jaw drops. "What good would that do? He needs the ring to open doors and buy things, and..."

I cut him off. "I didn't say leave it somewhere, I just said he should take it off." He looks blank. "They aren't active when you aren't wearing them. While it *might* be programmed to sound the alert even when deactivated, I'll bet he could just stick it in his pocket and walk out of here." Dame B would have had to hire someone to reprogram Nicolai's ring, and I doubt anyone currently on-station really understands how they work. Heaven knows I didn't!

"Let's try it!" Bobby says, rubbing his hands together.

"That won't help me," I say. "Mother has instructed the guards on 82 to 'watch for and physically detain' me if I try to leave. That's why I need your help. If you and Nicolai cause a distraction, I think I can get away."

"How?" he asks.

I smile. "That's my secret."

His eyes narrow. "OK, I'll help you, on one condition. Meet me down on 82 after you get out. I don't want you wandering around the station alone with a crazy on the loose. Dame Morgan would kill me if I help you escape and then something happens to you." He must sense my indecision because he goes on, "I'll escort you down to 10, and wait outside Ops to bring you back. I won't interfere."

"OK." I lie without hesitation.

He gives me another shrewd look. "I mean it," he says. "I'll see you in Radial 7, B Ring, in five minutes."

Sighing, I say, "I'll need ten."

I slip through the maintenance entry, camouflaged behind a large mirror. I have no intention of meeting Bobby Putin. Although he's undoubtedly in excellent condition, he's also, as I've previously mentioned, extremely hot, and I don't need him distracting me from my mission. Plus, as long as I stay in well-traveled areas, I should be perfectly safe from the psycho. And, of course, there's the fact that he's a top-lev brat, and you never know what he might decide to do while looking for entertainment.

Large, well-stocked maintenance closets sit at the corner of the entry Radial and the access Ring. I slip inside. Shelves containing cleaning supplies, vacuum hoses, sonic shampooers and trolleys to carry all of it line the walls. There's one for each of the six penthouses on this side of the station, neatly parked under labels bearing the suite's letter.

I pull cart C out and duck into the cart-sized charging cubby. The back wall is covered by an access panel secured with a digital lock. Crossing my fingers, I wave my holo-ring at the lock and the panel pops open. This top-lev ring really does have access to everything. It's frightening to think what kind of trouble Nicolai or Gloria can get into. I swing the panel open and lights glow to life, illuminating a narrow metal ladder.

When I step out onto the ladder, an alarm sounds, echoing through the narrow chamber. My arms clamp around the ladder. My mind spins: can I access and deactivate the alarm. Then I relax when I realize it's Bezos' alarm. I laugh. I can't believe Bobby believed taking a ring off would deactivate it.

I pull the panel closed behind me and start the short descent to Level 82. The ladder continues for the full length of the station, but I'm not in good enough shape to make the whole climb. Besides, why should I? From here I can exit into B Ring and take the float tube down. It will take ages for Bobby and Nicolai to get away from Board Sec agents at the 82 lobby. I laugh again. Maybe Ty will respond to the alarm. This day is looking up.

I stride out of Radial 3 and head toward the float tube. Halfway across the concourse, an iron hand grabs my arm.

"This isn't Radial 7," Bobby says, shaking his head in mock distress. "You promised to wait for me."

"How did you get away from the Board Secs?" I ask, astounded he evaded my trap.

He laughs. "Did you really think I'd fall for that? I've been wearing a holo-ring a lot longer than you have, sweetheart. I know exactly how they work. I told Nic to give me five minutes, then follow me down. He totally bought your 'take-it-off' scam." He ushers me into the float tube.

"Speaking of taking things off," he says with a roguish grin, "maybe you can show me what you wear under that uniform."

"Yeah, right," I say. "Can't you turn it off for a few minutes? I may have had a crush on you when we were kids, but I'm all grown up now. And I've got important things to do."

He manages to look hurt, and I laugh. "You aren't interested in what I have on under this uniform," I say, although the thought disappoints me just a little. I told you, he's really hot. "And you could have any girl on this station. Or beyond."

"Yeah, but none of them are any kind of challenge," he replies, pressing his hand against my lower back to urge me out of the float tube. "You, on the other hand, have made your indifference obvious, so challenge accepted."

I look around. "Why are we on Level 52? I need to go down to 10."

He shrugs apologetically. "You aren't in a hurry to get back topside, are you? I have an errand to run here and thought you wouldn't mind if we do that first. It won't take long."

We set off down Radial 2. He slides his arm through mine as we stroll along. It's such a relief to be out of the penthouse, and if he wants to play at gallant gentleman suitor, who am I to complain? I notice the envious looks on the faces of women we pass. There's also some surprise to see a top-lev with a Maint Tech. I smile to myself. One point for the lower-levs!

"Patrick's death was pretty convenient, wasn't it?" Bobby asks, in a conversational tone.

I cringe. "I wouldn't wish anyone dead, not even her," I say slowly. "But hopefully it will mean Rash is back in Ops, and I can get my job back."

He nods. "That's what I meant. And you didn't even have to lure her into a dark corner." He laughs.

"Where are we going?" I ask, hoping to change the subject.

He ignores my question. "It's almost as if this guy is on your side, isn't it? I mean, of all the people on this station, he picked her? You gotta wonder about his criteria, right?"

"Do we really need to discuss this?" I reply. I think about Hy-Mi's message and shiver. He can't be involved in this, can he? Surely Patrick's death was a coincidence. "The guy is obviously crazy. Let's just leave it at that."

"Do you think the other victims were hot?" he asks. "That Gonzeles girl was pretty sexy. And Candice is smokin'. Or at least she was before she got all messed up. I mean, if I were going to kill people, I'd pick hot girls, not dried up looking middle-aged station rats. Not that all station rats are dried up, of course. You're pretty hot."

I slow down and pull my arm away from him. There is definitely something wrong with Bobby. How could I have not noticed it before? I know money and appearance can blind people to the truth about a lot of top-levs, but I never thought it would affect me. Of course, I haven't seen him in six years. Maybe he wasn't this twisted when we were teens.

"You know, we can get things done a lot faster if we split up," I say. "You go take care of your errand while I pop down to 10, and I'll see you in a while. Maybe we can meet up for lunch or something?"

He snags my hand. "We're almost there," he says. He leads me down a mostly deserted hallway, unusually quiet even for A Ring in the middle of the day. "What's bothering you? I guess I shouldn't tell you how hot other girls are, should I? That's not very good manners, is it? My mother would kill me if she knew I'd done that."

I try to pull my hand away, but he's clamped on like a vacuum seal. "If we were a couple, I might object to you discussing other women's appearance," I say. "Since we're not, feel free to comment. But stop talking about killing people! It's creepy how you're analyzing his choice of victims. It's almost as if you admire this psycho."

He gives me a strange, sideways look. "That would make me as crazy as him," he says.

Yeah, it would. "How did you know Patrick was middle-aged?" I ask slowly.

He shrugs. "She's an inspector. I'm guessing they're all middle-aged."

"And Gonzeles," I continue. "I didn't think her name had been published. They haven't released the names of any of the victims."

He shrugs again as he stops to face me. "I must have heard it somewhere. Ah, here we are."

A door swooshes open behind me. When I turn to look, Bobby shoves me into a dark, narrow space. I frantically grab at anything, but I trip over the threshold. I twist my body as I scrabble, but I can't stop myself from falling back onto my butt. My landing is cushioned by something warm and lumpy.

"What the hell?" I yell, but he backhands me across the face and pain explodes into my head. Tears bursting from my eyes, I clamp my free hand onto my throbbing face. He reaches toward me, and I jerk back, fearing another assault. Instead, he grabs my wrist and yanks my holo-ring off my finger. I yelp as he wrenches it over the knuckle, taking skin with it.

"Don't worry," he croons to me. In the dim light from the hallway, he smiles at me as if I'm his favorite flavor of ice cream. "I won't leave you here long. But I have to make sure you don't run off."

Pocketing my holo-ring, he twists the arm he's still holding, forcing me over onto my stomach. I struggle, but the space we're in is tight, and there's no room for me to maneuver. My bruised cheek slams into something hard, and the pain explodes again. By the time I've fought through it, he's managed to get both my arms tied together.

He grabs my upper arm and flips me back over with frightening ease. I knew he was in good shape, but I never realized how strong he is. My heart pounds in my throat, making it impossible to talk and difficult to even breathe.

"You can try screaming if you want," he says in a conversational tone. Still holding my upper arm, he pulls me in close. "But this Level is being renovated and there's no one to hear you. Just relax for a while. I'll be back soon. Then we'll have some fun." I squeeze my eyes shut as he leans in and kisses me gently on the lips. Ew, creepy.

He stands over me, staring down. "Maybe I'll bring your friend. I'll bet she likes to have fun. What's her name? Kara?" He smiles.

"NO!"

The door shuts behind him, and I'm left alone in a narrow, pitch black space. In the few seconds of our fight, I recognized our location: an escape pod. The narrow vehicles are slotted in between compartments on the outer Ring of the station. Each one holds eight bunks, four on each side, with just enough space between to squeeze in. In the event of a station failure, residents would climb into these. The eight occupants would be put into deep-sleep so they could survive until rescue.

They've never been used, and who knows if they even work anymore. When I was a kid, we had drills in school. We'd line up in an orderly fashion outside our assigned pods. Of course, top-lev pods are much more spacious. And even then, we never went inside them. In fact, I think this is the first time I've ever seen one open.

I shift a little, trying to get more comfortable. With my hands tied behind me, my arms are starting to go to sleep, and I can't use them to lever myself up. I arch my back, trying to relieve the pressure. As I squirm, the odd, lumpy surface beneath me moves a little. Suddenly I realize I'm lying on top of a body.

THIRTY-FOUR

WITH A SHRIEK, I manage to roll off the body and up a few centimeters into the narrow bottom bunk. My shoulder slams into the wall and knocks the air out of me. After hyperventilating for a few minutes, I realize the body must be alive, since it moved, and was warm. I inch my way to the edge of the bunk.

I hold my breath and listen, but I can only hear my own heart pounding. "Hello?" I say, my voice barely a whisper.

Get a grip, Moore! If someone is here, it's because Bobby put her here. Chances are she's in no shape to hurt anyone. Besides, she barely moved when I landed on her, so she must be out cold. I clear my throat and try again. "Who's there? Are you awake?"

A low groan sounds loud in the tiny pod. It also sounds very masculine. Since all his previous victims were female, I assumed this one would be, too, but obviously, Bobby is branching out. I wrack my brains, trying to remember how to revive someone. On *Ancient TēVē*, the hero always throws a glass of water on the victim, or slaps their face, or puts something smelly under their nose. I don't have any water, my hands are tied behind my back, and if my stench of fear hasn't revived him, nothing will. I roll onto my back and settle in to wait.

Oh, who am I kidding? I wait about as patiently as that animated bird who drops anvils on the coyote. I nudge the body with my toe. "Hey, you. Yeah, you. The one passed out in the escape pod. Wake up!"

That's about as successful as the coyote's plans. "So, I'm just going to talk until you can't stand it anymore and wake up in self-defense," I tell him, nudging him with my knee this time. "Otherwise, I'll be a crazy, screaming mess in about thirty seconds, like that animated tornado-type creature. And you'll be even more bruised than you probably are now."

I roll back again and stare at the bunk above me. The one I can't see because it's like a black hole in here. My chest tightens up, my breathing gets faster, and sweat breaks out on my forehead. Quick, think about something else. Anything else!

"Bobby Putin," I say, aloud. "Yikes. I've known him pretty much since I was born. He's older than me, like five years older. So, we didn't go to school together or anything, but everyone knew him. There aren't that many top-lev kids. And he was hot, even then. I know I told Errol that he had acne, but that was a lie. He's always been gorgeous. I never realized the hot covered total insanity."

"Some people might say that about you," a hoarse voice whispers. I yelp.

"Ty?" I roll close to the edge of the bunk again, trying to see him.

"Here," he says with a groan. "God, it hurts!"

"What happened?" I ask.

"That—" he spits out a long stream of syllables in a language I don't recognize. Even so, I can tell he's swearing. "—murderous piece of zark! He stunned me and threw me in here. I think my head hit one of the bunks because that's all I remember until you started moaning about how beautiful he is."

I laugh a little, but tears are running down my face. "I'm so glad you're here," I choke out. "I didn't want to die alone."

He laughs and then swears again. "Please don't make me laugh, it hurts. He might have broken some ribs, too."

"I wasn't trying to be funny," I cry.

"Wouldn't you prefer I was out there somewhere so I could come to your rescue?" he asks.

"Yes, but then I'd be alone in here." I'm wailing like an idiot now. "And besides, you hate me, so you'd never rescue me."

"I don't hate you," he says. His voice is faint, but he says it like he means it. "I was mad for a while, but I'm over it now, believe me. We're going to get out of here, and I'm going to take all my mad out on Putin's beautiful face. And then I'm going to send him to a dirtside prison for the rest of his life."

"How are we going to get out of here?" I hiccup. I can't reach my face, so I wipe my cheeks on my shoulders.

"You're going to use your genius tech skills and get us out," he replies. "Anyone who can take a holo-ring off-grid—"

"Holy zark!" I yell. "I've got my old holo-ring!" My high evaporates immediately. "I can't get to it, though. My hands are tied behind my back. Are you free?"

I hear a little scuffling and then he says, "No, I'm tied up, too. Where's your ring? Surely he didn't leave it on your hand?"

I shake my head, then remember he can't see it. "No, he took that one. Annabelle's ring. I have *my* ring, my real-life, jacked up, Level 2 Maint Tech ring, in a locket around my neck. You'll have to get it. Can you roll on your side so your back is to me?"

"I'll try," he says. I hear more scuffing and scraping, and a few muttered curses.

"What language is that?" I ask as he struggles.

"I think it's Shinese," he says. "My grandmother taught me all the swear words. I need to rest a minute; my head is pounding. And my hands are asleep."

We lay there in the silence for a few minutes. His labored breathing gradually slows and smooths out. "Triana?" he asks.

"What?"

"Do you want me to call you that?"

"Yes! For the hundredth time," I say. "I am Triana."

"OK," I can hear a smile in his voice. "The day we met—when I showed you my ID—why were surprised by my name? At the time, I thought it was because you were from the lower Levels, and maybe you hadn't met anyone with as many names. But obviously, that wasn't it."

"You're kidding, right?" I ask.

"Kidding about what?" he asks.

"Tiberius. O'Neill. Mendoza," I say. When he doesn't respond, I go on. "Tariq? Reynolds? Those are all names of heroes on *Ancient TēVē* space shows."

He snorts a laugh and then groans again. "I should have known. Ok, I've got my back to you, and my fingers are mostly working. Now what?"

I roll onto my side, bend my knees and scooch about halfway down the bunk, then wiggle closer to him. When his hand brushes against my chin, I press my face against it for a second. His fingers are icy, but he curves them against my cheek. I wonder how long he's been in here. Tears start to leak out of my eyes again, so I slide up a little. "Ok," I say. "The ring is in a locket on my necklace. See if you can feel it."

His fingers slide across my upper chest, sending my heart rate into the stratosphere. His fingers may be cold, but warmth radiates from his back. I press my face against him.

"Uh, you're going to have to move back a couple centimeters," he says. "I can't move my arms if you're pressed so close."

"Oh, sorry." I wiggle a little. "How's that?" His fingers close around the chain, and he pulls the locket away from my sweat-sticky chest.

"It's warm," he says. "How do I open it?"

"Just pry it with a fingernail," I say. "Don't drop it! When you get the ring, put it on."

Somehow, he manages to get the ring out of the necklace. It lights up as he slides it on, and the faint glow makes me squint after so much time in the dark. I shove my feet against the bulkhead until I'm stretched out full length again. I roll in as close as I can get and kiss him on the side of his neck—the only bare skin I can reach. "Let me see if I can find something to get us loose. It looks like he used plas-ties."

Scooting down to the bottom of the bunk again, I wriggle around until I'm in the aisle between the bunks, kneeling over Ty's feet. "Do you want to roll into the bunk?" I ask him.

He shakes his head slightly, his eyes closed. He looks like hell. There's blood all over his head and shoulders, and under it, his skin is grey. His leg is twisted in what looks like an impossible angle. Nothing is actively bleeding, and there isn't much I could do if it was, so I start looking around the pod.

The eight bunks take up most of the pod. At the far end, a small cupboard fills the space between the top two pairs of bunks. I carefully step over Ty, so I'm standing astride his chest, and push my forehead against the cupboard door. Thankfully, the pressure activates the magnetic latch, and it swings open. I squint, trying to make out the objects inside. Just then, the holo-ring finishes its boot sequence and goes dark.

"Ty, can you flick the ring?" No answer. Don't panic. I take a couple deep breaths and lean down. "Ty?" I blow in his ear, and he jumps a little. "Flick the ring, Ty."

The glow comes back, and I stand quickly. My ring is set to a five-second fade, so I don't have much time. A quick glance in the cupboard. "Ah!" I press my chin against a panel on the inside of the door, and it glows to life. In the brighter light, Ty looks even closer to death. Tears threaten again, so I focus on inventory.

"Toolkit!" I exclaim. Now how the hell am I going to get it out of the cupboard without dropping it on Ty's head?

"Ty?" I lean down, whispering to him. "I know you're in pain, but I really need you to roll into the bunk. I don't want to drop anything on you."

His bruised eyes open and it takes a minute for him to focus on me. He blinks a couple times. "Yeah, sure. I can do that."

It takes longer than you can imagine to get him into the bunk. I try to help, but with my hands still tied, I can only nudge him along with my feet. He chokes down a scream when I jostle his leg. When he's finally sprawled across the bunk on his stomach, I kneel beside him. His face is so grey, and his breathing is so ragged, I'm afraid he'll die right here.

"Come here." His voice is barely a thread. I lean into the bunk, almost falling on my face since my hands aren't free to catch my weight. I wiggle around until I'm lying on the floor with my head on the bunk, face to face with him.

His eyes open briefly. "Closer," he says, his lips curving slightly as his eyelids drop.

I slide my head closer until my nose is touching his. It's cold. That's not good, right? Aren't people supposed to have warm noses? Or is that dogs? He pushes his chin forward, wincing as he does it, and his lips barely touch mine. A little spark jumps between us and he smiles again. "Now save our asses, ok?"

I gaze at him, willing him to get stronger. As I watch, his face relaxes a little, although the groove between his eyebrows stays in place. I lean toward him and kiss him a little more firmly, then roll off the bunk.

It's really hard to stand up when you're lying in a space less than forty centimeters wide and your hands are tied behind your back. Really, try it sometime. Eventually, I get to my feet. After cursing under my breath for a few minutes, I turn my back to the cupboard and put my right foot on the second bunk. I brace my shoulder back against the edge of the cupboard, then push up with my right leg. It takes me three or four tries, and I'm certain I'm going to lose my balance and end up on my face, but I finally get my left foot up onto the left bunk so I'm straddling the aisle.

I reach into the cupboard and wrap my fingers around the toolkit I saw in there. I pull on the box, but it doesn't move. I pull again, and still no joy. Did some moron glue the thing to the cupboard? I guess when you're designing escape pods, you want to make sure sharp implements are prevented from floating around in zero gravity. But when you're thrown into an escape pod by a psychopath with your arms tied behind your back, you just want a pair of freakin' scissors!

I grab the bottom edge of the cupboard, flex my legs, and with a scream of rage, I leap. My head smacks into the roof on my way up and my butt slams onto the shelf on the way back down. With a horrendous shriek of tearing metal, the toolkit, cupboard, and everything in it, including yours truly, plummet to the tiny strip of floor.

When the dust clears, my butt is still wedged into the remains of the cupboard, which is now where Ty's head was only a few minutes ago. My skull throbs from slamming into the ceiling, and pain shoots up my tailbone. Blood trickles down my arms, but I can't see how badly they're scraped. The middle two bunks on the left are collapsed onto the bottom one. The cupboard door, with its light panel aglow, somehow still hangs from the wall, swinging gently. Crazy shadows swoop back and forth across the pod. Dusty but safe on the bottom right bunk, Ty opens his eyes and gazes at the wreckage.

"Sweet." His eyes close again.

THIRTY-FIVE

WITH THE TWO BUNKS COLLAPSED, I'll have room to sit upright on the thin mattress. The bunk is still partially supported on the foot end, so I'll be sitting at an angle, but I'm trying to focus on the positives here. I shift from the crushed cupboard to the bunk and use a toe to flip the lid of the toolkit open. The magnet holding it shut fights me for a minute, but eventually, it lets go.

A couple minutes of squirming, and a few nicks and cuts later, my hands are free. Pins and needles shoot through my arms. I give myself a few minutes to regain my circulation. Then I lift Ty just enough to cut his bonds as well. He doesn't wake while I do it, and I'm not sure if this is ok or a medical crisis. When he's free, I carefully pull my holo-ring from his finger, then gently arrange his arms in the most comfortable position I can manage. I grab a blanket from the top bunk and spread it over him.

With my holo-ring back on, I feel more in control. I flick it to life and call Hy-Mi. Except the call doesn't go through. I try to connect to the web, but there's nothing. I run diagnostics, and the ring is working correctly. I run connection loops. Nothing. I rub my forehead, almost growling in frustration.

"Isolated system," Ty says. Does his voice sound stronger? Maybe the nap helped him. He still looks like crap.

I grab the first aid kit and attach the diagnosis cuff to his arm. "You mean the pods are isolated from the OS?" I ask as the device clicks and hums.

He nods, barely moving his head. The cuff chimes and I look at the readout.

Mild concussion, broken leg, two cracked ribs, minor blood loss. No internal bleeding, no brain injury. Thank God. But wait a minute; it also reports a sedative in his bloodstream. No wonder he's so zoned out; he's been drugged.

I use some antiseptic wipes to clean the blood from his face and neck. He swipes weakly at my hand. "Don't worry about that," he says. "Get us out of here."

I sit back on the bunk. "How?" I moan. "I was going to call Hy-Mi, or Board Sec, or even my mother, but I can't reach any of them with this piece of junk!" I wave my hand around. "I can't connect my ring to this pod; there's no ports or wireless access. These things are dinosaurs."

"Not the ring," he agrees. "You're smart; you'll figure it out." His eyes drift shut.

"Wow, you're a great help," I mutter.

"I heard that," he says, but his eyes don't open.

I sit on the bunk, with my feet up the slope and my head leaning against the wall. I shove my hands through my hair and pull on the tangled strands. Come on, Triana, think!

"Aargh!" I bang my head against the wall, then sit staring blankly at the hatch. Tears start leaking out of my eyes again and I blink hard. I'm going to save our asses; I don't have time for this!

That's when I notice the handle labeled 'Emergency Exit.'

―――――

IN MINUTES, we're free. If he were conscious, I know Ty would tell me to run and send help, but there's no way I'm leaving him where Bobby can find him. I pull one of the mattresses off the bunk and down onto the floor between the bunks. Bending over double, I grab his good ankle and pull. He moves fitfully but doesn't pull away.

"Come on, Ty, help me out here," I beg, grabbing his hips and pulling. He opens his eyes but doesn't really see me. "I need you to shift over to this mattress," I say loudly. "Come on O'Neill, move!" His eyes close again.

Knowing this will probably hurt, I take a new grip on his belt loops and pull him slowly onto the mattress. He moans but I keep pulling. Finally, his legs and hips are on the mattress.

"You weigh a tonne!" I groan. He doesn't respond.

It takes even longer to get his torso and head onto the mattress. I probably hurt him terribly, but I need to get him out of here. Once he's completely out of the bunk, I climb over him to the open door of the pod. I cram the first aid kit under his good leg to keep it from falling off the mattress and stack the toolkit next to it. Then I grasp the thick foam as tightly as I can and wrestle it out of the pod.

It's easier to pull him along the wide hallway. A few meters along, the toolkit falls off, but I don't stop to get it. I'm afraid if I stop I'll never get him started again. I drag him a few more meters until I reach the door to the first compartment.

"I'll put you in here," I say, using my holo-ring to open the door. Ty, still in a stupor, says nothing, so I drag my burden into the room. It's empty, with construction materials strewn about and thick dust on the floor. I shut the door behind us then push and shove the injured man into a corner. Crouching down, I whisper, "You stay here, and stay quiet. I'm going to call for help."

I sit down next to him and call Hy-Mi. But before I can connect, a flashing, red warning symbol pops up. The loop I attached to Kara's holo-ring reports the ring has been deactivated. "Zark!" I reach out and shake Ty's shoulder. "I think Bobby has grabbed Kara." He doesn't respond.

I was going to let him sleep it off, but Kara needs our help. I yank the first aid kit out from where I tucked it under his knees. Pawing through the contents, I throw the things we don't need onto the floor. Aspirin. Adhesive tape. Smelling salts. Hey, that might help. I crack the packet and wave it under Ty's nose. He swats my hand and turns away, eyes firmly shut.

Compression bandages. Muscle relaxers. Condoms. I shake my head and fling them across the room. "Come on!" Bee sting kit. Really? In an escape pod? Antihistamine. Cough drops. Buzzkill. Yes! I shake a couple tablets out into my hand and pinch Ty's nose shut. His mouth opens, and I pop the tablets in. They dissolve almost immediately.

"Blah! What was that?" Ty tries to sit up but stops with a groan. He falls back and wipes his tongue on his shirt sleeve.

"Buzzkill," I say. "I need you to be awake, not drugged out. Bobby must have drugged you."

"Do you at least have some water?" he asks. "Those taste vile."

I toss him a small water pac from the first aid kit. "I think they may have been expired," I say, looking around on the floor for the discarded packet. His color is better, and he's awake, so maybe he'll be ok. "Here it is. Yeah, they expired about twenty years ago. I think Buzzkill is one of those drugs that gets more potent with age. Do you feel more sober than usual?"

He rolls his eyes. "Help me up," he says.

"Let me put the splint on first, ok? Just because you're awake now doesn't mean you should be running around on a broken leg." I pull the auto splint out of the kit and unfold it. I wrap it around his leg. "Do you think I should straighten your leg out before I activate it?"

He shakes his head. "Just activate it." He grits his teeth.

I press the activation pad and the splint expands and forms around his leg. Ty makes a couple animal noises while it's adjusting, but when the light turns green, he relaxes. "That feels much better. Now help me up."

I get him to his feet, but it's a slow painful process. I only have one auto splint, so I can't immobilize his cracked ribs and getting him off the floor hurts. Finally, he's upright, and I find a discarded board about the right length for a crutch. We hobble out into the room and he leans against a sawhorse. "Did you call Security?"

"Not yet." I show him the warning on my holo-ring. "She'd never deactivate her holo; I think Bobby has grabbed her."

"Can you track him?" he asks.

I shake my head. "No. Well, I could, but it would take hours to set up. Who should we call? Anyone could be working for him. The Putins have more money than Mother, and Bobby has a huge trust fund from his maternal grandfather that he uses as fun money."

"May I?" he holds out his hand. I slip the ring off and hand it to him. Normally I wouldn't let anyone touch my holo, but Bobby must have taken Ty's. While he's placing the call, I go over to the control panel by the door.

This is one of the older models, and it doesn't connect to a holo-ring. Probably one of the reasons they're renovating this area. I press the power button, and the panel lights up. I activate the external cameras. If Bobby has taken Kara, he might be coming back up here.

"My team is on the way," Ty says. "I told them to look for Putin and a woman with purple hair."

"Lavender," I say.

"What?"

"Her hair isn't purple, it's lavender." Then I reconsider. "Of course, it's been a few days, she may have changed it by now. You should probably send them a pic of her. I've got some in my photo feed."

Ty mutters something under his breath, but I ignore him and turn back to the control panel. Suddenly, an ear-splitting shriek tears through the room. I know what this sound is, but I've never heard it broadcast through the station before.

"Attention! Attention! Meteor storm in progress. Proceed to the inner Rings." The calm, deep voice echoes through the compartment, somehow inspiring both calm and urgency.

Meteors are a fact of life in space. In the old days, they were a real threat. Station designers made the outer skin as strong as they could, but a meteor with enough velocity could punch right through. The station OS would monitor the surrounding area and warn occupants to move to the inner Rings when meteor activity was detected. Airlocks between A and B Rings would close to preserve station atmosphere in the event of a breach.

But no one has heard the meteor claxon in a hundred years. Not because meteors don't exist anymore, but because all stations were upgraded to include a meteor clearance system. Plasma lasers pulverize anything large enough to harm the station before it can get within a kilometer. After the Meteor Object Pulverizers, also known as MOPs (I know, how corny can you get?) were installed, the outer Ring compartments became the most prestigious. Before that, all the upper-levs wanted to live in the inner core.

Ty and I look at each other. "Putin!" he shouts just as I yell, "Bobby!"

"Do you think he really activated the Invacuation Sequence? Or just the alarm?" Ty hollers. In his palm, the holo of a ten-centimeter tall warning triangle flashes on and off. Instructions scroll across the bottom. All the while, the voice continues to urge us to move to the central concourse. "*Could* he activate it?"

"It's still an active part of the OS," I yell back. "That loop is partitioned off, but available in case of accidental depressurization. Like if a space liner crashed into the station."

"Or if a madman wanted to create mayhem," he replies. "If the system has been activated, the Radial blast doors are closing in—" He looks down at the holo which also displays a clock counting down. "—three seconds."

Something flashes on the door control panel, and I whip around. In the hallway, there's a flurry of movement. I use the controls to refocus the camera. As I try to zoom in, a muffled WHOMP sounds and the claxon stops. My ears are ringing.

"Guess we aren't going anywhere," Ty says, breaking the sudden silence. "At least not anywhere outside A Ring." He flicks a few commands on my holo-ring and swears. "My team is on the other side of the blast doors."

"Of course," I say. Bobby must have realized the Sec Agents were closing in on him and activated the Invacuation. As I watch on the control panel screen, he yanks Kara down the hallway toward the escape pod. She's clearly fighting him, but he just pulls her along like a parent dragging a toddler away from a birthday party. Zark, he's strong.

"You stay here," I tell Ty. "Bobby has Kara, and when he discovers we've broken out, who knows what he'll do? I'm going to draw him away. When we're clear, get Kara in here and lock the door. I'm guessing he has put some kind of kill command into the Resume loop, but even so, Ops should be able to get the blast doors open in about ten minutes. I wonder who did his programming?"

O'Neill grabs my arm. "You aren't going out there alone."

"You can barely stand," I say. "You sure as hell can't run. I know this station like the rebels know the death planet blaster thingy. Before they blew it up." Ty looks blank, so I wave my hands. "Never mind. I can lead him away for ten minutes, and then your guys can rescue me."

I jerk my arm out of his weakened grasp and stride to the door. Opening it takes every gram of courage I can muster up. I am scared to death of Bobby Putin, but he has Kara. I reach out a shaking hand and press the button to slide the door open.

Bobby has just reached the open pod door. I step away from the door and wave. "Hey, Bobby! Where've you been? I was getting tired of waiting!"

He looks into the pod, does a double take, and then looks back at me. Kara uses his distraction to slam her shin into his crotch. Bobby doubles over for a second, and Kara wrenches her arm free. She takes off down the hall toward me.

Bobby recovers faster than any man I've ever seen. Within a second, he's sprinting at us, his Multi-Grav conditioned body responding like a million-credit space yacht.

"Run, Kara, run!" I shriek.

Time slows down, and every detail burns into my brain. Fear widens Kara's eye so the white shows all around her violet irises. Sweat pours down her face, darkening her hair to purple. Her feet slap on the worn carpet and her chest heaves. Without apparent effort, Bobby puts on speed, gaining on Kara with every step. She pushes harder, her arms pumping like pistons.

With a yelp, she trips over something. Oh, God, it's the toolkit from the pod! Before he reaches her, I launch myself at him, screaming like a banshee.

Surprise flashes across his face as I plow into his shoulder, spinning him around with his own momentum. I must have hit him exactly right. He slams into the wall, and I keep going. His hand slides down my calf and ankle as he falls, but I pull away before he can get a grip. I race down the hallway, glancing quickly over my shoulder. Bobby pushes himself to his feet and behind him, Kara scrambles near the door to the compartment behind him.

A loud crack echoes down the hall. Still running, I look back. Kara is standing above Bobby, a long, broken board in her hands. The rest of the board crumbles over Bobby's head. He sits on the floor, shaking his head as Kara darts back into the compartment. I hear the door whoosh closed. Trusting her and Ty to keep each other safe, I sprint away.

In a few seconds, I've run far enough that the curve of the station has hidden Bobby from me. I can hear him cursing, so I keep running. I blast through a piece of plastek sheeting across the hallway, and burst out into a huge, echoing space.

The inner walls have all been removed, and this whole Slice of the Ring is just metal struts, ventilation ducts, and exposed wiring. The automatic lights don't come up, of course, but I don't know if it's because I'm without a holo-ring or because the power is off during construction. It doesn't slow me down much because light still filters in through the plastek and I really do know this station better than the rebels know the death planet blaster.

I hurdle over a pile of construction materials and veer inboard as Bobby rips through the plastek. He takes half the sheeting down as he rams through. I duck behind a duct barely wide enough to hide me. I hunch down, peeking around the metal sheeting at knee height.

Bobby has stopped just inside the area, his head swiveling around like a motion detecting camera.

"Annabelle?" he calls, his voice calm and pleasant. "Let's not play silly games. This whole Ring is locked down and it will take Ops several hours to figure out what I did. You can come out, or I can hunt you down. But I *will* find you."

I *so* want to answer him. A sarcastic response is burning on my tongue, but I bite it. It's possible he's right about how long it will take Ops to open the blast doors, but I'm not convinced. And I can hide from him for days if I can just get enough of a start. I just need a distraction. I look around, but there's nothing except construction debris.

With a shrug, I grab a chunk of something. I have a hereditary inability to play any sport that involves a ball, but I can heave a chunk of something across a room. I throw it as hard as I can, and it makes a satisfying ka-chunk on the other side of the space.

I peek out again. Bobby's eyes are locked across the room. He takes a couple of steps. It's so quiet, I can hear his slow footsteps, even over my pounding heartbeat. My breathing sounds loud in my ears. Staying hunched low, I creep across the floor toward the inner wall. His footfalls stop, and I freeze. My head turns slowly in his direction, and I realize he's staring right at me.

Like a shot, I'm across the floor and climbing the access ladder exposed on the inner wall. Lucky for me the construction crew demoed this space clear down to the frame or I wouldn't have been able to access it without my ring. I scramble up the rungs.

The lights flare on as I climb. The construction is limited to Level 52, and the walls close around me once I reach the ceiling. At Level 53 I glance down but Bobby isn't there yet. I kick open the access panel but keep climbing. With luck, I can get to the next one before he reaches the bottom of the ladder, and he won't know where I've gone.

Lungs heaving, legs screaming, I swarm up. Climbing in regular gravity is a piece of cake, right? Tell that to my body. My arms are already starting to ache when I finally reach 54. As I swing across to the access, I catch movement below. I ram my shoulder into the panel and dive through, praying he didn't see me.

I'm not taking any chances, though. I race toward the door and almost smack into it when it stubbornly refuses to open. ZARK!! No holo-ring, no auto-doors. Behind me, I can hear Bobby on the ladder. Given enough time, I can open this door, but unless Bobby checks out Level 53, I'm screwed. His voice drifts up the shaft, sounding so normal.

"Annabelle, why are you running away? I just want to help you. I took care of Patrick for you. Stop running and let me help you."

My eyes dart around the small closet, desperately seeking a hiding place. Large tanks of cleaning solvents with auto dispensers, two bots parked in their chargers, a small cupboard holding a few tools for when we need to do a manual clean-up. No place to hide.

A tiny creaking sound from the shaft. Is that Bobby exiting at 53? I hold my breath, but I can't hear anything over my pounding heart. When he doesn't emerge from the access shaft, I lunge for the nearest bot, my hand already scrabbling in my pocket for a screwdriver.

A quick twist pops open the programming port. I snap out a board, strip a wire in record speed and twist two others together then power up the bot. It trundles toward the door, which opens obediently, and I leap over the bot as it freezes in place. Without instructions, it will stand here forever.

I burst out of the maintenance closet and race down the hall. Level 54 is mostly residential, so I pass door after closed door all along the gently curving hall. I glance back, but the supply closet is already out of sight behind me. Bobby must have checked out Level 53, right? He's probably a Level below me right now, racing down a deserted hall, searching for me. I'm probably safe.

I should have jammed the access door shut before I left the closet. Zark.

There's nowhere to hide on 54. All the compartments have been evacuated, so there's no one to take me in and hide me. There are no greenhouses on this Level, no open shops, no conveniently open maintenance ducts. The blast doors on the radials are all still closed. I keep running, but I'm slowing. My legs drag like lead and a stitch pulls in my side.

I reach Radial 6, almost opposite the closet where I emerged. If I keep going, I risk running into Bobby if he chooses to come around the other direction. The blast doors are shut here, too, but across from the Radial corridor, instead of another compartment door, there's a wide alcove. Ancient plastek chairs line the outer edge of the space and discarded candy wrappers, cups, and empty water pacs litter the floor. In front of an airlock, a booth stands like a guard, the word Tondra emblazoned across the top. The BunG jump.

I stop dead. The idea of throwing myself out of a perfectly good space station has never appealed to me. But there is nowhere to hide on this Level. I could try to backtrack to the bot closet and climb back down to Ty and Kara, but I have a good chance of running into Bobby. If I'm quick, maybe I could get into the airlock and hide outside until the Ops crew gets the blast doors open.

My stomach lurches. I really don't want to go out there. I hold my breath. Is that footsteps I can hear, or just the blood pounding in my ears?

I take a deep breath. Scenes from every space decompression disaster vid flicker through my mind. I take another breath. Now I see visions of what will happen to me if Bobby Putin catches me. I take a third breath. OK, this isn't working. I clench my fists, grit my teeth, and march into the Tondra.

Then I march back out. I need to set the controls manually. If I survive this, I will never take off my holo-ring again. In fact, I might wear two of them, just to be safe. Of course, I *was* wearing two of them this morning, and clearly, that didn't stop me from losing both. I wonder if I can get one surgically attached to my hand?

I press the power button and the Tondra hums to life, its touch screen lighting up. I've never used this system before, but it's pretty basic. I enter my height and body mass, set a ten-second delay, press start, and slip into the booth. As the door slides closed, I catch a glimpse of Bobby Putin jogging into the alcove.

THIRTY-SIX

Zark. Zark. Zark! He was behind me! I should have kept running! I could be climbing back down to Ty right now. But no, instead, I'm trapped in a tiny box with a homicidal psychopath only twenty meters away. Fear clamps around my lungs and I can't breathe. I gasp, trying to get enough oxygen. My vision starts to darken. He's going to open the booth and kill me!

The pressure on my chest relaxes, and I realize it was the Tondra, not panic. It's dark inside the booth, but not as black as the pod. There is no window, so I don't know what Bobby's doing, but he must know I'm here. The machine isn't silent. Why isn't he stopping it and dragging me out?

The booth hums and squishes and tugs. I bite back a yelp when it pinches the underside of my arm. Claustrophobia grips me when the membrane folds around my face. I gulp in some air and it doesn't suck around my nose or mouth, so I relax a fraction. Pressure against the back of my neck and a click announce the attachment of the air tank. With a soft ding, the back of the booth opens directly into the airlock.

I step out of the booth. Although I did some ESA sims in school, I had no interest in pursuing a job that involved doing it regularly, so I haven't been in an airlock since arriving on-station two years ago. The training sims all required donning real vacuum suits, not Tondras. I look down at myself. A thin, flexible, translucent material covers me from the neck down, more or less form fitted to my body. It's a little tight around the torso; I guess I might have been a bit, hmm, optimistic when I entered my mass. The bubble around my head is clear and wavers as I move, making my vision a little blurry.

The airlock is about four meters square, with a station standard height ceiling. The inboard door connecting to the booth is normal sized, and the outer door is a little larger. They're completely automated, although there are red wheels for opening the doors by hand in the event of an emergency. The two doors are connected, so it's physically impossible to open both at the same time. A single, ridiculously large, red button marked Open/Close controls the doors.

There's a window in the external door, and a smaller one set next to the door to the booth. I step over to that window and cautiously peek out. Nothing. Could Bobby have jogged on by without even noticing the Tondra's noise? Or maybe he thought it always made that sound. I guess if he'd never been down here before, he might not—

"Aaargh!" I fling myself away from the window, my heart about ready to burst through the Tondra suit. Seriously, the suit vibrates in time to my racing pulse. I look at the window again, and the leering face turns out to be Bobby's. Not that recognizing him makes me feel any better. He laughs and points, although I can't hear him, of course.

He stops laughing and smiles, a nasty little smile with an evil glint to it. He points at himself and then through the window. He's coming in.

I lunge across the room and slap the door release. The outer pops open, and I'm sucked out into the void.

"Oh God, oh God, oh God, oh God!" I pray as I fly out into space at a pace that makes my eyes water even though there's no wind. Zark! I never checked my BunG! Please let it be automated like everything else! Surely it must be, right? They wouldn't let ignorant tourists fling themselves off the station without making sure they were attached. Losing tourists would be bad for business, and SK Corp wouldn't allow that.

I glance back. A thin cord snakes away from me up toward the station. I take a shuddering breath and look up. The huge bulk of the S'Ride liner looms in front of me. It's both so enormous that I'm sure I'll smash right into it before I reach the end of my tether, and so far away that I'm terrified I'll fly right past it and out into the beyond.

I look behind again, putting myself into a tumble. A sickening montage of station, space liner, stars, docking arms, station, space liner, stars, spins before my eyes. I clamp them shut and fling out my arms and legs just like the stupid tourists. It doesn't help.

THE VACUUM OF SPACE

My wild ride slows; the BunG must have reached the end of its length. I hover there in the stars for an instant and just have time to register how amazing it looks out here before I'm karooming back toward the station.

I thought the S'Ride liner looked big; the station is huge! I can't see either end of the thing, and as I race toward it, the bulk fills my field of vision. "I'm not going to crash. I'm not going to crash. Oh God! Oh God!" The primitive part of my mind that controls my will to survive crawls into a deep fold in my brain and hides. Pure panic floods through me as the station rushes at me. I can only squeeze my legs together and try not to wet myself.

And then it's over. Suddenly, I'm back in the airlock, collapsed on the floor. I press myself to the deck and suck in air. I will never leave this station again.

That's when the outer door starts to shut. I look at the panel by the Tondra booth door and realize Bobby is coming. Zark! What I just said about never leaving the station? It was a total lie.

I gently push off the floor and slip through the slowing closing door. I look frantically around for something to jam it with. If the door can't close, Bobby can't get out. I grab a fold of my BunG cord and flip it through the door like a cowgirl lassoing a horse on an *Ancient TēVē Westirn*. The door snags for a second, as if analyzing the material, then snaps shut, severing the cord in two places.

I manage to catch myself before I lunge for the other end of the BunG. I'm now floating free with a two-meter piece of string that's NO LONGER CONNECTED to the station. Every action has an equal and opposite reaction. Lunging would be a really bad idea.

If I survive this, not only am I going to have a holo-ring surgically implanted in my brain, I'm going to have to get a heart stress test. My blood is pounding in my ears again, and I swear the thumping in my chest is moving me away from the station. I start to hyperventilate, but the Tondra suit is made to handle that, and it lowers the oxygen level until my breathing evens out. Or maybe it raises the oxygen level. I have no idea, I just know it works.

I slowly stretch out my arm and grab the free end of the BunG. I use it to reel myself into the station. Pausing a second, I press a hand against the station, activating the minimally magnetic mitts to stop my drifting. Once I'm stable, I pop my hands away from the wall and quickly tie the severed cord back together.

OK, now I'm safe from the vacuum of space, at least for now. I pull myself to a ledge about a meter from the airlock door and take stock. The BunG is connected to the outside of the station, emerging from a groove in the metal skin not far from my perch. I'm still trying to work out how this is possible when a new BunG snakes out of the groove and across the airlock door. It seems to attach itself to the other side. I knew smart BunGs were smart, but this is kind of creepy. It almost seems to be alive.

As I watch, the door pops open, and a figure shoots out of the airlock. I catch a glimpse of Bobby's grinning face as he hurtles past me, the BunG somehow snapping around his waist. He points at me, in an "I'm coming for you" gesture, and flies out into the void.

With the door open, my survival instincts crawl back out of hiding and take over. I scramble into the airlock. Activating the magnetic booties, I stick my feet to the deck. I look back out at the stars. Bobby hurtles back toward me. Without thinking, I grab his now slack BunG, pull a loop into the lock with me and slam my hand onto the big red button.

THIRTY-SEVEN

BONG! reverberates through the room when he hits the station. With his BunG severed, there's nothing to slow him down. I don't know if he hit hard enough to kill him, but I don't care. A fog of calm enfolds me, and I step into the Tondra booth. I stand there while the booth does its magic, not noticing any sensations at all through my wonderful new cotton-wool numbness. When the door opens, I step out and walk to one of the plastek chairs. I drag it to the booth, wedge it in the open doorway, then slump to the floor.

I'm cold. So cold. It's all I can think about. I don't know if jamming the outer door of the Tondra will keep the inner door from opening. I don't know if Bobby will be able to get the airlock door open. I don't know if the Sec Agents will get here before those things can happen, but I just can't make myself care. I may have just killed a man. Or not. Don't care.

———

SOMETIME LATER, the fog begins to clear. I'm sitting in a huge reclining chair in my mother's office. I have two blankets wrapped around me, a heat pack for my feet, a huge cup of hot chocolate in my hands and a plateful of Dav's croissants on the table next to me. R'ger sits in a smaller chair on the other side of the table, and Mother is bustling around in a very uncharacteristic manner, making sure we both have everything we want. I look at R'ger and he grins.

"Going to jail was almost worth it for this," he says, taking a sip from his steaming mug. I can smell the orange and spices from his *api morado*, even over the aroma of my cocoa.

"What happened? Where are Ty and Kara?" I ask.

"Everyone is fine," Mother answers, settling her hips against the huge desk. This is her power position: apparently relaxed and casual, but carefully higher than everyone else in the room. She had the desk specially built to her exact leg length. To be fair, perching there is probably automatic after all these years.

"What about," I pause. Do I really want to know? I think I need to know. "What about Bobby?"

"He's fine, too," she replies. "They collected him a few minutes after they found you. He has a minor concussion, a broken arm, and three cracked ribs. He'll be treated and released."

"Released!?" I shriek. "He's a psychopathic killer! They can't release him!"

She looks down at me, "He's a top-lev," she says.

"I don't care if he's the king of the freaking universe!" I leap to my feet, blankets and heat pack tumbling to the ground. Cocoa splashes. I'm so angry spit flies out of my mouth. "He KILLED five people. Maybe more! He tried to kill Ty, Kara and me! He should be locked in an escape pod and shot out into deep space!"

"You don't mean that," Mother says, her voice calm and smooth, but I can hear the familiar edge of command. The signal to back down.

I automatically take a step backward, then stiffen my spine. No, it's time to stand up to her. Someone has to speak on behalf of those lower-levs he killed. I take a step forward, and my foot catches in the pile of blankets. Without looking, I shake them off and advance on the desk and her.

"Bobby Putin is going to prison," I grit out. I take another step until I'm looming over my mother like an avenging angel. "I don't care how much money Don Putin throws into his defense fund. I will testify against him every day for rest of my life if that's what it takes. I will press charges against him myself in the galactic court if necessary. This is one top-lev crime that will NOT. Go. Unpunished."

Mother shakes her head, a tiny smile on her lips. "I'm so proud of you," she says. What? But she goes on. "I agree, charges will be pressed. And if I find *any* evidence showing Don Putin helped cover up these crimes, he will be ejected from the board and charges will be pressed against him as well. But it won't matter." She takes my arm and leads me back to my chair.

"What do you mean?" Her response had taken the photons out of my solar panels. I plop back into the armchair and let her tuck the blankets back around me. A soggy patch of cocoa soaked fabric slaps against my arm, but I ignore it.

"You know how this works," she says, sitting down on the footstool near R'ger's chair. He shifts his feet over, and it looks like he rubs his toes against her hip. What's going on there?

"By now," she glances at the clock, "Bobby is off-station. Or if not, he's holed up somewhere in a shielded safe room. All of us," and her sweeping gesture takes in the entire Level, "have a bolt hole somewhere on this station, with easy access to a shuttle dock. Within a few days, he'll have a new identity and be living in some dirt-side estate that was purchased by a shell company owned by another company completely unrelated to Putin Enterprises. We'll press charges, but he'll never be found to stand trial."

I set the empty cocoa mug down, trying to swallow the bitter taste in my mouth. "But Don Putin can't want him free. He *kills* people. For fun! I know the Putins have little use for lower-levs, but the Don must realize he can't cover up something like that forever." I think of the *Księżna*. "It's not a long-term solution."

Mother rubs the bridge of her nose. "I know, and I think he knows, too. He'll have to keep Bobby under constant surveillance. In a way, he *will* be in prison. Just a very luxurious one."

"Not good enough," I mutter, but arguing at this point will fix nothing. I change the subject. "Where's Kara? And Ty?"

"They're in the clinic on 80, getting checked out," Mother replies. "I asked them to come up here when they're able."

I gather the blankets. "Ty had a broken leg and ribs. And I don't know what happened to Kara. I'm going down to see them."

Mother puts up a hand. "He is in the clinic right now. And Kara is in the psych spa. Give them a few hours to recover. They only let family in, anyway."

"They'd let me in," I grumble. Top-levs can get in anywhere. But Kara won't be able to talk to me if she's in a CalmPod, and I'm not sure if Ty will want to see me. I *did* rescue him, but sometimes guys are weird about that kind of thing. I settle back in my seat and focus on R'ger. "So, what's the deal with you? Why did the Hilltonne vids get deleted?"

R'ger gives me a sheepish grin and looks toward Mother. She meets his eyes and shrugs. He smiles at her, a kind of dopey smile that makes me squirm. "Your mother and I have established an informal relationship," he says slowly, not taking his eyes off her. "I needed a way to visit her without leaving any evidence of our, er, dalliance."

"Seriously?!" I ask. "You went to jail over a booty call?" I turn to Mother. "And you let him? What's with all the secrecy anyway? I can't remember how many different men you've contracted with over the years. Why the sudden modesty?"

Mother flushes. Like a teenager in love. What is happening?

"This was," she looks at R'ger and shrugs, "different. I wanted something private, protected. It was foolish to go to such lengths when I knew there was some kind of mayhem going on, but...." She shrugs again and pats R'ger's leg. Eww. Old people in love. Worse yet, my mother.

"Ok, ok," I hold up my hands, waving her off. "I don't need to hear about my mother's love life. I'm just glad R'ger got out and wasn't involved in anything illegal." I look at him through narrowed eyes. "You aren't involved in anything else illegal, are you?"

He laughs. "No, no more mafia dealings."

"What?" Mother asks.

"*Sprzężaj*," I say at the same time.

Mother gives me the narrowed eyes this time. "Did you introduce R'ger to the *Księżna*?" Her face is like steel.

"Not on purpose," I mutter. I fling my blankets aside again. "I'm going down to 80. But before I go, can you explain why Hy-Mi was talking to Patrick before she died?"

Mother has the grace to look embarrassed. Really, today is a day of firsts. "When he told me of your problem with her, I asked him to intervene on your behalf. It turns out Patrick thought you were Tereshkovan." She pauses.

I shrug. "That is what my records say."

"Yes. You might want to change that," she says. "The Tereshkovans have a bad reputation in a lot of places. Particularly among those of the Pra-taki sect. Like Patrick."

"Are you kidding me?! Hasn't she ever heard of anti-discrimination laws?" I demand.

Mother shakes her head. "I'm sure she'd heard of them. Enforced them even. But people like her don't believe those laws apply to their special prejudices. Anyway, Hy-Mi convinced her that you've never even been to Tereshkova, and she was ready to reinstate you immediately. Then he fired her. Well, he called her supervisor and got her fired."

I laugh, without humor. "Bobby thought he was doing me a favor by killing her." I shudder. Giving myself a mental shake, I get to my feet. I start toward the door, then turn back. "So where do we stand?" I ask, gesturing between her and me. "I intend to go back to the MCC."

Mother stands and puts a hand on my shoulder. She shakes it gently. "I know. That's why I asked Hy-Mi to step in. But I hope we can, er, stay in touch."

I stare at her, shocked, then throw my arms around her. "I'd like that," I whisper.

———

"CAN WE GET A BIGGER COMPARTMENT?" Kara asks, leaning back in a plush air chair. Her closed eyes are covered by slices of homber fruit, and she's wrapped in a thick, self-warming robe. She reaches out a hand, and an attendant places a warm mug in it. Kara takes a sip and smiles. "I could get used to this."

"We can probably afford a larger compartment, but they don't come with tea servers," I wink at the very attractive attendant and he smiles back. "Or air loungers. How's your state?"

"I feel like butter," she says. "I could almost thank that skeevy sleazeball; I'd never be here without him." She bolts upright, the fruit slices falling off her face. "I can't believe I said that! Those poor girls!"

The attendant presses her back into the chair and carefully lifts a neuro-net over her head. "Let's get some more happy thoughts going," he says.

"I'll see you at home, Kara," I say. "Stay here as long as you want; you deserve it."

The attendant follows me out the door. "She just needs a few more hours of neuro-counseling, and she'll be fine," he says. "You know, in the old days, people had to go to months of therapy with specially trained physicians." He shakes his head. "Now that's crazy."

I think some old-fashioned counseling would be better than letting a computer mess with my brain waves, but that's just me.

Ty's room is a couple doors down. I stand awkwardly outside, wondering if he will even want to see me. It seemed like he'd forgiven me when we were trapped in the pod, but then again, we were trapped in a pod. Who knows what he's feeling now? But if I can thwart a psycho killer and stand up to my mother, I can face Ty O'Neill, right?

He's sitting on the side of a lowered bed, nudging a pair of slippers onto his feet without using his hands. He looks stiff as if bending or moving might hurt. He turns as I enter, smiling that heart-stopping smile.

"Hey," I say. Brilliant conversationalist.

"Hey," he says back. He pats the bed beside him.

I perch on the edge of the bed. "How're the ribs? And the leg? Head?"

"It's all good," he says. "The bone knitter is amazing. I haven't broken anything since I got on-station. If I'd known it was this easy to fix a broken bone, I might have tried that BunG thing, too."

I narrow my eyes. "Are you on something?" I ask.

"Oh, sure," he says. "I think I'm hopped up on two or three different drugs. Bone knitting is painful if you don't dose up first. I think we should go dancing." He puts his arms up in a classic partner-dance position and slides his feet around on the floor without moving off the bed. "Woah! Enough spinning already! Maybe we should sit the next one out."

I pat his hand and agree. "I know it's not fair to ask you this when you're bombed, but I'm going to anyway. And I'm going to record it, in case there's any doubt later." I flick my holo-ring and turn on the recorder. "Are we good?"

He slides an arm around me and kisses my cheek. "We're great." Then he slumps down on the bed. I swing his feet back up, pull off the ridiculous slippers, tuck the blanket around him and tiptoe out of the room.

EPILOGUE

I TAKE a bite out of my half-eaten Tasti-bun and slap it back down on the console. Bot 56C reports a broken scrubber. I pull up the bot vid and swivel the camera around. A trail of slimy gunk spreads behind the bot as far as the camera can see. I shake my head, thankful it isn't gum.

Pushing my chair across the MCC, I log into another system and swipe a few commands. In a couple minutes, Bot 56 F trundles up behind its little brother, cleaning up the mess left behind. I route the two bots to work in tandem until they get back to the bot closet where I can run a full diagnostic. I check the time. I should be able to get it done this afternoon, before heading up to 83 for Mother's blasted cocktail party. I wouldn't go at all, but Ty invited me, and I can't turn down a date with someone that shiny.

I run a quick check on my search programs. They've been running non-stop since I got my job back. They comb through public records, media reports, public and private vid cams, and, when I can get them, classified government documents, looking for any trace of Bobby Putin. His father has retired and spends his time jetting between several of his thirty estates on fourteen different planets and stations. So far, none of them appear to be harboring Bobby, but I'll keep looking. In the meantime, I'm expanding my search to the rest of the galaxy.

My holo-ring buzzes. I flick the gold filigree and Kara's face pops up in my palm. Today she's pasty pale, with platinum hair and bright red lips. It's not a good look for her, but I'm not going to tell her.

"Ready for lunch?" she asks.

I check the clock again. "Yeah, but I'll have to make it quick. Got a bot repair this afternoon." I close the holo.

A few minutes later, the door chimes, and I pop it open. Kara comes in with two steaming containers of noodles. We spread lunch out across the consoles. I grab a bowl, take a bite, and smile. "This is the life."

The glamorous life of a space janitor.

Turn the page for an sneak peek at
Space Janitor Two: The Dust of Kaku

AN EXCERPT FROM SPACE JANITOR TWO

The crowd in the T-Bahn jockeys for position as the train approaches the station. Bodies press against me from all sides, elbows and luggage corners indistinguishable, and equally painful. Fortunately, I am tall; otherwise, this mass of people would have me reduced to a claustrophobic breakdown. Kind of ironic that a trip to the planet would cause a station dweller like me to feel closed in. I stretch my neck, tilting my nose up searching for slightly less funky air above most of the crowd.

The train stops, and the masses push against the doors, shoving me forward. As the doors slide open, the crowd surges, and I imagine the first few people popping out like corks from a champagne bottle. Nearly hysterical giggles bubble up through my throat, and I clamp down. Breathe deep. Only a few more minutes.

The crowd carries me along, my duffle clutched tightly to my chest for fear it will be ripped away. As we plunge across the station toward the slide ramps, I try to maneuver to the edge of the throng, but I am trapped by a large woman with a face set like iron, wielding a massive luggage float. Her multiple offspring march quickly behind, grimly clinging to the float in a line. All but the last one. A little girl of about five, she skips along at the end of the line of children, singing quietly, her eyes alight as she tries to see everything.

The woman barks something over her shoulder, and the little girl drops her head, slumping into the required trudge behind her siblings. After a second, she peeks up, her eyes still bright, and the bounce creeps back into her step. I catch her eye and wink. She grins back, then dips her head before the woman notices.

A shriek rings out over the crowd. Heads swivel wildly, looking for the source. A hand points, upward. "There!" We all stop to look.

Along the left wall, a pair of float tubes stretch up the wall and into the ceiling. Halfway up, a woman bobs in the tube, slowly rotating as she screams. The sound wavers in time to her spin, sounding like some kind of emergency siren. The little girl next to me giggles and claps a hand over her mouth. She glances up at me, and I make a face. Her shoulders shake with suppressed laughter.

"Stupid tourists," a man on my other side mutters to another man. "Everyone knows the float tubes have been flaking out for weeks. Better to take the slider." He grasps his friend's elbow and steers him to the right, ignoring the trapped woman. After a glance at the screamer, most of the crowd follows suit. My little friend watches over her shoulder as her family hauls her away.

A group of people dressed in beige coveralls arrows through the crowd like a ship through waves. As the rest of the travelers stream away from the tubes, the team sets up a rescue tramp and a crawler bot. Their moves are practiced, and their faces are weary, as if they've done this before, many times. I give a mental shrug and leave them to it.

The crowd bottlenecks against the slide ramp entrance, and I squirm between bodies to the edge of the room. A tiny gap opens up, and I dart between two business suits talking loudly into their holo-phones. Suddenly, I'm at the front of the group, and I dash onto the miraculously open ramp, just ahead of the older couple whose slow progress clearly annoys the entire crowd.

The slide ramp is mercifully quiet as it angles up toward the surface. The vid feed covering the walls shows happy, wealthy people enjoying a sun-filled day on Kaku. Tiny letters across the bottom of the holo give the real news: employment is down, erratic weather has caused crops to fail, a suicide bomber took out a small store in Frobisher Cove. The happy people party on, carefree.

I step out into a transit station. The trickle of people exiting the tubes feels so much less frantic than the crowd downstairs. Many of them peel off to other tubes that lead to connecting trains. Ahead, glass doors reveal a wide, green lawn, and a sign over the doors reads doors: Turing-Sassoon Technology Institute of Esthetics and Computing — Kaku.

I walk out of the transit station, sucking in the flower-scented air. The famous Kaku ti-cherry trees are in full blossom, clouds of brilliant orange color shading every walkway. A fountain burbles somewhere nearby but out of sight.

Students whiz by on hovercycles, stroll together through the quad, and nap on the grass while the sun beats down. The campus relations folks should be out here filming for their VR tours; they'll never get a more perfect day.

A woman, about my age, with a pert, lightly freckled nose, a slim build, and the most gorgeous burnished copper hair I've ever seen, smiles at me. How does she get her hair so straight? I self-consciously push my own flaming, frizzy corkscrews out of my eyes.

"Hi, I'm Lindsay! Welcome to TSTI! Are you here for the Admissions Rodeo?" she chirps. She cocks her head and scrolls through a list on her holo.

"No," I answer, hiking my bulging bag up on my shoulder. "Refresher course, COM 453. I know where to go."

Her smile dims a little, and I wonder if her performance rating is based on the number of students she helps. "I'm supposed to meet a friend here, though," I say. "Can you tell me where Whiloby Hall is? I think it's new."

"Of course!" The grin amps back up as she spins around, her copper locks flaring out around her head, and settling back into a perfect fall. She points across the lawn toward a distant, lavender building. "Across the quad, past Luberick Center—that's the purple one—then the second drop shaft on the right." Spinning back, she flicks a code slip at me. "There's a guide. Have a wonderful day!"

I mumble my thanks, but she's already moved on to the boy who followed me out of the station. I settle my bag more securely on my shoulder and start across the quad. The guide she flipped to me vibrates my holo-ring so that it feels like someone pulling on my hand, leading me toward my destination.

I walk and walk, my legs feeling like rubber. Living on a space station does not prepare one for a massive campus like the Techno-Inst. When I was working on my certification, I thought nothing of flitting across campus several times a day. Now, I'm daydreaming about a hover cart. With air conditioning. I don't remember it being this hot and muggy.

A group rushes by, all bare legs and hairy arms, revballs flying between them as they shout and laugh. More students surge up behind them, headed toward the sports fields. They must have just finished their exams; revball is a finals week tradition. I duck under a huge tree to avoid being swept away by the tide. The blossom-heavy branches droop down, creating a hidden refuge. During the term, these living domes are usually occupied by studying or amorous students. Today, it's a solitary refuge. Then suddenly, I'm alone on the quad.

I sit down on the ground, leaning against the tree trunk, enjoying the shade.

The drone of insects buzzing around the ti-cherry flowers lulls me, and I close my eyes, breathing in the heavy, sweet scent.

An angry whisper rouses me. "You need to make sure they don't get suspicious."

A higher voice responds. "What do you think I've been trying to do? But some of those idiots just won't keep their mouths shut."

"You should take care of that." The first voice is cold. "I will have them eliminated if necessary."

"What?" The second voice breaks mid-word. "Eliminated? You mean— don't do anything, uh..." The voice trails off.

Something about that voice rings a bell in my head, but I can't think what. Looking out under the branches, I can see two pairs of feet in the same sports shoes every other student wears. The thick flowers and foliage hide the speakers' faces from me.

The first voice speaks again, deadly intent obvious beneath the casual tone. "I'll do whatever needs to be done to protect my project. If that bothers you, then you should make sure I don't have to eliminate any problems." My breath catches in my throat. I have no idea who this guy is, but he is seriously frightening.

The second guy gulps so loudly I can actually hear it. "Don't worry, I'll keep everyone quiet until after the event."

The two men move away, and I stay in my safe little flower dome. I'm not relaxed anymore. In fact, I'm cold and sweaty at the same time. I hug my knees to my chest. The first guy sounded so dangerous—so unconcerned about doing violence. And he could be anyone! I have no idea what he looks like—I might have a class with him, and I'll never know unless I hear him whisper.

To keep reading, click here to buy
The Dust of Kaku: Space Janitor Two
Or get the whole series in one e-volume:
Triana Moore, Space Janitor
If you liked *The Vacuum of Space*, please leave a review on Amazon or Goodreads. Reviews help other readers find stories they'll like. They also tell me what you like, so I can write more of it.

If you'd like to be notified when my next book becomes available, sign up for my newsletter. I promise not to SPAM you, and you can download a couple of free short stories.

You can also find me and information on all my other books (three series and counting!) on my website:
juliahuni.com

ACKNOWLEDGMENTS

Every author knows there are tons (or tonnes, if we're going metric like Triana,) of people to whom we don't give enough appreciation. That's why we give them a page, or sometimes two, at the end of every book. Even though we know that isn't nearly enough.

First of all, thanks to my family. My husband, David, who puts up with me type-type-typing all the time when he'd rather be out doing something fun *with me*. Thanks to our three kids who are now in the "don't bother me until I really need some help" stage. Which is convenient—it makes it really easy for me to ignore them, most of the time. And thanks to Pippin the wonder dog who sits under my desk and barks like crazy when anyone comes in the front door but doesn't notice people coming in the back.

A big shout out to my sister, writer A.M. Scott, who reads all my crappy first drafts, and helps me figure out where the heck I went wrong. She also forged the way in this whole publishing thing. She writes space opera—if that's your thing, check her out!

Thanks to the great team at IPH Media: my editor Graham Erly, my tech support guy Dave Arthur, and the rest of the team. Thanks to Les at German-Creative for the awesome book cover. And a big shout-out to all the indie writers on 20BooksTo50K© and the Indie Cover Project Facebook pages. You folks gave me the confidence to forge ahead.

Special thanks to Douglas Adams, for creating some of Triana's favorite swear words.

And finally, thanks to the Big Dude for making all things possible.

ALSO BY JULIA HUNI

Space Janitor Series:
The Vacuum of Space
The Dust of Kaku
The Trouble with Tinsel
Orbital Operations
Glitter in the Stars
Sweeping S'Ride
Triana Moore, Space Janitor (the complete series)

Tales of a Former Space Janitor
The Rings of Grissom
Planetary Spin Cycle
Waxing the Moon of Lewei
Tales of a Former Space Janitor (books 1-3)
Changing the Speed of Light Bulbs

The Phoenix and Katie Li
Luna City Limited

Colonial Explorer Corps Series:
The Earth Concurrence
The Grissom Contention
The Saha Declination
Colonial Explorer Corps: The Academy Years (books 1-3)
The Darenti Paradox

Recycled World Series:
Recycled World
Reduced World

Krimson Empire (with Craig Martelle):

Krimson Run

Krimson Spark

Krimson Surge

Krimson Flare

Krimson Empire (the complete series)

ROMANTIC COMEDY (AS LIA HUNI)

Stolen Kisses

Stolen Love Song

Stolen Heart Strings

Printed in Great Britain
by Amazon